SHE LAY PERFECTLY STILL AND WONDERED IF SOMEONE WAS BREAKING INTO HER HOUSE.

She should have paid more attention to the feeling that her sister's murderer might decide to come after her. She had no security system, no lights outside save the ones on the porch, and no plan for escape if someone did break in.

The noise continued, but a different sound this time. *Ta-tap, ta-tap, ta-tap.* She couldn't pinpoint the location exactly.

She inched her way out of bed.

Ta-tap, ta-tap, ta-tap. The noise was louder now. It sounded like someone walking. It was inside the house and coming from one of the guest rooms down the hall. She pressed herself flat, with her back against the wall, and inched along it toward the door in the darkness. Then she heard a new sound. She held her breath. It sounded like water running. It, too, seemed to be coming from one of the bedrooms down the hall.

Something crashed downstairs.

When, after some time, she didn't hear another sound, she switched on the light and started down the hall. The sound of water was louder now, and she followed it until she opened the door to one of the b̶e̶d̶ ̶ ̶ ̶ ̶ ̶ ̶ ̶ ̶ ̶ e̶ turned on the light and ̶ ̶ ̶ ̶ ̶ ̶ ̶ ̶ ̶ ̶ ̶ ̶ ̶ t of the bathroom.

D1010215

SHE LAY PERFECTLY STILL, AND WONDERED IF SOMEONE WAS BREAKING INTO HER HOUSE

ALONE
in the
DARK

Elaine
Coffman

POCKET STAR BOOKS
New York London Toronto Sydney

An *Original* Publication of POCKET BOOKS

A Pocket Star Book published by
POCKET BOOKS, a division of Simon & Schuster, Inc.
1230 Avenue of the Americas, New York, NY 10020

This book is a work of fiction. Names, characters, places and incidents are products of the author's imagination or are used fictitiously. Any resemblance to actual events or locales or persons, living or dead, is entirely coincidental.

ISBN-13: 978-0-7434-7579-2
ISBN-10: 0-7434-7579-8

This Pocket Star Books paperback edition October 2006

10 9 8 7 6 5 4 3 2 1

POCKET STAR BOOKS and colophon are registered trademarks of Simon & Schuster, Inc.

Cover illustration by Larry Rostant

Manufactured in the United States of America

For information regarding special discounts for bulk purchases, please contact Simon & Schuster Special Sales at 1-800-456-6798 or business@simonandschuster.com

For Jackie Williamson
Dear friend, neighbor, partner in crime.
What one of us doesn't think of, the other one
does . . . Hasn't it been fun?

It is one of the blessings of old friends
that you can afford to be stupid with them
—*Ralph Waldo Emerson*,
American Poet, Lecturer and Essayist,
1803–1882

The more enlightened our houses are,
the more their walls ooze ghosts.

—Italo Calvino (1923–85), Italian author, critic.
"Cybernetics and Ghosts," lecture, November 1969, Turin
(published in *The Literature Machine,* 1987)

Prologue

SHE WAS LATE.

He wanted to make her disappear and she was not co-operating.

Ordinarily that would not set him on edge, but there was nothing ordinary about tonight. He had come here to kill her.

It was not supposed to be this way. He'd planned on her being home earlier—not because he willed it, but because he knew a great deal about her ordinary and predictable life. He knew her established patterns—all the comings and goings—where she went and whom she saw, and how long she usually stayed. He knew her brand of toothpaste and her addiction to Diet Coke. He could tell you the scent of her perfume and what size underwear she wore.

Her one amazing talent was her ability to maintain her boring life with almost no variation. She was as predictable as the sunrise; only she would not live long enough to see the next one.

He glanced at his watch and was amazed to see she was late and it set him on edge. He liked to be in control and it disturbed him when he was not. He wondered if he should give in to his anger when she arrived and kill her immediately, or be magnanimous and grant her a few more minutes to live.

Control your temper or it will control you . . .

He had read all the books. He knew how to control himself. He did not need to explode with anger to prove it. The final proof of his superiority, his omnipotence, came in knowing he could decide if someone lived or died—and if the latter, the precise moment and exact way they would go.

As the hand that held the knife relaxed, he was careful not to let the sharp edge of the blade cut the latex gloves he wore. He liked the weight of the knife in his hand, the perfect balance—so much, that for a moment he was unaware that his thumb stroked the hilt lovingly. Holding a knife like this was a powerful aphrodisiac. He thought of her slender body, the fair skin, the long legs. He did not need to imagine her naked. He had seen her that way many times, unbeknownst to her, which aroused him even more.

He heard the car before he saw the dull glow of automobile lights coming up the road. He knew it was her car before he saw the metallic blue color. Who else could it be? Hers was the last house at the end of the street.

His heart began to pound with anticipation. He had her now.

A flash of bright light snagged his attention. He observed the widening circle of light thrown in front of the car and knew the joy of rewarded patience. The head-lights were on high beam now. He must exercise caution. He stepped back into the dark shadows of the trees as the car drove up the drive and stopped in front of the house.

She got out of the car, graceful to the end. Although he had replaced the porch light with a burned-out bulb, she would have no trouble finding her way. The car's headlights would remain on long enough for her to get inside the house.

When she passed in front of the car, her figure was sil-houetted against the headlights and he breathed faster when he saw her perfect body outlined through the fab-ric of her floral print dress. Her legs were still fairly slim, he noticed, and well shaped all the way down to the straps of sandals fastened around trim ankles. He closed his eyes against painful impulses and desires, and blocked the pain of her rejection from his conscious mind.

Soon she would be dead and she would not know why it was necessary to kill her. The purest part of the joy of it was realizing no one would ever know, not even her.

She reached the front steps and paused long enough to turn and take a quick glance behind her. His grin was a sardonic one. What would she do if I jumped out and said, "Boo?"

He waited for her to unlock the door and step inside. He knew she would lock the door behind her, not that it would do any good.

With a snap, the car's lights went out. He waited until he saw the light go on in her upstairs bedroom, then he began to move toward the house. The grass provided a soundless cushion for his feet as he crossed the yard, his movement screened by thick shrubs. The windows he passed were all black and behind them the house was silent and dark. She had no alarms, no dogs, and the neighbors were far enough away they did not concern him.

Earlier he had unlocked the back door. She was the trusting type and not prone to rechecking the security of her house when she returned.

Another mistake in my favor . . .

He stepped into the house and quietly closed the door behind him. He was about to enter the kitchen when he heard her come downstairs. He remained hidden in the dark shadows while he watched her take a bottle of water out of the refrigerator, then pause and glance around before turning off the light and leaving the room quickly.

He waited a moment before moving. He knew how many steps it was to the stairs. He had practiced this walk in the dark many times. He approached the stairs slowly and stopped when he saw she was almost to the point where the stairs made a U-turn in front of the double windows, through which moonlight cast an eerie blue light over everything inside.

She wore a pale satin gown cut low in the back, and her long hair was silky and straight. He could tell by the rigid way she moved that she was afraid. She had good reason to be.

He waited until he heard her tread move slowly down the hallway overhead before he followed her. When he reached the second floor, he saw a pale glow coming from a lamp in her bedroom.

With one hand, he pushed the door open. The room was empty; the bathroom door ajar. He could hear the sound of water running and three taps of a toothbrush against the side of the basin. He heard movement in the bathroom. The door creaked as it was opened further. A diffused glow of light came into the room. He stepped to one side of the door and flattened himself against the wall so he was partially hidden behind it. His thumb caressed the hilt of the hunting knife clutched in his hand.

She stepped into the room and paused, alert as a deer sensing danger, then she began to turn slowly toward the door. He stepped forward out of shadow and into light.

Their gazes met. Her eyes widened. But instead of screaming, she simply stared at him, as if rendered mute by the sight of someone in her bedroom and the confusion of not understanding why he was here.

He knew she was trying to put it all together, to find answers by logic and reasoning, not yet understanding that there was no logic to this. Now, he was the one being unpredictable.

He listened to her rapid breathing and focused on the beads of sweat that appeared over her upper lip. She was scared and it fed his confidence.

He knew the exact moment when she saw the knife. At first, she simply stared dumbly at it, and then at him, her expression lost somewhere between puzzled and blank. Her poor mind had not reached the point of comprehending that he could be capable of using the knife on her or that he had come here for that explicit purpose. Ah, but he did love the element of surprise.

When comprehension settled over her, she shook her head as if disbelieving what her eyes and mind told her. He felt a rush of adrenaline when he saw the exact moment when she put it all together. First the indrawn breath, and then she held out her hand toward him and she began to back away—until she bumped against the bedroom chair.

"Why?" Her eyes were filled with terror now. Without lifting her gaze from his face, she moved her hand slightly behind her—to guide her until she was completely around the chair. Then, she turned quickly and he saw she intended to run. She bolted before he could grab her, but she tripped and fell to the floor. She had forgotten about the ottoman.

That one miscalculation had cost her dearly, and she knew it. She raised her hands as if that could protect her.

"Please . . . please don't do this. Don't hurt me."

"Too late for that, I'm afraid, but I will try to make it quick."

"No! Please! Oh God, no!"

"God doesn't make house calls."

He raised the knife and stabbed her, just as she shifted her body and made a move to get up. She screamed. The knife went in easily and plunged deep—all the way to the hilt—but her sudden movement caused him to miss his intended mark. The wound was too high and too near the shoulder to hit anything vital.

She screamed again when he yanked the knife out. The sight of her staring at the knife, the blade dripping with her own blood, distracted him for a moment. It gave her enough time to roll to her feet. This time, there was no hesitation before she ran from the room.

He followed her, careful not to step in the trail of blood. He caught up with her at the top of the stairs and yanked her around by the arm to face him. She was bleeding heavily from her wound. He raised the knife. Desperate now, she wrenched away from him and started down the stairs. He lunged after her. She screamed when he stabbed her again, in the back this time.

Once. Twice. Three times.

She kept moving. She was staggering and clinging to the banister along the wall, fighting for her life as she tried to get away. She was losing a lot of blood now and he could see she was weakening. He had plenty of time. He could afford to be magnanimous and let her live a bit longer.

He let her go, and felt oddly disconnected as he watched her struggle to make it down the stairs. It was only after she collapsed at the bottom that he began his slow descent, careful to keep to the unbloodied side of the stairway, away from the bloody footprints that marked her descent.

He couldn't have painted it better if he tried. Jackson Pollock would be envious . . .

When he reached the bottom, he paused. Blood was everywhere. His attention was drawn for a moment to a crimson stain that began to creep from beneath her body and soak into the long, silky hair that fanned around her. The pool of blood grew larger and larger still.

Who would think there could be so much blood in such a small woman?

He waited, his breathing only slightly elevated. He did not need to check her pulse to know she was dead. She almost looked like she was sleeping, but in death she was not as beautiful. He sighed with satisfaction. The deed was done.

She would never be late again.

One

WASHINGTON, D.C., WAS DARK. At five in the morning, the streets were quiet, almost empty. The way she liked it best.

A fine mist fell upon the black Lincoln as it made its way slowly up K Street before coming to a stop. She was sitting alone in the back seat, looking out the window. The meager gray light from the street lamp cast a shadow on the familiar face of one of D.C.'s most popular newscasters, the face of a woman whose life was not her own.

The door opened and she stepped onto the wet pavement. She handed the driver a voucher, then fastened the buttons of her black raincoat before stepping over the curb. Her steps were long and brisk. She did not seem to notice the sleek lines of the building that shot up ten stories to end with a helicopter pad on top. Nor did she glance at her reflection in the polished façade of gray granite as she passed.

The mist was changing to a hard rain that began to pelt the pavement. She tucked her head down and quickened her pace. It was not hard to see she was a woman with a mission.

It was only when she came to the polished brass plaque that she glanced at the words AMERICAN BROAD-CASTING, and below that, WMDC-TV CHANNEL 6. Seeing her approach, the doorman jumped up from his stool and adjusted the jacket of his uniform before he opened the door and held it wide. "Good morning, Ms. O'Brien."

She greeted him with a brief smile. "Good morning, George."

The rhythm of her shoes tapped a message of pressing importance, yet she moved like a dancer over the glossy marble floors, her body supple and bearing the assurance of a woman in control of her emotions and her body.

Before George made it back to his stool she disappeared behind the closing elevator doors.

At 5:01 A.M., the elevator doors opened and Ellery O'Brien stepped off and wondered if her blond hair was damp from rain, or if her makeup needed a touch-up. Not that she needed makeup, for she was the kind of woman people accused of waking up beautiful.

Her cohost, Chad Newberry, came whistling down the hall—a good indication that he was in prime form for the WMDC-TV morning news show, *Starting Point*. He had a cup of coffee and five doughnuts in his hands.

When he saw her, Chad held up his left hand, where a doughnut dangled from each finger. He extended his hand toward her. "Sweets for the sweet?"

She laughed and shook her head. "You know better than to wave those at me. I don't understand how you stay so slim eating all those sweets."

"I don't understand either," he said, "but I'm thankful." With a quick smile, he ducked into a room a few doors away.

She stopped by her desk long enough to drop off her purse and two leather tote bags before she took a compact from the drawer and checked the condition of her hair and face. Satisfied, she flipped the compact closed and went into the break room to grab a cup of black coffee.

She carried the coffee back down the hall to the newsroom. Before she had a chance to read over the news updates Bill Gaither, the executive producer, stopped by to see how things were going.

At 5:50 A.M., she was behind her computer reading the headlines when Chad walked toward her. "Anything earth-shattering happen during the night?"

"I bet you always asked your friends if you could copy their homework when you were in school."

"Nope, I asked them to do it for me. But seriously, did anything newsworthy happen last night?"

"Yes, the producer killed your story."

His face paled and Ellery laughed. "For once I got one over on you."

"That definitely isn't like you." He started to sit down next to her, then paused to give her a considering look. "Are you feeling okay?"

"I'm fine." He did not look like he believed her, so she added, "Really, I am."

"You look pale."

"I'm just a little tired, that's all. It's been a long, trying week."

"You're worried about your father, aren't you?"

"Do I look that bad?"

"You could never look bad, but I know you well enough to know you aren't the Ellery I see every morning. So, is it your father, or something else?"

"Yes, I'm worried about my father." She stared at the computer screen, then after several seconds she said, "But I'd rather not talk about it now, Chad."

There must have been something in the tone of her voice, because his face took on a grave expression. "You aren't thinking of quitting, are you?"

Her face registered surprise. "Quitting? Television? No, it never entered my mind." She decided not to elaborate further.

He studied her face, watching her with those brown eyes beneath a shock of unruly red hair. She felt sorry for Chad. She had never seen him look so bewildered. She tried to reassure him. "Truly, I'm not leaving the show. I am going through a difficult time right now, but it won't last forever."

He seemed to wilt with relief. "Thank God for that," he said after a moment's consideration. "For a moment there, I heard the whizzing sound of our ratings plummeting along with my future in broadcasting."

He was watching her as if he still weren't completely convinced. "You worry about ratings too much," she said, shaking her head.

He looked at her incredulously. "Ratings are what this business is about. If that was supposed to make me feel more secure, it didn't." He stroked his chin, the concerned look back on his face. "Are you moving to a more challenging position? Are you changing stations? My God! You aren't going to New York to do cable network news, are you?"

She almost laughed at that because she had been offered a job with Fox in New York only a couple of weeks ago, but she turned it down. "No, I'm not going anywhere. I'm simply searching for something in my life that has more purpose," she said and hoped that reassured him.

Something about the way he looked at her said he understood what she was trying to say and she couldn't help smiling.

He released a long sigh. "Well, I can't deny I'm relieved to hear you say you aren't leaving. I have to tell you that for a moment there, I thought my days were limited. I could easily be replaced without it having any effect on the show, but if you left . . . Hell, I can't think of anyone who could replace you," he said. "We would drop to the worst-rated morning news team around before we found anyone to even come close to taking your place. You are the darling of D.C. news and you can't deny you can get interviews when no one else in this city can."

She shook her head. "That's a glowing tribute, but it's pure nonsense. Besides, why should you worry about losing me, when you and Margo are great together?" She couldn't repress the humor in her voice when she said, "I know she would jump at the chance to work with you."

"Margo? You mean Margo Garza? She's a lightweight. She's got about as much hold as a paper clip. She won't bolster our ratings. How could she possibly carry this show the way you have for any length of time?"

"Has it ever occurred to you that you don't need any-one to carry the show because you carried it for years, long before I came on the scene?"

"Oh yes, I carried it all right . . . in the number two spot, which plummeted, as you know, to number three after Jackie Tam left. And don't forget dear old Cassandra. When they brought her in to replace Jackie, we dropped so low we fell off the charts. For a while I thought they'd change the name to *Ending Point*. Thank God she had enough sense to quit after three months."

"The two of you didn't work together long enough. You needed more time to gel."

"Gel? Listen, sweet cakes, Cassandra Mandell and I wouldn't gel if they left us sitting in a vat of gelatin for a hundred years."

She smiled at him without trying to hide the humor that danced in her eyes. "You gel with Margo."

His expression was as gloomy as his voice. "Yeah, and any more gelling with Margo and my marriage is over. The last time she filled in for you Alexis threatened to di-vorce me."

She reached over and popped one of his suspenders. "Then you better learn how to put a lid on that efferves-cence of yours."

He went down on one knee and took her hand in his. "Say you'll never leave me. What about our five children? The mortgage on the house?"

She couldn't help laughing as she reached out, grabbed him by the suspenders, and tugged. "Will you get up? Do you want people to start talking? Alexis might not be so easy to convince next time."

He shot to his feet, grabbed her hand, and held it against his heart. "Think what a rumor of that magnitude would do to the ratings!"

Behind them Mignon, the sales director, cleared her throat. "When you've finished auditioning for Shakespeare, and rather pathetically, will you stop by my desk? I've got something I want to show you."

"I'd sign the Declaration of Independence if it would impress you, Mignon."

"Idiot. It's already been signed. Didn't you take history?"

"Yes, but I was absent the day they studied that."

Mignon laughed and Chad watched her leave before he turned back to Ellery. "Why are you looking at me like that?"

Ellery shook her head. "I was waiting for you to tell me she has a nice derrière."

"What she has is a nice ass."

"You're impossible! And by the way, did you know the editing is running late?" Ellery was still laughing as she started from the room.

"Wait! How late?"

"They promise to have it ready by the time we go on the air," she said.

She started to leave and he asked, "Where are you going?"

"To call Alexis and tell her she better get down here." She blew him a kiss and left him speechless for once.

It was 6:30 A.M. by the time she was through changing clothes and walked to the set. She saw Bill motion for her to come over, so she headed in his direction.

He gave her a concerned look. "Any news about your father's condition?"

She nodded. "The results of his tests came back last Friday. Yesterday I took him to Johns Hopkins to see an oncologist. He has a melanoma, a malignant tumor on the skin."

"Serious?"

She swallowed against the painful lump that formed in her throat and reminded herself that she could not cry now. "It's fatal, Bill. He has a month at the most."

"Lord, I'm so sorry, Ellery. You know how much all of us here think of Dr. O'Brien. If you need time off to be with him . . ."

"Thanks, but you know my father—he wouldn't hear of it, but I will let you know if it comes to that. Right now, I can handle things. Just spending my afternoons with him will help a lot. I've hired a nurse who will start next Monday and I know he isn't going to like that."

"He will if you explain it is for you as much as for him. Don't worry about anything. We can always get Margo to fill in for you if you need to be away. Otherwise, I want you to be out of here by noon each day. Chad can take over any interviews you have scheduled. If there's anything else any of us can do to help, just say the word."

"I know, and thank you, Bill . . . for the offer . . . for everything. I think having my afternoons with him will be enough."

"Keep me updated," he said, and glanced at his watch. "Guess you better find Chad. He was looking lost as a lamb this morning."

"I was with him a moment ago. I think he was going to

speak with Jack about some technical problem. It may interest you to know that I left him in brighter spirits than when he came in."

"I'm glad. He thought you were leaving WMDC. Did he tell you that?"

"Yes, although I don't know where he got that idea. I assured him that I was not going anywhere."

"Good," he said. "Good."

It was 6:45 A.M., when she met up with Chad again. She saw the show producers were in position just as the technical crew gave the signal that the control room and the floor were "all set."

She took her place behind the news desk next to Chad and her earphone fell out. There was a mad scramble to get it in place and she breathed a sigh of relief when she heard the stage manager's voice in her earphone. She listened as he gave the countdown: Five . . . four . . . three . . . two . . . one . . .

At precisely 7:00 A.M., they were on the air.

"Good morning, D.C.! Here's your favorite team of hosts, O'Brien and Newberry . . ."

She opened, giving the morning greeting, then led into a quick briefing of the local breaking news, which she read from the monitors.

It was 7:15 A.M. when the opening segment ended, and the show went to its first commercial break. Bill called the control room with a couple of comments. In the control room, the producer relayed the information to the director, who made a few changes in video segments.

For the next hour and fifteen minutes everything went as smoothly as it always did.

At 8:40 A.M., she returned to her desk, worked until noon, and then left for her father's house in Chevy Chase. On her way, she stopped by Whole Foods on Wisconsin Avenue to buy fruit and a container of the tomato bisque soup he liked.

Sam was asleep when she arrived. She put the food away, then went to sit with him for a while. Sam woke up around three-thirty and they visited while he ate the fruit and soup. That evening he felt like watching television, so she watched *The Godfather* with him, and they talked about Marlon Brando's remarkable talent during the commercials. He fell asleep before the movie ended and she kissed his cheek and slipped quietly from the room.

Later that evening, she lay in bed and wondered why she felt as if someone had nailed one of her shoes to the floor. She was in motion but going nowhere, like a compass that could not find its magnetic north. She felt strange. Her hands trembled. A headache began to build at the back of her head, pounding . . . pounding . . .

Two

She dreamed of the house again . . .

It was obvious no one lived there. It stood desolate and barren at the end of a dead-end street, grass and weeds wild in the midst of a circular gravel drive.

A gabled roof frowned at anyone who approached. The wind swirled around it, a brooding echo of nameless deeds. An ornamental gate had rusted off its hinges and leaned against one of the stone columns that flanked the drive. Long, prickly fingers of pyracantha poked through the iron bars, and its fiery thorns grabbed at her clothes as she passed, as if warning her to stay away.

The large oak door was ajar, and beyond it stood a curving staircase. Voices called from deserted rooms above, where flickering shadows of truth danced eerily across the rafters. Once, it had been someone's home, but something tragic had happened here. Now it was the abode of abandoned hopes, unborn children, and dreams cut short.

Silent and mysterious, it was a place where sin whispered and murder cried out, and she recoiled with shock at the violence she could feel reaching out to her. She feared it would darken to something worse. What had happened here, and to those who had inhabited it? Where had they gone?

There were no answers, only the long shadows of evening creeping across the floor, accompanied by the mournful sigh of the wind. Somewhere in the house a voice cried out and the sound of it went over her, chilling and cold as the fingers of death. She realized she was inside the house now, trapped in a nightmare—a dream within a dream.

From somewhere above the staircase came a solitary scream followed by a bubbling cry. A bleeding woman stumbled down the stairs and fell a few feet from where she stood, her eyes filled with unshed tears.

A low, keening cry came from deep in Ellery's throat, and her body recoiled with horror. For it was not a stranger's face she saw, but her own. At the top of the stairs she heard footsteps, and saw the shroudlike shadow of a man, a bloody knife raised in his hand. He started down the stairs, the lower half of his face sufficiently illuminated to reveal an evil smile that said she was next. Ellery screamed and kept on screaming until the shadowy figure began to fade, and there was nothing left but his evil grin, which remained for some time after everything else was gone.

Her body jerked. Ellery rolled to the side of the bed and sat up. She put her feet on the floor and leaned her head forward, while she gasped to catch her breath. Her skin was damp, her nerves shattered, and her muscles tightly coiled. Around her, the house was deathly quiet and she snapped on the radio, needing some small assurance that she was alive and in her own house in Washington, D.C.

Her head still pounded with a headache. She turned on the bedside lamp, but the image of the grin remained, fluorescent and surreal, and superimposed over everything in her mind. Was it a dream, or was she going mad? She could not seem to tell the difference anymore, between the world she knew when she was awake, and the one she stepped into when she slept.

By now, she knew it was only a dream . . . the same recurring dream that had plagued her sleep since childhood. In the beginning, it was nothing more than dreams about a strange house, but as the years passed, the dream became more detailed and more frightening. When they first began, she had the dream no more than two or three times a year, but they had increased in frequency until now they were coming a month or two apart.

Although this same dream had come to her many times before, this was the first time she'd seen the man with the knife grin at her.

Three

As her father's illness progressed, Ellery could see that he needed someone with him all the time, but Sam refused to move into Ellery's home on Woodland Drive in the District.

"I've lived in Chevy Chase since your mother and I moved here. This is where I plan to die . . . in my own house. Once I'm gone, you can park me anywhere you like."

Stubbornness like his . . . She sighed and decided to let it go, relieved about the full-time registered nurse named Irene Davenport she'd hired to live with him so he would have around-the-clock care. At first, Sam wasn't too happy about it. "I don't need a nurse's coddling, or her sitting around watching me sleep," he said. "I can die just fine on my own, without any help."

"I wish you could see that I am not doing it for you, Dad. I know how independent you are and how you believe you can take care of yourself. I wish you would try to understand that I'm doing it for me. I hired Mrs. Davenport because I want someone with you when I can't be here. Call it the purchase price for peace of mind."

"Well, why didn't you say so?"

She smiled, knowing that was as close as Sam O'Brien was going to come to relenting.

Ellery spent time with him every day, sometimes reading to him, other times listening to him talk about the past. He was a well-respected dentist, a brilliant man with a fine mind, and his wisdom had no end. He was her father, her mentor, and her friend. She considered herself fortunate to have this time with him.

It was a warm afternoon, late in March, when her father said, "I know I don't have much longer."

"Don't say that. It sounds like you're giving up."

"We have to be able to talk about it, Ellery. Talking and grieving . . . it's all part of the process. But don't let me get started on that because it's not where I want to go right now. I have something to tell you . . . something I should have told you before now; something that will affect you greatly."

He stopped for a fit of coughing. With each day that passed it became more difficult for him to breathe. She could see he was pushing himself just to organize his thoughts. "I want you to listen without saying anything until I have finished. I want to be certain you comprehend everything before you unleash all the questions I know you will have. Do you understand?"

Puzzled by the urgency in his tone, she nodded. "I understand."

"I have always tried to be completely truthful and honest with you, Ellery, but I confess it did not always work out that way. Sometimes things happen unintentionally, but in this one instance it was intentional. What I have to say will shock you but I don't know any way to soften it. I am not your real father."

It took a moment for the impact of the words to hit her. *I am not your real father . . .*

"What do you mean, you aren't my real father?" she asked. "You're joking, right?"

Her father looked at her but remained silent.

"I don't understand. If you aren't my father, why didn't you tell me before now? How could you keep something like this from me? Didn't you think I had a right to know?"

"I know you're angry."

She shook her head. "No . . . not angry . . . at least, not yet. Right now, I'm just shocked. Are you telling me that you raised me after my mother died, although I was not your child?"

"Not being your birth father does not mean I cared less for you because you were not the child of my body. No father could have loved his daughter more and I think you know that. I also hope you realize this is the most difficult thing I have ever done, just as I know hearing it is equally devastating to you."

Ellery couldn't believe her wonderful, loving father was capable of such deceit. "I can't understand how you let me live a lie all these years thinking my mother died and that you were my father. Now, I find out that neither of you were my parents."

"That is not completely true. Claudia was your birth mother. Have no doubt about that.

"I made a vow to your mother before she died. She pleaded with me until I promised that I would raise you as my own; that I would never tell you the truth."

"You had no right—"

"Believe me, I have regretted that promise since the day I made it. The only thing worse than not telling you the truth was living with the guilt of it all these years. There were so many times I came close to telling you, but once you were older, I was afraid the truth of my not being blood kin would cause you to turn away from me. I couldn't bear the thought of losing you . . . you were my life."

She ignored that because she did not want to deal with it right now. She wanted answers. "Then who is my father? Where I was born? Where is my father now?" She gave him a confused look. "Why would you do such a thing? I could understand you holding back when I was young, but you should have told me when I grew up!"

"I know. I'm guilty as charged. I made a vow to my dying wife without thinking about the hurt it would cause you. If you will bear with me I will try to explain. All right?"

She was too overwhelmed to do much more than nod. Although her heart pounded furiously, she was so hurt and shocked she was afraid she might say something she would regret. She tried to focus on the fact that he was dying, and if he died with her at the peak of anger, she would have a difficult time forgiving herself. She wanted the truth, so she sat down and forced herself to listen to what he had to say.

"You were born before your mother and I met. The

first time I saw her was in Dallas. She was working at a bank and I was finishing my last year of dental school at Baylor. She didn't take a shine to me at first, but I was persistent. She was the prettiest thing I had ever seen, and it didn't matter one whit to me that she had borne a child out of wedlock."

So, now I'm illegitimate on top of everything else, Ellery thought. Lovely . . . Just how much worse can this get? My life has become a freaking soap opera.

"Times were different back then," he continued, "and a woman who had a child outside of marriage was a blight to the family, an outcast. This affected your mother more than I realized at the time. I asked her to marry me, and afterward we moved here. I knew Claudia loved me just as I knew she adored you, but there was something in her past that tormented her; something she called the 'sin she could not speak about.' She kept that secret to herself, locked away in her own dark dungeon. In the end, she told me about it shortly before she died. Then she asked me to promise I would never tell you. I kept my promise, but I can't die without telling you the truth."

He paused and Ellery closed her eyes for a moment. Grief filled the room and came to sit down beside her. Tears ran down her face. Her heart felt ripped apart with sadness and pain, for her mother, for Sam, and for herself. She thought of the Scripture in Ecclesiastes: "In much wisdom is much grief: and he that increaseth knowledge increaseth sorrow."

She was wondering how things could get much worse when Sam spoke. "There's a small chest in my closet filled with a few things that belonged to your mother. It's locked, but you will find the key in the top drawer of my bureau. Tied to the key is a bit of yarn. I want you to bring it in here."

Ellery went to the drawer and found the key. She opened the closet and carried the chest back to Sam's bed, where she sat down with the chest in her lap.

"Go ahead . . . open it," Sam said.

The first thing she saw were two sets of baby shoes, two white crocheted baby gowns, and two matching bonnets. She picked up one of the bonnets, awed that she could have ever been so small.

She replaced the bonnet, unable to stop smiling, for she saw her mother as a bit eccentric for buying two of everything—not that Ellery hadn't done the same thing occasionally.

As she sorted through the contents, her hands were shaking. It was the closest to her mother she had ever come. She prayed these relics would tell her something about her history. "It's strange that she has two of everything," she said, noticing the expression on Sam's face—an expression of both anguish and expectation.

"You are a twin, Ellery."

"What? Oh, my God! Surely this isn't true." But when she looked at Sam's face, she saw the truth in his eyes. She shook her head. It was too much. Her life was suddenly turned upside down and within a few short minutes she had gone from being Sam's daughter, to an illegitimate child he adopted, only to learn a moment later that she was a twin.

"Ellery . . ."

"No . . . this is too much." Shock, then disbelief; the

words jammed in her throat. She felt as if she had suddenly been sucked into the whirling vortex of a tornado that sent flashes of lightning shooting through her skull. She was numbed to the point that her entire brain felt detached, as if to protect her from the shattering pain tearing at her senses.

It can't be true. She wanted to scream. *It can't be true . . .*

Before she could say anything, Sam spoke with a voice that sounded as broken as she knew his spirit must be at this moment. "They say the body has an infinite capacity for grief, and yet I find I only have such a capacity for remorse. There are, I know, no words that I can utter to compensate for the anger, anguish, and suffering you must be feeling at this moment. I can see it on your face. I wish to God I hadn't kept this from you. If I could only change what I have done."

Her mind was scrambled like eggs and all she felt right now was deep, searing pain. Yes, there were questions but she could not ask them now because she no longer knew who she was. She was an imposter; a fake; a person with no past; a nameless void.

Her mother had never been more than a fleeting shadow, a figment in a child's lonely mind, a smiling face that looked out at her from an old photograph. But now the word "mother" had a different connotation. She was a visitor who came calling, and left nothing behind save a bequest of sorrow and a keepsake of hurt.

"Is my sister alive?"

"I don't know if she is still alive, but she was alive when you were separated."

"What is her name?"

"Claudia named you Laura Ellery and your sister was Mary Ellen."

"And you don't know anything about what happened to her?"

"As I said, your mother didn't like to talk about it. All she said was 'I took one and the father took the other one.'"

A sharp, stabbing pain lodged in her heart. "The father? You mean my biological father took my sister and my mother took me . . . so we were split between our birth parents— Illegitimate and separated at birth?"

Sick as he was, Sam did manage a little humor. "You aren't illegitimate. Your birth parents just didn't marry."

It was good to laugh and when they stopped it was easier to talk about Sam's stunning revelations. "Why didn't they marry?"

"He was already married."

"Oh, this is too much! It's beginning to sound like something from *Days of Our Lives* or *Macbeth*." She thought about her next question. "If he was married, why did he want one of us? Didn't he have other children?"

"Claudia said they couldn't have children."

"Why did my father take only one twin? I can't believe neither he nor my mother wanted to keep both of us."

"Oh, Claudia wanted both of you and losing one is what killed her. All she ever said when I asked that same question was, 'He was a wealthy man, a banker, and he had lots of money and fancy lawyers. I was young. I didn't know any better when he said if I tried to keep both babies he would get his lawyers and he would take both twins from me. I knew he would do it, and I couldn't bear to lose them both.' I asked her how she decided which twin to keep and she said, 'Mary Ellen started crying the day he came to take one of them, so I told the nurse to take the one that cried.' "

It was almost too much . . . to think it came down to choosing a child by whether she cried or not. Ellery suddenly felt drained, mentally exhausted. She realized at this point that she couldn't talk about this anymore. It was as if all her psychological wiring had run amok and blown out a fuse.

"Where was I born?"

"In the Edna Gladney Home in Fort Worth."

"Texas," she said. "Was my mother from Fort Worth?"

"No, she was from a little town near Austin called Agarita Springs."

"Spanish," she said.

"Yes, agarita is a native shrub common to the area."

"Do you think my sister might live there?"

"Anything is possible, although I did try to locate her a year or so after your mother died, just to have the information for you when you were old enough to know the truth. But I never could find out what happened to her. I was informed the Edna Gladney Home allows the birth parent to choose the type of postplacement relationship between the birth parent and child. Your mother chose 'no contact.' I was informed that the family who adopted your sister—your birth father and his wife—requested the same thing."

"I was only three when Mother died. You could have married again. Why didn't you? Why did you keep me?"

"I kept you because you were my daughter, and the

thought of anything else never entered my mind." He glanced at the Bible sitting on the table beside him. "Hand that to me, will you?"

She gave the Bible to him and watched silently as he opened it and removed an envelope from the Book of Genesis. He held it out to her. "I intended for you to find this after I was gone, but perhaps it's better for you to read it now."

She opened the envelope and began to read.

Dear Ellery,

I have decided never to tell you I was not your father only because I know in my heart that I am your real father, if not your biological one. I adopted you when Claudia and I married and you were the daughter of my heart.

Understanding you as I do, and knowing how you have a nose for investigating, I believe you won't waste any time trying to locate Mary Ellen yourself. Although you were probably too young to remember, it was always apparent that you had some inkling that you were a twin, or at least separated from a sibling. I don't know how you could have known about your twin sister, and to think you did leaves me with an eerie feeling. When you were quite small, you would often ask me where your sister went. For years, whenever you drew a picture of our family, or yourself, there were always two of you. Later, when you stopped drawing two, you would say, "There used to be two of me, but now there is only one."

Claudia never got over the burden of separating you and your sister. Her grief and the guilt she felt are what eventually destroyed her. She always said you knew, and I think that added to her grief. From the very beginning, she would wake up at night and say she could hear another baby crying. Gradually she began to believe there were two of you here with us instead of one.

I know you will follow your heart, and if it is to be, you will find your sister. I hope, as well, that you can find it in that same heart to forgive me for waiting so long to tell you.

Your loving father,
Sam

With her hands shaking, Ellery continued to stare down at the words in her father's shaky scrawl. She folded the note and placed it back in the envelope. Tears rose from deep within her and fell, one after the other.

"There used to be two of me, but now there is only one" . . .

When she looked at her father she saw the apprehension on his face. She thought of the man who had raised her and the life he could have had with someone else—a life he abandoned to fulfill his promise to her mother. She leaned over and gave him a kiss. "I could not love you more if you were my birth father."

Later that evening when she was back home, she thought about everything that had happened that day. She had a twin. She was illegitimate. Her biological father had never wanted to know her. Her own mother had betrayed her. The man she loved and adored as her real father had betrayed her as well.

She was overwhelmed by it all. Dear Lord, she thought, I'll need hip waders to make my way through all of this.

There was something tragic about human sacrifice no matter what the form. She knew it was time to release all the pent-up emotion she had been holding back because she didn't want to upset her father. When she cried, there were so many things that kept coming into her mind. She cried for herself and the mother she never really knew, and the tragic way she had died; for the father who selfishly split his twin daughters apart, denying them the right to know each other. She cried for the twin sister who had not existed for her until a few hours ago. She cried for the loss of that special human relationship they'd come into the world sharing—the unexplainable bond of closeness between those who are twinborn. Lastly, she cried for her father and the hurt Sam had inadvertently caused her by keeping her identity a secret, and the burden he must have carried all these years because of it.

By the time she was all cried out, she felt better. She also had several more questions she wanted to ask him. She picked up the phone to call him, but when she glanced at her watch it was later than she thought. Ten-thirty, and past the time her father went to sleep. Tomorrow would be soon enough for answers.

Ellery never got the answers to her questions because that night Sam O'Brien died in his sleep.

Four

A MONTH AFTER SAM'S FUNERAL, Ellery sat on the front steps of a big clapboard house that stood on a shady, tree-lined street in Chevy Chase, Maryland—the home where all of her memories of childhood resided, her yellow Lab, Bertha, stretched out at her feet. Was she really going to sell the house? A quick glance at the SOLD sign in the yard made her realize that another part of her life would soon be gone.

Since learning she had a twin sister, decision-making had been difficult for her. Inside, she felt an aching dullness in a place that did not exist, just as an amputee feels pain where a limb used to be. Something was missing, yet a part of it still lingered. The only way to deal with it was to find her sister. It sounded simple enough, but in truth, Ellery didn't know where to begin. So many questions remained unanswered. If only Sam were still alive to fill in the gaping holes.

All her life she was as sure of Sam as she was of the North Star. His was the shadow that followed her through life, reminding her of all that she was and everything she had been taught. When he died, the stars seemed to shine a little less brightly.

It was hard to lose such a father. The fact that he wasn't her birth father made him all the more remarkable. That one fact made his life and his devotion to her shine with greater significance. It was the first time she really looked at him in adult terms. By keeping her mother's secret, he had done what he thought best. In a bittersweet moment, she remembered how he always said, "All my mistakes are well thought out."

Later that evening, after she arrived back at her house in the District, she was thinking about her decision to go to Texas. She knew life was a chain of events where each present moment was connected to some future one. When she'd made up her mind to go to Texas, she'd known it was nothing more than a beginning, a place to start. She might learn what she wanted to know, or the trip could be a total waste. For now it was full of possibility; just as every raindrop was a potential puddle. Only time would tell at which point hope and reality would meet.

She would find her sister. Then she would learn the truth about her mother's past. She was not daunted in the least. She had faced tougher assignments than this her first year as a reporter, when she'd managed to ferret her way into numerous stories.

She'd asked for a leave of absence from her job and allowed Bill Gaither, her executive producer, to persuade her to do a documentary about her search for her sister. She thought about the house she'd rented from a photo—or rather a photo and a few encouraging words from a zealous real estate agent in Agarita Springs.

"Rental property in Agarita Springs is as scarce as hen's teeth, and a house of this magnitude . . . well, I am sure I don't need to tell you that they don't come available too often."

"Could you send me a few photos of the house, inside and out?"

"I'll send them, but I can't guarantee the house will still be available by the time they get there."

Ellery ended up faxing the agent a FedEx airbill so she could send the house pictures overnight. When they arrived the next morning, she took one look at the white clapboard house with its wraparound porch and was enchanted.

Even her neighbor Merrily liked it. "Reminds me of houses in Alabama," she said.

Ellery laughed. "I knew you would say that."

Most charming of all was the conservatory with its tangle of grapevines growing up over the door. That's what sent her to the phone in a great rush to tell the real estate agent she would take it.

"I think you will be very pleased and quite comfortable there. It's a lovely house. It's been completely redone with new paint and carpet. My only concern is that it might be too large for just one person."

"I have quite a large house now, so I'm accustomed to having a lot of space. Do you have any idea how old it is?"

"It was built around the end of the war."

"Oh, in the mid-forties," Ellery said.

"Wrong war," the realtor replied. "I place it as having been built between 1865 and '70."

A smile settled over Ellery's face when she remembered telling Merrily about "the war."

Merrily laughed. "Honey, any self-respecting Southerner would know that 'the *wahr*' was the Civil War. Now, don't you go poking fun at that either when you get to Texas. You've gotta do your mama proud, you hear?" Merrily looked at the photo again. "You know, I swear I saw this house in a Bette Midler movie . . . The one about the three sisters who were witches . . . *Hocus Pocus*! That was it."

A shudder passed through Ellery and she said, "Gee, thanks. Now I have to worry about living in a haunted house." She studied the photos again. "How could you say such a thing about such a sweet old house?"

"How do you know it's sweet?" Merrily replied.

Ellery was still studying the picture of the house when she felt another chill. "I can tell."

"From a little three-by-five?"

"That, and a feeling I have. I don't know why, but already I feel attached to it—almost like I've been there before. I'd like to look into its history."

Even now, she could see Merrily shiver as she said, "Well, that gives me the willies. It looks to me like it was built by someone who cured colds with cobweb tea, and grew man-eating plants in the garden. Don't they have any *new* houses for rent?"

"I don't know, I didn't think to ask. Besides, this is exactly what I wanted . . . a house that's been lived in."

Ellery smiled to herself as she visualized the sweet, big

old house. In three days she'd begin her trip to Texas, right after she signed the papers on Sam's house.

She was going to Agarita Springs to find Mary Ellen and then she would begin to put the missing pieces of her life back together. She found it unbelievable how promising the world looks once you decide to have what you want. Otherwise, why would she feel as if she'd fallen into a snowdrift in the Italian Alps, and a Saint Bernard had suddenly appeared with a keg of brandy around its neck?

She leaned down and scratched Bertha's head, thinking about all the times she'd yearned for a brother or sister, literally begging her father to adopt one. She wondered if perhaps unconsciously she'd needed to heal the deep wound left from the experience of starting life as a twin and growing up alone. Uncanny is what she called it now, when she thought back on the interest, the fascination, she'd always had for twins—almost to the point of obsession. She remembered something she'd read about twins. Was there truly an impact on a lone twin separated at birth? Was the bonding of twins so profound even before birth that if separated, they sensed the loss for the rest of their lives?

She took a deep breath, as if clearing her lungs would somehow have the same effect upon her brain. She felt completely drained. Only an eerie sensation of some sort of loss for her twin remained. Mary Ellen, she thought, and felt a cold shiver touch her, as if a sudden chill swept over the room.

Every doll she had ever owned she'd named Mary Ellen.

Five

AGARITA SPRINGS WAS built on the old railroad grid system with streets running north and south, or east and west. It seemed to be a town where the influences of German settlers and the Anglo-Saxons came together.

Most of the buildings still retained the tradition of its German and Bohemian founders, while a collection of fine, old homes, in the more graceful and timeworn tradition of the Southern plantation house, settled in comfortably among them.

In the center of town, a lovely park took up an entire city block. The fountain in the center was outlined with flower beds and shaded by huge live oak trees. An old water tower, its sign proclaiming it was built in 1881, still stood on one corner of the block, while on the other stood a small brass cannon that bore a plaque claiming it was used during the fight for Texas independence.

It was a strange feeling to be in the town where her mother had spent most of her life. This was where Ellery and her sister had been conceived, and where she hoped

Mary Ellen resided still. She wondered if anyone would notice the resemblance between herself and Mary Ellen, although she was not expecting it to happen. Too many things other than genetics could influence the physical characteristics of twins. After hours on the Internet, she was some sort of an expert on the subject now. That caused her to recall those first awkward attempts at Internet research, when she was overwhelmed with so much data on twins: monozygotic twins, dizygotic twins, mirror-image twins . . . even the Minnesota Twins.

But disappointingly, she'd found little information about twins separated at birth.

She was curious about the uncanny things that she read twins separated at birth often had in common—things each of them had no way of knowing about the other. What would their common peculiarities be? Did Ellen hold a job in communications? Did she harbor a fondness for chocolate-covered raisins and Jordan almonds? Was her favorite color green? Did she drink Diet Coke? Had all of her cars been black? Did she love big dogs, seaside vacations, and Johnny Depp? Was she still single? Unlimited possibilities played on in her head, and her excitement increased in direct proportion to her escalating heartbeat. She was filled with anticipation, and thinking about the unknown that awaited her was like a free fall—exhilarating and terrifying at the same time.

There were doubts and misgivings as well. What if she never found Mary Ellen; what if her twin sister did not want to be found? Perhaps she didn't know she was illegitimate or a twin and didn't want to know. What if they had nothing in common, or hated each other on sight?

Still, she refused to feel downhearted now that she was here, where it all began, at the point where the past and future intersect, the place where the answers had lain hidden for too many years.

She noticed a 7-Eleven just ahead. It would be a good place to stop for a cold drink and to get directions, in spite of having a map and directions the realtor had sent. Ellery had never been very good at reading maps or following directions. Her friends used to say she couldn't find her way down a straight hall with no doors.

She rolled the windows down for Bertha and hoped neither her khaki shorts nor her white sleeveless shirt was too wrinkled. She glanced in the mirror, thought about pulling her hair back, then decided against it. She did run her fingers through it and reminded herself it was only a convenience store. She wasn't going to see anyone who cared what she looked like.

There were only five or six people inside the store when Ellery entered. Two toddlers were trying to make a decision over ice-cream bars, while their father was pouring enough sugar in a cup of coffee to turn it to syrup. She continued on, to the back of the store, where she took a Diet Coke out of the case. She arrived at the register at about the same time three teenagers turned to leave.

Ellery put her Coke down and noticed the dark-haired girl behind the counter who was staring at her. "Are you Sharon Stone?"

Ellery smiled. "No, I'm not."

"You sure do look like Sharon Stone. Has anyone ever told you that?"

"Yes, they have."

The girl rang up the Coke.

Ellery saw a rack of newspapers and she picked up a copy of the *Austin American Statesman* and the *Agarita Springs Register*. She placed them next to the Coke and handed the girl five dollars.

The girl still didn't look too convinced that Ellery wasn't Sharon Stone. "Will there be anything else?"

"Yes, could you give me directions to Live Oak Street?"

"Oh, sure! It's not far from here," she said. "When you leave the store, make a left onto Main Street. Go down to the third light. That's Live Oak. You have to make a right because Live Oak begins right there. If you turn left, you'll end up in the parking lot of the First Baptist Church."

Ellery paid for her Coke. "Three lights . . . then turn right."

"Yeah, you can't miss it. You'll see the First Baptist Church before you get there. They've got a tall, white steeple with a bell."

Ellery flashed her a smile. "Thanks again."

A big man with a shaggy red beard came up to the counter, a six-pack of beer in each hand. He put the beer on the counter. When Ellery saw the beer, she was reminded she needed to buy a few things. "Could you tell me where I might find a grocery store?"

"We have groceries here," the girl said, and handed Ellery her change.

A middle-aged woman put a carton of milk down next to the man's six-packs. "She means a big grocery store." The woman turned to Ellery. "For a little town, we've got quite a few choices. There's B and B . . . No, that's too small, and Garcia's sells mostly Latino foods. Agarita Springs Food and Gas . . ." She paused and gave Ellery the once-over. "Forget that. You don't look like the type to shop there. Where do you hail from?"

"Hail? Oh, I'm from Washington, D.C." She was suddenly aware of the drop in noise, and the curious gazes of several patrons.

Red must have been anxious to pay for his beer and leave because he said, "H.E.B. You should try H.E.B."

"Yes, that's a good choice," the woman said. "Don't know why I didn't think of it. It's about eight blocks from here. When you leave here, make a right onto Main Street, and keep going until you come to Church Street. H.E.B. is on the corner. You can't miss it. There's a big sign next to the street."

Ellery thanked them and returned to her car. When she opened the door and tossed the newspapers on the passenger seat, she was hit in the face with Bertha's barking and a blast of hot air. She started the car and put the AC on high, but it didn't help, as only hot air was coming out the vents. She turned all of them toward her, popped the tab on the Diet Coke and took a long drink. She was trying to remember a time when she had been this hot and thirsty, and recalled the time she rode a camel in the Sahara on her way to an interview.

She put the can on the dash, so she could fasten her seat belt. She put the Land Cruiser in reverse, turned to look behind her when she remembered the Coke . . . but it was too late. The can went sliding off the dash. She was not certain about the order of things after that, because it all seemed to spin forward in a rapid blur. She remembered the Coke sliding, and heard herself say, "Oh no!" as she made a grab for it.

Somehow, her sudden movement caused her foot to slam against the gas pedal and the Land Cruiser shot in reverse.

All hell broke loose after that.

The wheels dug into the ground, screeching and throwing up a cloud of dirt, gravel, and microscopic dust. Everything seemed to happen at once . . . The Coke can flew off the dash and spilled icy soda all over her hot skin, and just about the time she got her foot on the brake, she heard a sickening crash followed by a jolt.

She threw the car into drive and pulled forward, forced to listen to the horrible crunching sound of metal scraping against metal. "Dear Lord above, please tell me I didn't hit someone on my first day in town!" She glanced heavenward and said, "I don't need this."

She put the car in park and glanced in her rearview mirror. Red had his baseball cap off and was scratching his head, shaking it slowly while he said something to one of the men in the small group that was fast growing into a rather large one.

She was greeted by an angry voice. "Where in the name of hell did you learn to drive?"

For only an instant, she had an inkling of what made a person a hit-and-run driver. Only her fingers moved as she tapped them against the steering wheel and repeated to herself, "I really, really don't need this." She would rather be shot at sunrise than step out and face the owner of that voice. There was also the matter of discovering what exactly she'd run into . . . through . . . or over.

Her feet felt like lead, but she managed to swing them out and down to the ground. She glanced at her dog. Bertha was lying in the back with her head between her paws. "Coward," Ellery said, while wishing she could join her.

She walked toward the group, noticing they were all men, and wished she had chosen something other than shorts to wear today. Time to think like a television personality, not a woman, she told herself.

It occurred to her that it would help her case a great deal if she had some small injury, some diversion like a bump on her head or a bloody nose. She put her hand to her head. No bump, no pain, and no blood.

And no excuse either.

Preoccupied with settling into her new home and finding her sister, she wasn't feeling very confrontational. She didn't feel like locking horns with a few of the locals who might possess more testosterone than brains. She supposed it was too much to ask that she be fortunate enough to encounter a preacher among the bystanders, just to temper things a bit.

"Boy, oh boy, would you look at that," one of the men was saying. "She sure did a bang-up job. Squashed it flatter than Ruth Ann Sudberry's rear end."

The men were standing in a semicircle, near the . . . She paused, uncertain what it had been, or what she should call it now, but when she saw the mangled ball of chrome and shiny red metal, she asked herself, Just what did I run over?

"Well, it just proves a motorcycle ain't no match for a Land Cruiser," one of the men said.

Ellery barely heard. She was too busy studying the heap, trying to visualize a motorcycle, but all she saw was a twisted pile of metal.

She scanned the group, looking for the owner of the motorcycle. The moment she saw the back of a slender man with dark brown hair, wearing a pair of jeans and a white dress shirt, she guessed he was the owner, since he was hunkered down over the remains of what had been his means of transportation. But he didn't look like the type to ride a motorcycle.

Horses looked more his speed.

However, this was Texas, and they did things differently here. "I'm terribly sorry about your—"

"It started out as a motorcycle," he said, without turning to look at her. As she approached him, she was distracted by something that glinted in the sun. She picked it up and realized it was a shiny chrome mirror. It had to come from the cycle, she guessed. Ironically, it didn't have a scratch.

He still had his back to her, and she paused just behind him. It was a bit awkward and left her feeling quite inept as she observed his tanned fingers moving over the metal. She couldn't imagine what he was looking for. She decided he must have bonded with this particular motorcycle, and was having a hard time disassociating himself from it.

"Was it your motorcycle?" she asked. No one bothered to answer her. Well, she wasn't going to feel guilty. Motorcycles were a dime a dozen. She would buy him another one—redder, shinier, and newer. She didn't understand why the men began to squat down beside him, to poke and prod at the pile of metal. She watched for a moment, then decided that dropping down on one's haunches and staring at the remains of some inert object must be some sort of male separation ritual around these parts.

"I was just thinking what a nice-looking bike that was, when the next thing I knew, it was a goner," Red said.

"Well, one thing's for certain," an older man said, "it's beyond repair now."

"Yeah," said a teenage boy, "it's not good for anything but scrap metal."

She was suspended in a moment of disbelief. Six grown men were gathered around the deformed remains of a wrecked motorcycle, speaking fondly and staring at it with sad regard. She had seen less emotion at a wake.

If that had been a group of women, they would have had the whole mess cleaned up by now, and be on their way to town to shop for a replacement.

"It looked to me like it was pretty new," one of the men said.

"It was new," the one in the white shirt and jeans said, and stood.

When he turned around, her first impression was of a young Clint Eastwood, with darker hair. He had that tall, lanky Eastwood build, exhibited the same silent, man-of-few-words demeanor, and his blue eyes were remarkably similar, squinting against the sun as he took in everything and said nothing.

His straw cowboy hat shaded his face. She had never

seen a man in a cowboy hat before and she found it much more impressive in real life than on television. She might have been impressed with his six-foot height and masculine good looks if he had given her a reason to be, but the look he gave her was anything but friendly. And that scowl looked to be permanently etched between those dark brows.

A cool breeze whispered over her hot skin, caressing her face in a way that left her feeling strange. Her legs were heavy and stonelike, as if her mind and body knew something, some reason to hold her here, a reason the rest of her did not understand. What she did understand was that this cowboy was not a happy camper and he did not try to hide it.

In spite of the intense heat, gooseflesh erupted along her arms, and she could feel the escalation of her own heartbeat. She felt trapped in a small square of time, unable to move forward, or go back to where she had been a moment ago. It was as if she were observing what was going on around her, and understood it, but she was not part of it. She was removed; an observer rather than a participant, unable to connect in this place that was as foreign to her as frozen Siberia.

"Look, I'm sorry about your motorcycle. I put my Coke on the dash, and when I backed up, it fell off. I tried to catch it. It spilled. I don't know how my foot hit the gas pedal."

A middle-aged man with kind brown eyes glanced at her in a sympathetic manner and said, "Go easy on her. She said it was an accident."

Her body tensed. *Go easy on her?* She bristled at that

and noticed Clint Eastwood did not look at her with kind eyes. "Listen, I said I was sorry and I am, but there isn't anything either of us can do about it now. There is no need to act as if I committed murder. It was not intentional," she said, emphasizing each word.

"Lady, when you find yourself in a hole, stop digging."

"I will buy you another motorcycle."

"That isn't the point," he said.

"I'm sorry, but I don't have time to get into a tangle over this." She began going through her purse. "I'll give you my insurance information." She found her insurance card and wrote the information on the back of her WMDC-TV business card. She handed it to him.

He took the card and shoved it into his shirt pocket without reading it.

She sighed, anxious to be away from here and feeling horribly conspicuous with her out-of-state license plates and the shorts she was wearing. "I will see that you are fully reimbursed."

"I'm sure you will, but that isn't the problem."

"Oh, of course! You don't have a way to get home." She tried to ignore the guffaws from all the onlookers. "I'll be glad to rent a car for you."

"I don't need a car, ma'am. I have five or six cars. What I need is this motorcycle, but you seem to have trouble understanding that. I bet you have to touch a fire to be sure it's hot."

She could feel her face turning red. "I think you are being difficult on purpose." That was a true statement. The way she figured it, he was holding her up for ridicule in front of all these men to pay her back for smashing his cycle. "I didn't run over your cycle on purpose. It was an accident. I've apologized. I've given you my insurance information. I've said I would see that the cycle was replaced. I've offered to rent you a car. Now, what else do you want me to do? Throw myself in front of a truck?"

"Disaster follows some people like a pet dog," he said, shaking his head. "Anyone would be a fool to get within ten blocks of you. And that includes truck drivers."

She put her hands on her hips and made eye contact. "So what does that make you for parking your motorcycle behind my car?"

One of the men slapped him on the shoulder. "She got you on that one, Clint."

Clint . . . she might have known. "This isn't a contest," she said, quelling any further comment. She decided to try one last time. "I'm trying to do the right thing here, but I don't seem to be having a lot of luck, so why don't you tell me what you want me to do?"

"I don't care what you do. It's a moot point since it's impossible to replace this motorcycle in time. So, why don't you get in your Land Cruiser and go wherever it was you were going, and I'll take care of things here."

"I'm sure my insurance company can get you a new one in a week or so."

He shook his head. "Lady, you persist in misunderstanding. A week or two will be too late. Next week is too late. I need it tomorrow. Now do you get it?"

"Yes, you want a new motorcycle tomorrow . . . but I don't know why. It isn't as if it's a matter of life or death."

"*That* depends on your point of view. The motorcycle

is a surprise for my nephew Brad. I was taking it over to my sister's for his birthday tomorrow."

"Does Margie know about it?" the man asked.

"Margie is the one buying it," Clint said. "I've been keeping it over at the feed store for her until his birthday."

"Maybe you should have held on to it a bit longer," the brown-eyed man said, and everyone laughed.

Another man offered his two cents' worth. "I can't figure Margie doing something as foolish as that. I always thought she was pretty levelheaded. Guess that just shows you never know what's going on in a woman's mind."

"Taking to the highway on one of these little contraptions is a good way to get yourself killed," someone said.

"It's a dirt bike," Clint said. "Brad's been told he can only ride it when he's working at the ranch."

"His birthday is tomorrow?" she asked.

"Yes, and you can't replace the motorcycle by then. It's impossible. Now do you comprende?"

She stared into his face and saw a rugged, solitary cowboy, articulate, educated, and looking quite like he could turn around and star in a Marlboro commercial without missing a beat. In the midst of it all, Ellery was beginning to feel like Scrooge for robbing all the joy from some unfortunate kid's Christmas. "I really feel terrible about this being a birthday present. Is there a motorcycle shop around here someplace? I'll be glad to buy you another one, right now."

"I'm sure you're accustomed to buying your way out of anything, but this one was a special order."

Of course it was . . . "Okay, how fast can I get another one?"

"This one took over six months."

"Oh." She could feel the intense pressure exerted by six pairs of eyes all focused on her. She was at a loss for something to say. Already, she had repeated "I'm sorry" so many times she was beginning to sound like a hung CD. "My name is Ellery O'Brien. And you are?"

"Clint Littleton."

She pulled out a notepad and a pen, and wrote down a number. "This is my telephone number, Mr. Littleton, in case you need to get in touch with me."

He glanced down at the piece of paper. His face registered surprise. "This is a local number. Are you visiting someone who lives here?"

"No, I've rented a house. I'm moving here."

"You're moving *here* . . . from Washington, D.C.?"

He spoke with such a tone of horror that she almost laughed. For a moment, she was tempted to tell him she was moving in next door to him. "Let's just say I'm trying it out for a while."

"Why?"

She was taken aback by his questions, which she found more than just a little out of line. "For personal reasons and I don't think that is any of your business."

"And I don't think Agarita Springs is the town for someone like you."

"I prefer to make my own decisions, thank you."

"I doubt you will like it here."

"Why would you think that?"

"I bet if you think real hard, you can come up with the answer yourself." He glanced at his watch. "I've got to go." He shoved the paper in his pocket. He turned to one of the men. "Carl, could you give me a ride back to the feed store so I can get my pickup?"

"Sure can. Do you need any help loading the motorcycle?"

"No, I'll send a couple of hands over to pick it up."

By this time Ellery was on her way back to the Land Cruiser, happy to see Bertha's head poking out the window.

A hand came around her and scratched Bertha's head. "What's her name?"

Ellery looked Clint Littleton in the eye. "Bertha," she said. She knew the look before he gave it to her. It was always like that, whenever she told someone her dog's name. She knew what he would say next: Where did you get a name like Bertha?

"Where did you get a name like Bertha?"

"I named her after Bertha von Suttner. And before you ask, she was the first woman to win the Nobel peace prize."

"Why her?"

"Because my dog is a yellow Lab and I wanted her to have a name that didn't sound like a blonde joke."

"Are you sensitive about blonde jokes?"

"Let's just say I've heard all the blonde jokes I care to hear in one lifetime."

She turned and was about to open the door, when a hand cut in front of her and opened the door.

"Allow me, ma'am."

She gave him a startled look.

"You seem surprised. Don't men open doors for ladies where you come from?"

"Yes, but they generally do it before they cut them down to size." She climbed into the Land Cruiser and turned the key in the ignition.

Six

Ellery put the motorcycle out of her mind and decided to forget the grocery store for now. She wanted to find her house, unpack, and take a bath.

She was heading down Main Street, following the directions she'd been given and counting streetlights. At the third one, she saw the sign for Live Oak Street. Across the street was the Baptist church. She wondered if this was the same Baptist church where her grandfather had been the minister.

When she made a right turn onto Live Oak, she was in another world. This was a street that belonged in *Southern Living*, or along the graceful banks of the Savannah River, shaded by live oaks, and scented with the heavy perfume of magnolias and lemon trees.

She thought the pace of life here had to be slow, and the living easy in these whitewashed houses draped with creeping vines. She could almost feel herself wrapped in the coolness of peaches-and-cream bed linens made of silk and taffeta; or sitting in the twilight of a summer evening on a veranda, sipping tea made with fresh mint and eating sponge cake topped with lemon curd. She didn't have time to let her imagination go any further, because she was at the end of the street.

She saw the address 619 Live Oak Street, and recognized the house from the photos the realtor had sent her. She considered herself fortunate to have found such a lovely house to rent.

Her thoughts were interrupted by an uncanny feeling that left her dumbfounded by the idea that somewhere or sometime she had seen this particular house before—something separate and different from the photo. With its gabled roof and the balcony on the second floor, the house seemed as familiar as her bedroom back home.

She knew it was absurd for she had never been to this town and therefore could not have seen the house. And yet for a moment she was wedged in a peculiar state of mind where one is teased with the memory of a previous experience that somehow had become intertwined with something she was seeing now—almost like a mental echo.

She pushed the feeling away. Of course she had never seen this house other than in the photo.

Made of native stone, with its white trim gleaming in the bright sunlight, the house looked as splendid as a wedding cake. It was quite a bit more than she expected, but perhaps that was because it looked much better now that the grounds had been cleaned up and the trim painted. It was a stately house, and tall—with a gabled roof, two stories, and an attic on the third floor. A yellow climbing rose clambered up the side of the house past the green shutters on the second floor, to inch its way along the balcony railing.

The moment she stepped through the front door, Bertha following close behind her, she had a strange feeling—the same peculiar feeling of familiarity she'd had outside, which was ridiculous. Yet it kept coming back. Like the slow trickle of a faucet, it came in small, annoying drips—nothing more than prickly reminders that made her shiver when she remembered that she had not seen any photos of the inside of the house or its furnishings.

She blamed it on stress. She knew conscious, rational minds teetered on top of the complex unconscious, which caused strange and bizarre thoughts in everyone at one time or another.

The furnishings were as delightful and quaint as the house itself. Every room was saturated in light and subdued color—inviting as a warm smile and

Familiar . . .

This is impossible, she thought, yet her head was in a whirl. There had to be some sort of explanation. There had to be, because if there wasn't, she was losing her grip on reality. This eerie feeling has got to stop, she told herself. I'm starting to think like Stephen King.

The kitchen was decidedly her favorite room in the house, simply because it opened magically onto the conservatory through French doors at one end. Happy, and full of light, it looked lived in rather than used. It was also where she was struck with another sense of déjà vu, for she had a strong feeling that those who had lived here before her had found this room to be the very heart of the house.

The creamy color scheme complemented the dark floors and trussed, high ceiling. She ran her hand along the big table that ran almost the entire length of the kitchen.

She could easily visualize the Christmases that had seen a goose or turkey trussed here, or Easter eggs colored, and the floured hands of a woman rolling out dough and canning peaches.

She examined the moldings and hardware, the glass in the cabinet doors that rippled as only handblown glass will do. Inside the cabinets, she found the dishes to be as quaint and full of charm as the kitchen.

She toured the rest of the house and found every room as inviting as a warm smile, and familiar. She sat down in the family room, in a buttery yellow wing chair, bursting with green leaves and blooms of red and white roses. She propped her feet on the ottoman and leaned back with a satisfied sigh as she looked about the room.

All she needed were her slippers and a newspaper.

Bertha padded over and poked her nose against Ellery's hand. "Okay," she said, patting Bertha on the head. "All I need are my slippers, a paper, and a big yellow dog."

Carrying in all the luggage was a chore that she finished late in the afternoon. It was only when her stomach growled that she realized she hadn't eaten since her coffee and granola bar at six A.M.

She changed into a loose-fitting beige linen dress with a long hemline. She dabbed on light pink lipstick, and rummaged through a box marked SHOES, until she found the Ralph Lauren sandals she liked to wear with the dress.

She hopped across the room on one foot and then the other, as she slipped on each sandal. As she left her bedroom, she grabbed her purse off the doorknob then went downstairs to the kitchen.

Ellery remembered the directions to the store and followed them to the letter, only the store wasn't where it was supposed to be. It was beyond her how anyone could lose their way in a one-horse town.

She stopped at a gas station and asked for directions. "Could you tell me how to get to H.E.B?"

The man looked at her oddly and said, "Yes, ma'am, it's right next door."

In his office at the feed store, Clint Littleton was on the phone explaining to his sister Margie how she wasn't going to be giving her son, Brad, a motorcycle for his birthday.

"What are you talking about?"

He barely finished saying, "A lady ran over it at the 7-Eleven," before Margie cried, "What do you mean someone ran over it?"

"I'll explain it to you when I see you tomorrow."

"What am I going to tell Brad? Sorry, but you get nothing from your mother on your birthday?"

"I'll explain to Brad what happened. You just take care of the party."

"Okay. Are you going to bring Mama?"

"Yes."

"Don't be late, you hear?"

On his way home, he stopped at the convenience store to put gas in his pickup. When he went inside to pay, the first thing he saw was Ms. Motorcycle Smasher standing at the checkout.

"I didn't expect to see you here," she said.

"Obviously, or you would have gone somewhere else for gas."

"I don't run from people or confrontations, Mr. Littleton."

"No, I suppose not. Head-on would be more to your liking." He put a twenty-dollar bill on the counter. "How are things today, Joe?"

"A little slow," Joe said. "Will you be needing anything else, Clint?"

"No, that'll just about do it, I guess."

"I heard that motorcycle you'd been keeping for Brad's birthday got smashed. Is that true?"

"Unfortunately, yes."

Joe was shaking his head. "Sure is a shame. I remember Brad wanting a motorcycle way back when. How'd that happen?"

Clint moved his gaze from Joe to Ellery. He saw the look of regret mixed with one of guilt on her face, but she was a television performer and probably had more contrite expressions than he had cows. Still, it wasn't part of his code to be ornery to a woman—but this one was an exception. He was about to change the subject, when she spoke up.

"I'm afraid I'm the villain in this scenario," she said. "I ran over it."

Joe looked a little embarrassed. "Well, I'm sure it wasn't intentional."

Ellery ignored that and turned to Clint. "Did you have time to check the Internet for another motorcycle?"

Clint had seen mosquitoes with less persistence. He started to tell her she still didn't get it, but she started up again and he didn't get the chance.

"I know you said there was no way to replace it, but I've never been one to give up easily."

Now why didn't he have any trouble believing that? This had to be the pushiest female he had ever seen, bar none. "I haven't tried the Internet for two reasons: I haven't had time and I know another one is not available. It was a limited edition special order. They sold out almost immediately. My nephew always wanted one of those but now he'll have to choose another model."

"Who was the manufacturer?"

"I'm not trying to be rude, but it's pretty apparent you're still stuck a few dozen sentences back. So let me see if I can put it in terms a first-grader would understand. They're all gone. Out of stock. Sold. There are no more of them. Nada. Nil. Zip. Zero. Zilch."

"Do you have a problem with telling me the name of the manufacturer?"

He shook his head. "It was a Suzuki, but you can't get another one, no matter who you are, or what you think you can do. Out of stock means out of stock . . ." He just gave up at that point. He was finished with trying to get through to this woman.

"I know it's a bad habit of mine, but I never take no for

an answer. There is always another way to go about things. I believe in exhausting all avenues, Mr. Littleton."

"Well, if it's exhausted you want, that's where I am right about now." He did not like the way she looked at him, as if she could see into his head and read what he was thinking.

"Are you a Republican, Mr. Littleton?"

He glanced at Joe, who was holding back a laugh. What in the hell has my political affiliation got to do with anything? he wondered. Clint nooded. "Yes, ma'am, I am," he answered, trying to figure out just where she was going with this.

"I believe it was Richard Nixon who said, 'A man is not finished when he's defeated. He's finished when he quits.' I never quit."

"And if I said I was a Democrat, what would you have said then?"

"I would have given you Hubert Humphrey. 'The heroes of the world are not those who withdraw . . . but those who stand the heat of battle.' "

This had to be the most hardheaded, stubborn woman God ever created, and he sure wanted to tell her that, but he didn't. Normally, Clint didn't belabor a point with anyone, especially a woman. He made an exception in this case. "This is the last thing I am going to say on this subject. If you want to pursue this, you have my blessing. You are welcome to try the Internet, the telephone, or carrier pigeons, if that suits you." He reached into his pocket and withdrew his card. "Here's my card. Call me when you find it, and have a nice life."

She took the card, and handed it back to him. "Would you mind writing your sister's name, address, and phone number on the back, so I'll know where to send the motorcycle . . . in case I find one?"

Clint wrote the information down and offered her the card.

"I almost forgot. Write the model number on there too."

There were people in this world that let their will override their intelligence, and he was up against one of them right now. He wrote down "red 1500LC, Special Edition Suzuki" and handed the card back to her. "Good luck with your search."

"I don't believe in luck, Mr. Littleton. I believe in hard work. And don't look so skeptical. You might be in for a big surprise."

He remembered she had given him a business card from a Washington, D.C., television station. "Are you a television reporter?"

"No, I coanchor the morning news."

He watched her walk away, while he thought about all the reasons why he had never met a reporter he liked. When he worked for the commissioner of agriculture he'd been around them a lot, and he'd never enjoyed a moment of their company. He knew their wiles and their dishonest maneuvers, and no one could convince him they didn't know that ninety percent of what they did was morally indefensible. They wrote more fiction than novelists; they betrayed confidences and wrote things you asked them not to print without remorse; they were masters of ruthless deception, and to disguise their intent and prove their trustworthiness, they preyed upon the ignorance and pride of others.

And they never knew when to quit.

He realized he was still watching her. She had her faults, but looks wasn't one of them. And she had great legs.

Seven

AFTER SHE FINISHED her first breakfast in her sweet, old house, Ellery dialed the number for the First Baptist Church.

"Reverend Sterling's office," a cheerful voice said.

"Hi, this is Ellery O'Brien. I'm searching for members of my family. I wonder if you could tell me if you had a minister at one time by the name of Claude Eubanks. It would have been about thirty years ago."

"If you don't mind holding, I can find out for you."

"Thank you. I'll wait."

The woman was not gone long. "Yes, we did. Reverend Eubanks was the minister here for over twenty years."

"Do you have any more information on him?"

"Oh, I'm certain we do. We have the records going back as far as 1850."

"Would you mind if I came by to look at what you have?"

"No, that would be fine. I'll be happy to help you. How are you related to him?"

"He was my grandfather."

"Oh, well, you just come by anytime. Just ask for me—Diane Broadhurst. I'm Reverend Sterling's secretary—he's the minister now."

"Thank you, Diane. I'll try to drop by before noon."

Diane Broadhurst turned out to be the archangel of information. She not only had a fat file on the Reverend Claude Aaron Eubanks, but copies of old church newsletters and a Book of Church History, all of which gave information on his family. An hour later, Ellery had several pages of notes, and reproductions of dozens of pages where she hoped to find something useful. But the most important thing she had was the name of her mother's sister, Margaret Ledbetter.

"Margaret Ledbetter's daughter, Hazel, goes to church here," Diane said. "If you hold on a minute, I can give you her address and Margaret's too, while I'm at it." She typed a few strokes on her computer keyboard and said, "Here it is . . . 1313 Thirteenth Street." She shuddered and rubbed her arms as if chilled. "Terrible street address, isn't it? Too many thirteens to suit my blood. Here, I'll print it for you."

Ellery waited while the sheet printed and Diane handed it to her.

"I appreciate your help very much."

"I should mention that you won't be able to call Hazel. She's on a month-long tour of Europe with some ladies from her Sunday school class. They've been raising money for the trip this past year . . . pie sales, babysitting, tutoring, that sort of thing. Such a sweet bunch of ladies . . . all of them old maids, widows, or divorced, but good as the day is long. You just missed them, since they left a week ago."

Ellery thanked her again and headed for home. With each block that passed, her excitement mounted. Once back home, she located Margaret Ledbetter's telephone number on the sheet Diane gave her. Her hands began shaking the moment she started dialing Margaret's number.

A female voice with a Spanish accent answered the phone. "Ledbetter residence."

"I'd like to speak to Margaret Ledbetter, please."

"Mrs. Ledbetter does not speak to strangers."

"I'm her niece, Ellery O'Brien."

Sigh . . . "Just a minute."

After a short wait she heard the sound of approaching footfalls, and a clanking noise when the phone was picked up. "She said you are mistaken. She does not have a niece named Ellery O'Brien."

"Yes she does. Tell her I'm one of the twin daughters of her sister Claudia Eubanks."

A loud sigh . . . "Just a minute."

The same routine played again, and after the footfalls the phone was picked up. "She does not wish to speak with you, no matter who you say you are."

"Then you tell her I will talk to the editor at the newspaper. I'm sure he would be interested in running a story about my connection to Margaret and her family, and the rude reception I have received."

This time there was no sigh, just a few mumbled words in Spanish. Ellery smiled, imagining what names she had just been called. This time the woman did not say "just a minute," but Ellery heard the clunk of the phone when she laid it down.

She was back quickly this time. "She said you may come over at four o'clock, and you should bring proof of who you are. And don't be late."

"Tell her thank you. I'll be there at four." She was speaking to a dial tone.

It was almost four o'clock when Ellery drove slowly down North Orchard Street, while she searched for the house number among some very nice homes. About the time she began to wonder if she had copied the address wrong, she saw it. The number 1610 almost leaped off the polished brass plaque. She drove around the corner to the side street, and parked behind a van with CEN-TEX POOL SERVICE written on the door. She sat in the car for a moment to give herself time to collect her thoughts and decide how she would approach her aunt, and the questions she would ask.

A wrought-iron gate enabled her to see into the backyard, where a man in a blue uniform was cleaning the pool. She got out of the car and walked up the curved flagstone walk that led to the front door. In the center of the door, an enormous brass knocker was engraved with the name Ledbetter.

When she pressed the doorbell, she heard the melodious ringing of St. Michael's chimes. A small Hispanic woman in a white uniform opened the door. "Yes?"

"Hi, I'm Ellery O'Brien. I spoke to you earlier and Ms. Ledbetter told me to come at four."

"Just a moment, señora," she said, and closed the door. Ellery wondered if she was going to be left standing there until she petrified, when she heard a dry, rasping scrape, as if a window were being opened.

Above her, she heard the sound of a woman's severe voice. "I don't know you and we are not related. You have obviously confused me with someone else."

Ellery took a step back and almost fell over an excessively red bougainvillea before she craned her neck and slowly searched the façade of the house. Through an open window, almost indiscernible in shadows, she saw a figure in somber dress, indistinct against the flat, deep brown of the dusky interior.

She lifted her hand to block the sun's glare, hoping it would give clarity to the poorly defined face. She could see the woman's gray hair outlining a thin face that showed traces of lost beauty. She looked anything but friendly. Oh great, Ellery thought. I'm going to interview Mrs. DeWinter.

Ellery had defused eccentrics before and survived. She had tried nice. Now, she would try something different. "My name is Ellery O'Brien . . . Ellery Eubanks O'Brien. My mother, Claudia Eubanks, was your sister, but of course you know that. I wanted to speak to you about my mother's family."

"I think you should leave. I don't want to talk about your family, or your mother."

"All right, tell me about my twin sister, Mary Ellen. Where is she? How can I find her? Can you give me her last name?"

"No, I can't. You need to learn to leave things alone. Stop prying into other people's business. I haven't a thing to say to you."

As the acid-tipped words found their mark, Ellery felt suddenly short of breath, as if the walls were closing in around her. Why was her aunt turning her away?

"Where did you get my name? Who told you about me?" the woman asked, fairly spitting the words out.

Before Ellery could answer, she said, "Go away. I have no way of knowing who you really are."

Ellery held up the folder in her hand. "I have ample proof, if that's what you need—copies of my parents' birth and marriage certificates. My mother was the daughter of the Reverend Claude Eubanks and his wife, Lydia. She had two sisters, Margaret and Ruth Anne. There were two brothers, Bud and Walt."

The woman began to close the window, and Ellery shouted out a desperate plea. "Wait! Please! Tell me what happened to my sister!"

The window slammed shut and the woman retreated into the shadows of her house.

Ellery returned to her car, and sat there for a while, devastated. The rude reception had shaken her and left her feeling terribly alone. "What was the harm?" she asked herself. "Why wouldn't that hatchet-faced woman give me even a tiny thread that might change my life—past, present, and future?"

By the time she reached home and calmed down, she wondered if there was more to this than simply a crotchety old woman displaying her haughty indifference. Perhaps Margaret Ledbetter was someone with an antisocial personality disorder. Or was there another reason, which no one other than Margaret knew about?

*　　*　　*

Clint arrived at Margie's house with his mother. Before he could sit down, Margie handed him a FedEx envelope. "This is for you. It was delivered this morning."

He glanced at his name on the packet. "Why was it delivered here instead of the store?"

"I wondered the same thing," she said. "Well, aren't you going to open it and find out?"

Clint opened the envelope and found a notice of shipment for a red 1500LC Special Edition Suzuki that was scheduled for delivery to Bradley Cooper in two weeks. "Well, I'll be damned." He shook his head. "I'd sure like to know how in the hell she pulled this one off."

"Who? What did they pull off? What's going on, Clint? Are you in some kind of trouble?"

Clint laughed. "You don't know the half of it. You might say I ran into a little female trouble yesterday morning," he said, and went on to explain his run-in with the hard-nosed newswoman from Washington, D.C. "I'm sorry the motorcycle won't be here in time for the party."

"Brad will be so excited to see this delivery notice he won't give the delivery date a second thought. You're sure the cycle was damaged beyond repair?"

"Oh yes. It's a heap of twisted metal."

"I'm sorry she had to buy a new one."

"She looked like she could afford it."

"Well, it was still nice of her to do that rather than make us haggle with her insurance company. I hope you thanked her for her offer to replace it."

Clint didn't say anything.

That made his mother chime in to say, "Clint Littleton,

that kind of rude behavior isn't characteristic of you. I can't believe you were such an ingrate. How could you do such a thing?"

"If you met her, you'd understand."

"We weren't raised that way, Clint," Margie said. "Give me her phone number and I'll call and thank her for her kind generosity. Maybe she'd like to come to Brad's birthday party."

"She didn't look like the kind who would enjoy a small-town birthday party for a teenager."

"My, she must have rubbed you the wrong way. You aren't usually so negative about people."

"I don't normally run into relentlessly aggressive, stubborn, or domineering women like this ball-busting newswoman from Washington, D.C."

"Aren't you being a bit unfair?"

"She is a television newswoman in Washington, D.C., which means she's at the top of her league and loving every minute of it. I bet she only runs news items that show the woman always comes out on top."

Margie laughed. "You know what I think, Clint? I think that in making love or business, no woman wants to be on top all the time."

Eight

Her emotions entwined like ivy around a column, Ellery felt hopelessly at war with the powers of her mind. She awoke feeling disjointed and disembodied because of a strange dream she'd had during the night. For some time afterward, she sat on the side of the bed and struggled for the elusive meaning by stumbling through her emotional entanglements in an effort to separate the seen from the unseen.

What she saw in the dark of night was by daylight all tight and twisted knots that she feared she could never undo. What did it all mean? Who was the woman robed in blue mist that appeared to her—an image too far away for Ellery to make out her face? What did the sweet scent that accompanied her mean? Ellery felt strongly that the woman wanted to tell her something and then her image faded and she was left with her curiosity aroused by the inexplicable.

It was at this point that she became aware that the scent from her dream lingered in the room, only now there was an element of familiarity connected with it. A feeling of uneasiness enveloped her. Suddenly, her heart began to pound and it was a laborious effort for her to breathe. She sprang from her bed and rushed into the bathroom where she splashed cold water on her face. She dried her face, took a deep breath, and realized the faint smell of perfume followed . . . a perfume she recognized because it was the same one she wore, Ma Liberté by Jean Patou.

I'm losing it, she thought. I'm really losing it . . . freaked out by the scent of my own damn perfume. She tossed the towel on the counter and decided she needed to get out of the house for some fresh air and exercise.

At seven-thirty she was in her running duds and took off toward town, with her trusty dog Bertha loping along beside her, tongue lolling and looking equally happy to be out and about. She jogged past Ace hardware, where a rack of shovels, rakes, and the like was displayed by the door, then Pepperdine's Drugs & Sundries—a sign that brought a smile to her face. She wondered just how many people in town even remembered what sundries were, or cared, for that matter. The Greyhound Bus Station was quiet; Chic Boutique was dark inside; Harvey Lanier was unlocking the door to his law office and waved at a friend who drove by and honked.

She checked the time and saw her thirty minutes were up, so she circled the high school football stadium and headed back home. She was almost to the gravel drive that led up to her house when she noticed an old, pink T-bird, beautifully preserved, coming down the street.

It turned into the driveway next door, bumped over

the curb, and lurched to a stop. Ellery went around the side of the house and put Bertha into the backyard, then went back to the front walk. She was about to go up the steps when she heard a car door slam, then the sound of a female voice as it called out.

"Are you the new neighbor?"

Ellery stopped and turned around. The owner of that voice appeared to be in her fifties, but her red hair didn't show any gray. She wore a pair of white coveralls, and pink sunglasses were suspended by a chain around her neck.

The real clincher was the leather purse hanging from her shoulder. Ellery tried not to stare, but it was difficult, since she had never, ever seen a purse shaped like a cow-boy saddle—stirrups and all.

An expanse of lawn lay between their two houses and Ellery decided it would be the neighborly thing to at least meet her halfway.

"Hi," Ellery said when she stopped to watch the woman come toward her, a fat English bulldog slobbering along behind her.

"I'm glad I saw you run by." The woman had a round pleasant face that reminded Ellery of Judith Dench. She turned back to her dog. "Webster, go home."

Webster sat down and turned his head to one side, as if any intention of going home was not what he had in mind. She pointed toward the house. "Webster, get back in your own yard."

Webster snorted and lay down.

"I saw you put your dog in the backyard. I don't suppose you want another dog, do you?"

Ellery laughed and shook her head. "No, I don't, thank you. Webster's a cute dog though."

"I named him Webster after the dictionary, because words can't describe him." She was looking at the dog again. "I should have named him Worthless because that's what he is."

"I think Webster is a nice name. It seems to fit him," Ellery said, somewhat distracted by the way the woman was looking at her.

"I don't mean to stare, but you sure look familiar to me. Have we met somewhere before?"

"No, I don't think so, unless you've spent some time in Washington, D.C." Ellery's heart was already beating faster because she hoped the woman noticed some resemblance between her and her sister. Maybe her next words would point out the likeness.

"I've never been there, so I guess that takes care of that. I'm Shirley Van Meter, by the way."

Ellery's hopes sank and she was filled with such disappointment that she almost forgot to introduce herself. "Ellery O'Brien," she said, and then added, "I hope you're going to tell me you live in that house, so I can say I've met my next-door neighbor."

"Yes, I've lived there since it was built. I'm sorry I haven't been over to welcome you before now, but I was in San Miguel with my sister." She stopped a few feet away, and Ellery noticed how her gaze kept coming back to her face.

"I've only arrived this week."

Across the street, a door slammed, and a woman came outside. She waved at them and opened her garage. As she backed out of the drive, Shirley said, "Looks like you've met Lorraine."

"She introduced herself yesterday. She seems very nice."

"She is nice and has a heart of gold. I hope you go to church."

"I do," Ellery said.

"Well, I go once or twice a year and she worries about me. She hinted once that lost sheep that remained lost were in danger of going to hell and I might want to consider changing my ways."

"Did you change?"

She seemed amused by that. "Hell no!"

Ellery nodded and tried not to smile.

"I guess you haven't had much time to socialize, but you will. People are very friendly here."

"I did meet one man. It wasn't under the best circumstances, I'm afraid."

"Who was that?"

"Clint Littleton. Do you know him?"

"Clint? Why, heavens yes. I've known Clint since he was a little boy. He's as nice as they come and held in very high regard around here. I bet he enjoyed making your acquaintance."

"I doubt that. I ran over his motorcycle at 7-Eleven."

She laughed. "I wish I'd seen that, although I don't quite picture Clint riding a motorcycle."

"It was for his nephew's birthday."

"Oh, that would be Margie's boy, Brad. The way I see it, you did everyone a favor by running over that dangerous contraption. As for Clint, don't go worrying yourself sick about the motorcycle. He isn't the kind to carry a grudge. He should count himself lucky if that's the worst that ever happens to him."

"What does he do?"

"He has a nice-sized ranch outside of town, but he makes his living from his feed store, Agarita Feed and Seed. He's never been married. His sister Margie has been shoving women at him for years. He'll take women to dinner and such, but after a while, he always moves on. Everyone around here considers Clint quite a catch, but no one seems to know how to go about getting the right bait to do it. Plenty have tried. Guess he hasn't met the right woman. Are you looking for a husband?"

"No, I'm not."

"If you don't mind my asking, what made you move to a place like Agarita Springs? You seem far too glamorous for a town like this."

"I'm doing some family research."

"What's the name you're interested in?"

"Eubanks."

"Eubanks," she repeated slowly. "I knew some Eubanks, but that was a while back. There haven't been any Eubanks here for quite a spell."

"What happened to them?"

"Died . . . married, moved away . . . There are some kinfolks here though, but none with the Eubanks name."

Shirley's rosy and wholesome countenance screwed itself into an expression of sincere and dedicated thought. "I sure wish I could think of someone," she said, her voice trailing off, only to rally faster than the Dow. "How could I forget about Ruth Anne Sizemore? I'm positive her maiden name was Eubanks."

Ellery almost choked at the sound of that name. Ruth Anne . . . The name vibrated with hammerlike force in her head. "My mother had a sister named Ruth Anne. Does she still live here?"

"Last I heard, she was living in a nursing home . . . in Bastrop, I think it was."

"Perhaps I'll give her a call and inquire about her family."

"I don't want to dash your hopes, but it wouldn't do any good. Ruth Anne couldn't tell you her own name, let alone anything about her family. She has Alzheimer's and it's quite advanced."

Ellery deflated like a balloon. There were bound to be ups and downs, and there was nothing to do in a case like this but keep on trying. "How about the name Mary Ellen Eubanks?"

"No, I can't say I recall that name. I'm sorry. I can tell by your expression she must be someone special."

"My sister." She knew Shirley was probably wondering what kind of woman would be searching for her own sister. She decided to save her the trouble of asking. "She's my twin sister."

She watched the play of emotion on Shirley's face. It was all there: surprise, wonder, puzzlement. "How do you have a twin and you don't know where she is? I thought twins were close to each other."

"They are close . . . when they're raised together. Mary Ellen and I were separated at birth."

She looked genuinely sorry. "That's a pure shame . . . a crime, really. Things like that shouldn't happen. Families ought to be together."

"Yes, they should, but for some of us it doesn't work out that way."

"I guess I should say welcome to the neighborhood and shut up, so you can get on with your rat-killing. Come on home, Webster, or I'm going to call the dog-catcher."

"It was nice meeting you," Ellery said, but Shirley had already turned away.

Once inside, Ellery fed Bertha and ate a bowl of cereal. She went upstairs, showered, dressed in jeans and a yellow linen shirt, and drove toward town with a to-do list lying next to her purse. She went to the post office, stopped at the hardware store, and then the pet store to buy doggie treats and a larger water bowl for Bertha. From there she went to the drugstore to pick up a prescription for allergy medicine transferred from D.C. While she waited, she wandered around the store and browsed through a display of antique jewelry. The aroma from an old-fashioned soda fountain was too good to resist and she soon found herself seated at the counter enjoying the best BLT she had ever eaten, along with a vanilla milkshake and a reminder that next time she'd have to jog twice as far.

Her last stop was H.E.B., to buy the items on her grocery list, plus a bouquet of fresh flowers that she considered an impulse item.

Back home, she put the groceries away then spent two hours on the computer answering e-mail and doing research on twins. Merrily called, and after they talked for over an hour, Ellery decided to enjoy the last bit of daylight. She poured herself a glass of wine and carried it through the conservatory, where she stopped long enough to pick up the copy of the *Agarita Springs Register* she'd purchased at H.E.B. and carry it with her to the backyard.

There were several white Nantucket-style chairs on the porch and in the yard, with wide wooden arms—just the right size to hold a glass. As soon as she settled herself into one of the chairs, Bertha came to lie at her feet. Ellery gave her a few loving pats before she leaned back with a deep sigh, kicked off her sandals, and propped her feet on Bertha's broad back.

With a relaxed sigh, she allowed her gaze to roam around the lovely yard with pink azalea bushes running along the fence and a fairy statue in a lovely little pond near a weeping willow. Something about the area around the willow and pond was almost depressing when compared with all the colorful pink blooms on the azaleas and the bright spring flowers that edged the porch.

She made a mental note to brighten up the area around the willow. It wouldn't take much . . . just a few colorful flowers.

With the setting sun warming her face, and her toes curled in Bertha's soft golden coat, she reached for her wine, but was interrupted by the sound of Shirley's voice.

"That's it! You'll be sorry, you worthless hunk of dog hair and slobber. You better enjoy this because it is the dog pound for you tomorrow. My mind is made up. Let go of my shoe! Let go! These are my new house shoes. Dagnab it! I'm taking you back home. You can sleep in the yard until the dogcatcher comes in the morning."

The voice was too close to come from Shirley's house,

so Ellery got up and went to peer over the back gate. She saw Shirley and Webster some distance away tangled together, with the leash wrapped around Shirley's legs and Webster tugging on her rabbit house shoes.

She smiled and returned to her chair. She sipped the wine and thought how she had decided, while driving to Texas, that she would need a few days to settle in before she started the search for her sister. She found herself going back over everything she'd done before she came here, mentally checking each one off.

To date, most of her search had involved phone calls—to Agarita Springs and the Edna Gladney Home in Fort Worth, where she learned the law in Texas regarding closed birth records had not changed since Sam had inquired years ago. That meant she would not be getting any information other than what was written on her birth certificate. Disappointed, she reminded herself there were going to be plenty of frustrations before she located Mary Ellen.

She knew she shouldn't expect this sort of search to move rapidly along. Searches of this type could take years. It was slow going, tedious, and all too often unfruitful.

That was part of the reason she'd decided to come to Texas. Her years in reporting taught her the importance of running a hands-on investigation. She was glad for the experience in reporting and happy she wasn't a well-known newscaster in Texas, which enabled her to do the search herself and would protect her privacy.

The moment some reporter or tabloid had the slightest inkling of what she was about, it would be on every television station in the D.C. area.

She didn't care if it was considered "newsworthy" or a "human interest story." She was dealing with something personal and private, and she would use great caution to keep it that way.

She watched the sun sink slowly and smiled when she remembered how, as a child, she asked her father where it went after it went down.

"It is sitting on the beach in Hawaii," he would say.

The exquisite wash of pink, gold, and blue that tinted the sky began to fade. It was either the warm, relaxing feeling of being outside that was beginning to work its magic, or the drowsy effect of the wine, because Ellery closed her eyes and let herself doze off on the back porch of her peaceful new Texas home.

Nine

SHE WAS AWAKENED a short time later by Webster's bark in the distance and imagined Shirley would soon be giving him a stern reprimand and an order to come into the house. He won't go, she thought, and smiled at the image of Shirley and Webster in a Mexican standoff.

Shirley apparently did not know the first thing about dog whispering. The mental image was too much to resist and she smiled. Someone else must have thought so too, because she heard a soft chuckle.

She jerked her head around.

"Mind if I join you?"

She was surprised to see Clint Littleton standing in her backyard, somewhere between the pink azaleas and the willow tree. She brought her hand up to her chest. "You gave me a fright. I didn't hear you come through the gate."

He gave her a nod, in that silent way men around here had of communicating. Something about him seemed almost embarrassed. She guessed he was at least aware of his intrusion.

Webster's bark cut through the silence.

He glanced in the direction of Shirley's house.

"I don't know how you get any peace and quiet with that dog next door," he said.

"Webster is cute and full of personality, and no, I don't mind if you join me, since you are already here. I'll even be polite and invite you to sit down."

She was a little annoyed that he'd simply walked into her backyard. She watched in that relaxed way people sometimes do when they are trying to decide if they should be offended or let the matter slide. She decided to simply watch.

His walk was slow moving and graceful, in a way that made her think these rancher types were bred, not made. He was wearing jeans and a blue long-sleeved shirt that magnified his baby blue eyes to the max. She wondered if it was intentional, and decided he didn't look the type.

He held a straw cowboy hat in his hand. The breeze kept playing with his hair, and as he drew closer, she could see the crease where his hat had been. Cute guy any way you looked at it, she thought. She tried to imagine the reaction of the women at WMDC-TV if he were to walk into the newsroom. She knew her assistant, Leigh, would rattle off her favorite line: "Now doesn't he look good enough to roll up and have with coffee."

Ellery was curious as to why he had come, but she decided to wait and see what he had to say.

Webster barked again, she glanced at Clint, and they

both dissolved in laughter. His laugh was as unexpected as it was appealing. She was thinking he should give in to it more often, when she moved her hand and knocked the glass off the arm of the chair. The glass shattered and she reached down to pick up the pieces and place them on the arm of her chair, when she cut her thumb.

It was just a small poke, so she wiped the small drop of blood on her napkin. She felt as graceful as a waddling goose when she was around Clint Littleton. "I guess I'll be a bit jumpy until I adjust to being in a new and unfamiliar place. Have you ever moved, Mr. Littleton?"

"Call me Clint. No, I've never moved. I'm still living in the same house where I was born."

She was definitely feeling a prick of envy, but tried to hide it when she noticed Bertha standing close beside him. Ellery narrowed her eyes at her dog's faithless behavior. "Traitor," she said, laughing. "What happened to alarmed barking?"

Clint gave a chuckle and patted Bertha on the head. "She's a friendly dog."

"Which is small compensation for being a lousy watchdog," Ellery replied.

"How's your hand?"

She glanced down at the napkin. "Faring better than my pride, I think. This is becoming quite embarrassing. Every time I see you, I put my worst foot forward."

"Or *two* worst feet," he said.

"I know you must think me a completely inept klutz."

He gave her a lazy grin and said, "Oh, I wouldn't go so far as to call you a klutz. I'd say you're more like a horse that's been penned up too long. He shows he's eager to run by the way he shakes his head and stamps his feet. Confinement does that."

"Do you think I'm confined?"

"I think you know your restrictions and you stay within your bounds."

"Is that bad?"

"That depends."

"On what?"

"On whether you want to be free."

"You obviously think I do."

"Like I said, you're eager to run."

The warm shot of heat she felt on her face meant it was turning red, but there wasn't much she could do about it. She looked down at her hands, thankful the sun was dropping in the sky. "Well, this is a first. I've just been compared to a horse and I don't find it insulting."

Apparently sensing her discomfort, he changed the subject. "I do apologize for barging in on you like this. I saw your car was in the drive, so I stopped and rang the bell. When you didn't answer, I figured you might be out here."

"I guess it's a good thing it's not the middle of the afternoon and I'm not into nude sunbathing."

He grinned. "Well now, that all depends on how you look at it. From where I stand, I'd say it was more of a disappointment."

The lights illuminating the trees came on and he glanced at the broken glass beside her. "Want me to throw that away for you?"

"I'll get it," she said, and stood to carefully put the broken pieces in the napkin. "Looks like I'll have to start over. Can I offer you a glass?"

"Never was known to turn down a pretty woman, or a good glass of wine."

Ellery laughed. "I didn't say it was good."

"Fair enough. I'll let you know what I think."

He picked up the napkin and she walked with him into the house. It hit her that some of the tension she felt earlier was easing off a bit.

He opened the screen door and held it for her to enter. She was beginning to see bits and pieces of a life that was slower, and more genteel. It made her feel awkward, and she wondered how long it would take her to become accustomed to it. And the slow, lazy manner of speech . . . Lord, she could brush her teeth faster than people here could say "good morning." She removed two wine glasses from the cabinet and handed one to him.

"Is the wine in here, or in the bar?" he asked. She did not try to hide her surprise. "How did you know there was a bar?"

There was an odd look on his face, not exactly embarrassed, and not exactly secretive, but somewhere in between. "I came to a party here once."

"Oh," she said, but she sensed there was more to it than he let on. She decided to give him the benefit of the doubt, since she was thinking he'd probably been sleeping with some woman who'd lived here before her. The thought was distracting and she stammered, "The . . . the wine is here. I bought a copy of *Wine Spectator* and decided to try some of the Wines of the Year. I'm not too good at remembering the ranking, so I marked it on the bottles." She picked up one and read the label. "I'm drinking this one—a number four, a Brunello di Montalcino, which I'm partial to, but then I love Italian wine, especially the Antinoris and Frescobaldis. Or, if you prefer something different, I bought about eight bottles. Pick what you like." She pointed at another one. "This Columbia Crest is the only white wine I have."

"I'll have the one you're drinking."

She laughed. "I didn't claim to be an expert, you understand."

He poured the wine. "We have a few wineries in Texas."

She gave him a look that told him what she thought of that. "I think I'll stick with the Italian ones, or a good Argentine shiraz."

He shrugged. "Maybe you should broaden your horizons a bit and try the local wines . . . 'When in Rome' . . ."

She gave him a flirtatious smile. "Maybe I will." She paused to turn on the porch light before she crossed the porch and stepped into the yard. She sat at the table this time and he took the chair opposite hers.

"I suppose you're wondering why I dropped by."

"I know it isn't a social call, so you could say my curiosity is aroused."

"I wanted to thank you for the Suzuki. I don't know how you did it, but you sure made Brad's birthday one he'll remember. I think he'll sleep with that letter."

"I hope it was the right one."

"It's the same model number, so it must be."

"I got lucky with a phone call, although I wish it could have been here for his birthday. I really do feel bad about what happened."

"Brad doesn't care. He's happy and excited, and I don't know how you did it."

"I made a quite a few unsuccessful phone calls before I decided to go to the top, and I called the chairman."

"Of what?"

"Suzuki."

"And he spoke to you?"

She laughed at the expression on his face and the almost awed tone of his voice. "Actually, I cheated a bit. A few years ago, I went to Japan to do a special report on Suzuki. They were so pleased that the CEO, Yoshio Saito, said I was invited to dinner at the home of Osamu Suzuki."

"This Suzuki—he owns the company?"

"Officially, he's the chairman."

"Did you go to dinner?"

"Of course . . . and I had a delightful time. They are such gracious people. As a token of gratitude, he offered me a Suzuki motorcycle of my choice."

He was smiling at her now. "You didn't."

She smiled back. "I certainly did. An offer is an offer."

He was laughing when he said, "Not when you wait a few years to accept it."

"There was no time limit on Osamu's offer. He couldn't have been more charming or more helpful. After our conversation, it wasn't long before I received a call from someone in Houston who told me that a red 1500LC, Special Edition, was on its way to your nephew, but it wouldn't arrive for a couple of weeks. I'm glad the FedEx arrived in time."

"The timing couldn't have been better; although it

made everyone think I was a Certified Master Liar for saying you couldn't replace it."

She ignored that and said, "I understand you ranch and own a feed store."

"You've been busy."

"My neighbors Lorraine and Shirley told me all about you."

"Then you probably heard I'm not cut out to sit behind a desk, choked by a tie, for ten hours a day."

"You say that like you have a personal grudge against ties."

"I'm not opposed to wearing a suit and tie when the occasion calls for it, but I wouldn't want a steady dose of it from the backside of a desk. If I'm going to sit somewhere, I'd rather it be in a pickup or on a horse."

"If you could describe ranching in one word, what would it be?"

"Unprofitable."

She laughed and realized how he had a knack for making people feel comfortable. He also had a sense of humor, which she considered a very good thing. The evening was still warm, and there wasn't the slightest breeze anywhere. But the sky overhead was clear and deeply blue, the air was warm, and Webster must have gone to bed. She smiled at the thought.

"What are you thinking that made you smile?"

"Thinking about Webster makes me smile."

Clint laughed at that. "Shirley thinks Webster's sole purpose in life is to torment her."

"Well, he does, but she asks for it," Ellery said.

"She doesn't know the first thing about dogs," he said.

"She was an only child and never had children of her own, so you might say she is lacking experience when it comes to obedience."

They both laughed, but their gazes caught and held—until he smiled and she returned it, and then quickly looked down at her hands.

"Before you ask, no, I've never been married, but I know a great deal about people and animals. So, tell me, what makes a woman like you walk away from the kind of success you had in television? Why would you give it all up for obscurity in a town like Agarita Springs?"

His voice was warm and caressing and she bet he had used it to his advantage more times than he could count. She had to admit it was pretty effective and had her feeling all buttery inside. To mask what she felt, she kept her tone cool and businesslike. "I didn't walk away from it. I took a leave of absence, to get away from it all for a while. I'm documenting everything in journals and when I return I'll do a documentary on my experiences here."

Apparently, he was good at seeing through "cool and businesslike" because his light blue eyes were brimming with mischief, and that smile—oh my, he was a charmer and she knew she was ripe for charming . . .

And she'd always thought of herself as immune to charming men and that included cowboys. Her next thought was cut off when he said, "I'm still wondering why an Ivy Leaguer would put a lucrative career on hold to move to a little town like this."

"What makes you think I went to an Ivy League school?"

"Didn't you?"

He was clever, she would hand him that, and he looked awfully good in jeans. "I went to Brown," she said. "And you? Did you go to an Ivy League school?" She didn't know why she asked that. It made her sound like a snob and she didn't want to make him feel bad if he hadn't gone to college, let alone to an Ivy League school. She was ashamed to put him on the spot like that and was about to apologize when he spoke.

"I went to Yale and majored in business, but I attended for only two years. After my father died, I transferred to Texas A and M. I decided on a double major in business and farm and ranch management."

The conversation broke down after that and a lull arose. She was thinking conversation was such a fickle creature, for it was likely to dry up without notice. And speaking of notice, she was suddenly aware that he was observing her with an odd expression . . . expectant, almost. "You're looking at me like you're still curious about something. Is there anything else you want to know?"

"Yes, tell me the real reason you came to Agarita Springs."

A shadow of indecision passed over her face and she knew it was obvious that she was wrestling with what, or how much, to tell. Not that he should expect her to reveal anything. They were, after all, little more than strangers. But she wanted answers and to get them she had to ask questions. "I came here to find my sister."

"Who is?"

"Her name is Mary Ellen Eubanks."

"Eubanks . . . I don't recall any Eubanks . . . I take that back. There was a Ruth Eubanks Sizemore."

"She's my aunt."

"Then you know about the Alzheimer's?"

She nodded. "Shirley told me she was in a nursing home in Bastrop, but it wouldn't do me any good to see her."

"No, it wouldn't. She's at what they call the late stage. She doesn't even recognize her daughter."

Ellery lifted her head off the back of the chair and looked at him. "Her daughter? Now, that I did not know. Does she live here?"

He nodded. "Lucy Sizemore Todd. She married Daryl Todd, but they're separated now."

"Thank you for telling me."

"I'm not sure how much good it will do. If I've never heard of your sister, I doubt Lucy has. How long has it been since you saw her?"

"We were twins, separated at birth."

"I'm sorry to hear that. How did it happen?"

She was so busy explaining how that came about that she didn't pay much attention to the odd way he was looking at her. She knew he was attracted to her, so she assumed that was the reason he seemed so interested in her face.

When she finished her story, he said, "You don't have much to go on, do you? What about your father's family? Are they from here as well?"

"They were when we were born, but I'm afraid I don't know much about my real father. I don't even know his name. All I know is he was the president of a bank and supposedly he was well off. His wife couldn't have children. That's why he wanted one of us."

"That isn't much to go on, is it?"

"No," she said, distracted a bit by his demeanor. There was something about the expression on his face, and the manner in which he spoke almost apologetically, that made her think he wasn't being totally honest with her. She hadn't been around him a great deal, but suddenly he seemed different, a little more reserved. Maybe he did know the name of her father. This town couldn't have had too many banks back then. Perhaps he knew even more than the name and didn't want to share it with her. It was also possible that he knew a great deal more than that.

"I realize I don't have much to go on," she said, "but there probably weren't too many bank presidents here thirty years ago, so finding one who had a daughter who is my age and favors me shouldn't be all that difficult."

"Thirty years is a long time and not everyone is as curious as you. It's possible, too, that if they are here, they might not welcome such an intrusion into their lives."

"I've thought of that, of course. But the opposite is also true."

"I'm sorry I can't be more help." He looked at his watch and came to his feet.

Clint's relaxed, easygoing manner was completely gone now. She realized it had been ebbing gradually since she mentioned her sister. Now she knew he was being intentionally vague. It was also obvious he was in a hurry to leave. She could not help but wonder why.

"I've stayed longer than I intended. Thank you for what you did for Brad, for the glass of wine, and an incredible story."

She walked to the front of the house with him. She waited until he was in his pickup, then she said, "Thank you for telling me about Lucy Todd. I'm going to give her a call."

A muscle flexed in his jaw. He started the car, and brought his fingers up to the brim of his hat. He nodded and said, "Sometimes you can stir the embers of a fire until it burns out of control."

It wasn't until much later that she fully grasped the meaning of that enigmatic comment.

Sherman T. DeWitt considered himself a brilliant sleuth and he prowled the political and media mixers in Washington, D.C., with his nose for gossip finely tuned for anything he could overhear or anyone he could persuade to disclose sensitive information.

Tonight he was prowling around the bar at Tequila Grill on K Street, when he happened to see someone he knew from his days at WMDC-TV. Monica Singleton had had a big mouth when he'd worked there, and that was a few years ago. He hoped age had loosened her tongue even more.

She was standing alone, so he acted happy to see her and said, "Hey, Monica . . . good to see you again. You're looking younger than you did back at WMDC! Let me buy you a drink."

That was all it took. Monica was always ready for a drink, so he bought her a few more and asked her how everyone at old WMDC television was doing. By the third drink she was revealing something she should have kept secret.

It wasn't until the next day that she realized she had placed her job in jeopardy when she'd violated the secrecy agreement she'd signed when she'd been hired. Desperate, she made a few phone calls, hoping to track down where Sherman T. DeWitt was working now. When she learned he worked for the *Daily Snoop* she put in a call to him, only to discover he was investigating a story in Texas.

Monica was terrified because she knew which story he was investigating. He was on his way to Agarita Springs, Texas, and he would be up to no good when he got there. She realized she should tell someone or at least place a call to Ellery O'Brien to warn her, but she couldn't afford to lose her job. Besides, there was always a chance nothing would ever come of it, she thought, but in her heart she knew that was not going to be the case.

Sherman T. hated Ellery O'Brien and Sherman T. was a vengeful man.

Ten

W HEN ELLERY FOUND Lucy Todd's name in the telephone book the next morning, she was jubilant. She
could barely contain herself. She wanted to shout, or at
least break open a bottle of champagne to celebrate. This
was it: This was the long-awaited link to the sister and
the family she never knew.

She had a feeling that Lucy Todd was going to be the
key person in all of this, and Ellery hoped she wasn't
going to turn out to be another Margaret Ledbetter.

Ellery sat back in the chair to allow her excitement to
settle down to an occasional bubble. It wouldn't do to call
Lucy sounding like a revved-up Ferrari. Calm down, she
told herself . . . calm down; deep breath; compose self.

After a few minutes, she took another deep breath,
picked up the phone, and dialed.

A woman answered on the third ring. "Hello?"

"May I speak to Lucy Todd?"

"This is Lucy."

"Lucy, my name is Ellery O'Brien. I have recently

moved to Agarita Springs for the sole purpose of finding my twin sister. I believe we are related. My mother's maiden name was Claudia Eubanks. I've been told she was a sister to your mother, Ruth Anne."

"Well, yes, my mother did have a sister named Claudia, but I don't remember . . ." She paused suddenly. "Oh, my God . . . if this is about what I think it's about . . . Oh my, this isn't something we should discuss over the phone."

"You tell me where we can meet and I'll be there. I realize you don't know me. I'll be glad to give you credentials . . . names of reputable people in Washington, D.C., you can call to verify I'm legit."

"Oh, I'm not worried about that. You can't imagine how happy I am to talk to you! It's not every day that a long-lost relative calls me out of the blue. Why don't we meet at Starbucks? Do you know where the one is down on the square?"

"Yes, I know it. I've stopped there a few times after my morning run."

"Wonderful! How about I meet you there in fifteen minutes, or do you need more time?"

"No, fifteen minutes is perfect. Thank you for agreeing to do this, Lucy. You have no way of knowing what this means to me."

"If you're who I think you are, I know exactly what it means." She paused. "I'm embarrassed to ask this, but could you tell me your name again? I got so rattled over what you said afterward, I've completely forgotten."

"I hope I'm not too rattled to remember it too," Ellery said, and they both laughed. "It's Ellery O'Brien."

"Ellery . . . you mean like the detective Ellery Queen in those wonderful old whodunit mysteries?"

"My father said my mother was a huge fan and read every book."

"Must be a family trait because my mother loved them as well. I grew up reading them. *The Greek Coffin Mystery* was always my favorite."

"I'm ashamed to say I never read one."

"We'll have to remedy that. I'll see you in fifteen minutes. Oh, by the way, I'm petite and blond."

"I'm blond too, but not petite."

Starbucks was practically empty when Ellery walked in. She saw a cute blonde sitting alone in a club chair near the window almost immediately.

She smiled at Ellery and waved.

Ellery smiled and headed in her direction. "Hi, you have to be Lucy," she said. "I'm Ellery and you have no idea how happy I am to find you, Lucy."

"Likewise, I assure you. You can't imagine how excited I was when I saw you pull up and I saw your Land Cruiser had D.C. plates. I knew it had to be you."

Ellery didn't know what she expected Lucy to be like, but she was surprised by what she found. Lucy was younger than she sounded on the phone. Ellery guessed they were about the same age. "Thank you for giving me this chance to speak with you."

"I hope I can be of help. Shall we get our coffee?"

They walked together to the counter. Lucy ordered, "One Splenda, grande latte."

Ellery felt she needed something stronger. "I'll have a doppio macchiato."

Lucy shuddered. "Brrr . . . a doppio macchiato? You drink 'em strong where you're from. By the way, where are you from originally?"

"I was born in Fort Worth. I live and work in Washington, D.C., but I grew up in Chevy Chase, Maryland." They made small talk for a few minutes and Ellery filled Lucy in on where she lived, what she did for a living, and the usual first-meeting banter.

Lucy then told Ellery a few things about herself. "Like a lot of local kids, I went to the University of Texas and got my degree in early childhood education. I taught kindergarten for several years and then I opened my own private kindergarten, Hill Country School, with all certified teachers. It's been a godsend, especially after my husband and I separated."

Their orders were ready, so they took them back to the club chairs in front of the window. Lucy took a few sips before she put her cup down and said, "So, where do you want to begin with your story?"

Ellery had both hands curled around the cup in front of her. "It's a long one."

Lucy smiled. "They're open until midnight."

Ellery started with the death of her father, the last-minute revelations about her birth, and the existence of a twin sister. "There were still so many things I wanted to ask him but I never got the chance. Finding you . . . well, I'm sure you can understand what it means to me."

"Oh, I do, but please go on."

Ellery filled her in on a few more details and when she finished she sat back and took a drink of coffee. "That's about the extent of what I know. Anything you can add to it will be helpful, and most appreciated."

Lucy looked as if she were about to burst with excitement. "Oh, I can add to it, all right. I can add a whole lot. This is truly your lucky day because you won't believe what I can tell you. I'm trying to find the best place to start. Maybe I should simply say I'm positive we are cousins. When you called today, I didn't at first make any connection, but then I remembered a long time ago, before the Alzheimer's, I asked my mother about her sister Claudia, and where she was. She told me what had happened—about the twins and all. You know our grandfather was a minister here?"

"Yes, that's where I found information on the members of my mother's family."

The golden light coming through the window fell directly upon Lucy's angelic face and to Ellery she was instantly elevated to archangel status. Truly, she fit the bill with her all-American good looks, the intense blue eyes, and lovely smile.

"According to my mother, our grandparents were not what you would call compassionate Christians, especially toward Claudia, even though Claude was a minister. When they found out she was pregnant, they hustled her off to Edna Gladney's in Fort Worth. It sounded like they basically abandoned her there. They told her not to call them. They did not go to visit her. My mother said the two of them exchanged letters for a while, but Claudia stopped answering them a few months after the twins were born."

"Do you know anything about my father?"

She laughed. "I know a lot, but whether it's worth going through all the cobwebs in my head to get it is another question. Your father's name was Nathan Wilkerson, or Nathaniel Wilkerson to be correct. He was president of First State Bank. His wife's name was Lydia. They had two kids, Emily Susan and Daniel."

"Emily Susan?"

"Yes. My mother said Susan was a twin, so I'm almost positive she has to be your sister."

Ellery had been about to pick up her coffee but when she heard the name she fell back in her chair. "I can't believe this," she said, so overwhelmed by finding her sister, she was speechless. She never dreamed she would find her so quickly and she was blown away by the impact of having her sister somewhere in this town, just a phone call away. Thirty years separated, she thought. We spent the first nine months of our existence together, only to be separated for thirty years. Now, at last, I will finally get to see her for the first time.

For a moment, Ellery was too overwhelmed to speak. Inside, she was a jumble of emotions . . . thrilled to find her sister at last; sad to have been separated; broken-hearted that she hadn't known about her twin until recently. She was happy the search was over, yet she hurt whenever she thought of what those thirty years would have been like if things had been different.

Emily Susan . . . She also felt like an idiot. She wanted to smack herself. All the trouble she had put herself through, the searching, all that time spent looking for the *wrong name*! "I feel like a fool."

Lucy looked stunned. "Why? What happened? Did I say something wrong?"

Ellery released a sigh and gave Lucy a reassuring smile. "No, you've been an angel. I was dumbfounded by the name Emily Susan and then I realized that, of course, her name was changed. What an idiot I am. I should have figured that one out from the beginning. Naturally that's why no one ever made the connection when I mentioned my sister's name."

"What do you mean changed?"

"When we were born our mother named us Mary Ellen and Laura Ellery. Naturally, all my inquiries have been after Mary Ellen Eubanks, when the person I was trying to find was Emily Susan Wilkerson."

"Hmmm. You know, I wouldn't have thought about that either. I suppose the Wilkersons wanted to give her a different name. I probably would have done the same thing if I adopted a child." She sipped her coffee. "They adopted Daniel a year after Susan was born. You look a lot like her, by the way. I saw the resemblance the moment you walked through the door. Of course, I already knew you were her twin, so that probably made a difference. Now that I think about it, I might not have noticed the resemblance otherwise."

"How do you mean?"

Lucy paused, thoughtful for a moment. "Just that there are a lot of things that are different about your appearance and the way you look."

"Like what, for instance?" Ellery asked, thirsty for every scrap of knowledge about Susan.

"Susan had long brown hair and blue eyes."

"My eyes are blue, but my contacts are tinted green. My hairdresser helps me with the blond part. What other things do you notice?"

"You said you wear contacts. Susan wore glasses and no makeup. She was pretty much a small-town girl. Don't get me wrong, she wasn't ignorant or without class. She went to SMU—sorry, Southern Methodist University in Dallas—graduated with a degree in fine arts and music. She played the piano and the harp and had a beautiful voice. Like you, Susan was very pretty, but she didn't know how to accentuate it the way you do."

Suddenly, Ellery became tense, alert, as if she were walking on quicksand. "You speak in the past tense. When did she move away? Do you know where she is now?"

Lucy looked startled. "She's dead. Oh Lord . . . I'm so sorry. Forgive me, I didn't mean to blurt it out like that. I forgot that you didn't know about what happened to her. I didn't mean for you to learn it that way. I wasn't thinking! I didn't think before I opened my big, fat mouth. God, I'm such a dolt."

Ellery could only stare at Lucy in a grave way, then she swallowed and looked away to stare into space, needing the break to hide the sudden sparkle of tears gathering in her eyes. She sighed deeply, feeling utter hopelessness while striving to fill the peculiar emptiness inside her; somewhere a cautionary voice called out but she was too distressed to pay it heed. How could she have been so euphoric a moment ago and now completely filled with despair? God, how could she explain the wrenching ache inside her? For a moment in time, she was so close, so damn close, and now nothing . . . nothing but a gaping void, black and empty, where once shone the light of hope.

All her expectations . . . dashed. The family connection she dreamed of . . . gone. The bright future she saw ahead of her . . . faded completely away and forever out of reach.

Lucy put her hand on Ellery's arm. "Forgive me. I really mucked this up. I feel like the worst louse. I'm so very, very sorry. I shouldn't have spoken impulsively. I don't know why I burst out with it like that."

"It's nothing you did. I had to find out sooner or later and I'm glad it was now. I don't suppose there is a *nice* way of telling someone something like that. I'm not upset with you. I'm upset that I never got to meet her. I had such hopes . . . I feel completely shattered inside."

"I know."

Ellery bit her lower lip, needing the sharp infusion of physical pain to offset the throbbing ache within her. She tilted the empty cup and stared at the bottom. "What other way is there to say it? I'm devastated, of course, and a little numb, but it isn't anything you caused. Perhaps I was just born under an unlucky star, or the planets weren't aligned right . . . who knows why heartaches tend to follow heartaches and each of life's disappointments rides on the tail of another disappointment?"

"I know this must all seem like a wonderful dream that you didn't get to finish," Lucy said gently.

Ellery had to smile at her cousin's sad smile. She really liked Lucy—a sunny blonde, charming, affable, and gracious. And the best part about her, Ellery thought, was she was so accepting. It was obvious her desire to help was genuine and so was her sorrow over her revelation of something that caused another pain.

"Yes, that's exactly how it feels." As if I've been cheated, she thought. Like I reached for a star and came up with nothing but vapor. The prize I won has been taken away and given to someone else. The groom bolted at the altar.

The sister she never knew was dead and she could never bridge that gap . . . not now, not tomorrow, not ever. Death was the one thing that she had no hope of overcoming.

She'd never known until now that one did not have to know someone to feel their absence in their heart and in their life. Learning Susan was dead left an empty hole inside her that she feared nothing would ever fill. "Tell me how she died; when she died."

"Oh, Ellery, it isn't pleasant. Are you sure you want to hear it now?"

"Yes, I'm sure." After all, she thought, there must be a threshold of pain and I have already crossed mine. Susan is dead. How much worse can it get?

"She was murdered."

Ellery buried her face in her hands. She needed some time to absorb these revelations that were coming at her way too fast. She had no concept of how much time elapsed before she removed her hands and said, "Tell me the rest of it."

Lucy looked a bit uncertain, but Ellery assured her, "Please . . . go on."

"It occurred almost two years ago. No one knows exactly what happened or why. It wasn't a robbery because there wasn't anything missing. In fact, the house was not disturbed at all, save for all the blood everywhere. Your sister didn't have an enemy in the world. Everyone loved her. We were all shocked to hear one of the neighbors had called the police, concerned about Susan when she didn't respond to the neighbor's ringing the doorbell and pounding on the door."

Lucy talked on about how a light was on upstairs, the car was in the driveway, and how the police came and found a large pool of blood at the bottom of the stairs. "But they never found her."

"What?" Ellery sat up straight and leaned forward. "You mean her body wasn't there . . . they never found her body?"

Lucy nodded. "It disappeared without a trace. It was a murder scene without a murder . . . a bodiless murder. There was all this talk about no one being convicted even if the police could determine who killed Susan, because there was no corpus delicti, but then I read in the paper that you don't have to have the actual body, you only have to prove a murder was committed. Two days after that, some lawyer in Austin wrote that only the state of Texas requires that the body of the deceased be found and identified. He did mention that the legislature had repealed the requirement of having a body, but apparently some courts still invoke it and some don't. Guess that means it's not very clear or else it's left up to each judge's interpretation. Who knows?"

"Perhaps she was wounded and got away," Ellery said.

"They thought of that, and checked everywhere for

anyone who might have treated an injured woman, but they came up with nothing. Not that they expected to. From the beginning they thought it unlikely anyone could survive such blood loss, and there were no bloody prints anywhere else, except in the bedroom and down the staircase. Anyone injured that badly would have left a trail of blood if they'd managed to leave the house. They decided it had to be some weirdo who killed her and buried her body elsewhere . . . or did something worse with it. You know the kind of horrible things we see on television with all the forensic and crime shows."

Ellery nodded. "I start off every morning reporting on that sort of thing in the District." She paused, then asked, "After almost two years they still don't know any more than they did back then?"

"No. The case went cold, but it was never closed as far as I know. No body. No murder weapon. No suspects. Not even a motive. Most believe it was some homeless drifter, or someone freaked out on drugs. No one wants to think it could have been someone who lived here."

"This all seems so strange, bizarre even."

"Oh, it gets more bizarre, believe me."

A shiver of cool air passed over her and Ellery had a feeling that she should leave well enough alone—ridiculous though it was, because being a newsperson she never let a sleeping dog lie. "Then tell me the rest of it."

"You're sure you want me to go on?"

Ellery nodded. What's a little more pain? How numbed can a body get before a fuse blows and everything shuts down?

"About three years ago Susan's husband was killed. He was found with a shotgun hole in his chest. They ruled it an accident, but Clint contested the ruling. He said his brother . . ."

Ellery wasn't listening. Everything suddenly began shifting into reverse after Lucy mentioned the name Clint. "Wait . . . wait a minute. Did you say Clint?"

"Yes. Clint Littleton's brother, Clay . . . he was the one who was killed."

"What?"

"Clay Littleton was Clint's older brother. Clay was married to Susan."

Ellery wasn't concentrating on the brother connection right now. Her mind had already zeroed in on something else. "Clint must have known Susan's father was the president of First State Bank, right?"

Lucy's expression said she was a bit dumbfounded by Ellery's question. "Of course he knew who Nathan was. Everyone in town knew. Gracious, Clint was the best man at Susan and Clay's wedding and it was held in the Wilkerson's backyard."

Clint's words came back to her. *Sometimes you can stir the embers of a fire until it burns out of control.*

Was that what she was doing now—stirring the embers with her questions? Good, she thought angrily. It's high time someone stirred something enough to get some answers. Oddly enough, her anger at Clint Littleton for not telling her that her long-lost twin sister had been his sister-in-law energized her. She sat up straighter and said, "Tell me about the Wilkersons. Do they still live here?"

"No, they're both dead. Lydia died when Susan was in

high school. Nathan died about three years ago. After he died, the First State Bank had a lousy president and the bank lost a lot of its customers. Finally, it merged with Bank First. I'm sure Nathan rolled over in his grave when he learned that all his hard work had turned to dust." Lucy stopped to look at her. "Did you know he was very rich . . . ? I mean rich, rich?"

"I was told he was a wealthy banker. That's all my mother told my father about him before she died."

"Well, he was wealthy all right, but he got even more so . . . but all that money couldn't save him from a massive heart attack."

Ellery barely heard what Lucy said. Her mind was trying to arrange everything she had learned in an orderly sequence. Her sister was dead. Her biological father was dead. So many disappointments; so many deaths; so many murders. Strange that one family was suddenly stricken with such ill fortune in a relatively short period of time. She was having trouble assimilating it all.

"Are you okay?" Lucy asked.

"I'm a bit overwhelmed. I was so optimistic a few hours ago, just thinking about the family I would have. And before I knew it I was back to having no family at all."

"That isn't exactly true," Lucy said. "There is Susan's adopted brother, Daniel. He lives in Austin. I mentioned him a moment ago, but you were probably too wrapped up in what I was saying about Susan that you didn't pay it much attention."

"Yes, I remember, but Susan's adoptive brother isn't any blood relation to me."

"And a poor substitute for your twin sister."

Ellery nodded.

As if wanting to get Ellery's mind off the loss of family, Lucy said, "A quick change of subject, but I meant to ask you something earlier. What is the perfume you're wearing? It's familiar but I can't place why."

"It's Ma Liberté by Jean Patou. It's all I ever wear. I've worn it since I was a freshman in college, in fact. So that tells you how old a fragrance it is." Ellery gave her a hesitant smile before she noticed Lucy did not seem to be listening. She wondered at the shocked expression on Lucy's face.

"Lordy me, I knew it was familiar," Lucy said, "and you won't believe why. It's the only perfume Susan ever wore. I know, because I gave it to her for her birthday several times. Quite a coincidence, isn't it?"

Ellery felt carried away beyond the bounds of her normal sensibility. She felt the same constricting tightness in her chest that she'd experienced this morning, and as then, she was gasping for breath.

Seized by sudden panic, she stood up quickly and bumped the table as she did. She picked up her purse. She saw the startled look on Lucy's face. "I'm terribly sorry."

"What's wrong?" Lucy asked. "Did I say something wrong? Did the comment about the perfume upset you?"

She put her hand on Lucy's arm. "Thank you for telling me all of this, but I have to go now. It's been quite a blow to hear all of this . . . my sister murdered, her body never found, all the other deaths . . . I can't seem to absorb it all. Don't think that it's your fault. You can't imagine how grateful I am to you for telling me the truth. I want to see you again, Lucy—truly I do. You are the only family I have right now. I'll call you. I do want to see you again, but I need some time to deal with all of this. I just can't talk about this anymore. Not right now."

Lucy put her hand over Ellery's. "You don't have to tell me anything, Ellery. I saw it all on your face. I'm here . . . whenever you want to talk just pick up the phone."

Eleven

As he drove toward the ranch, Clint thought about the conversation he'd had with his mother a short while ago when he stopped by her house in town. Even now, he couldn't believe she'd said, "You ought to be married, Clint."

His answer was evasive. "I've got a peaceful life."

"That's what you have when you're six feet under. You're too young for that. You don't need peace. You need excitement. You need a wife. I want to see you happy, Clint, before I die. And I wouldn't mind a couple of grandkids thrown in."

How could he tell her that kind of happiness was like a foreign word to him now, or that he could barely remember what it was like? Oh, there were times—like tonight—when he was haunted with the memory of making love to a woman he loved. He remembered the way it had been afterward, when they lay together joking and teasing, and he would recall what it had been like to laugh.

Clint pinned his gaze on the horizon at the end of the dusty road that lay ahead of him and a flood of reminiscences came pouring into his mind. He recalled Travis Franklin and Sarah Godwin. They had been friends since the age of five; Travis was his best friend and Sarah was his sweetheart. For most of his life, Clint planned on two things: to go to Texas A&M, and to marry Sarah.

His father sent him to Yale instead, but he still planned to marry Sarah when school was out. Everything changed when his father had a heart attack, and by the time he died, Sarah was tired of waiting, and she eloped with his best friend, Travis. Clint was nineteen at the time and he thought he would never forget it. Only now, he had trouble remembering the details correctly—had it really been thirteen years?

He recalled that night a year or so after Clay died, when Sarah called to say she'd read about Clay's death and how difficult it had been for her to call.

"It's taken me a while to get up the courage to call and say how sorry I am about Clay. I have such wonderful memories of him. I know how close you were. I feel so sad for you and your family, but you know I never was very good at expressing myself that way."

He remembered there was one time when she didn't have any difficulty expressing herself and the words floated out of their hiding place and rang in his memory as clearly as they had that day when he came home from college and asked her to marry him and she uttered the words that shattered his life.

"I'm married, Clint. Travis and I eloped not long after your father's funeral."

He closed his eyes and waited a moment, allowing time for the voices to fade back into the silence of memory. Even now, he could hear the sound of her soft breathing and another memory stirred—a memory of her apology for not waiting for him to finish the semester at Yale. He remembered his terse reply and how he told her there was no need to apologize, that it was all a matter of perspective. They were young. They'd been kids together. She was the first girl he ever kissed; the first woman he made love to. When she married Travis it shot a hole in his heart the size of Alaska, but he got over it . . . eventually.

He never tried to block that part of the past from his memory. Why should he? It was part of him, part of his life, and part of what made him the man he was. It hadn't worked out for them, but that did not mean it never happened, that he couldn't cherish the memory or that he should look back and say it was never love because it ended. He was sorry to hear her ask if he thought there could ever be a second chance for them; apparently, her and Travis's marriage wasn't working out well. He regretted the reply that still burned like a brand in his heart. "When you married Travis it shattered us and what we were. I no longer love you, but that doesn't mean I don't remember the reasons why I once did."

He wondered if he would ever feel that way again about another woman or if he would marry and start a family. He knew the desire was still there, but damn, he just hadn't met a woman who drew him strongly enough to make a lifelong commitment to her.

He thought about the two young women who'd called

him last week to invite him to a Founder's Day picnic and how, before the week was out, he had turned down six invitations because none of them interested him. What was it going to take to spur him to go out and find the right woman? He sure didn't want to wake up one morning and realize he had grown old and that he would never know the laughter of the children he wanted.

He turned through the gate and stopped by the foreman's house to check on how many acres of hay had been cut that day and if the farrier had come to shoe the horses.

"Josh Hopper put new shoes on two of the cow horses and replaced a couple of shoes on one of the mares," the foreman said. "We should finish cutting the hay in the north pasture tomorrow. In this heat we should be able to turn it in a few days. We've got a problem with some feral hogs rooting and wallowing in the east pasture. Someone must've released some Russian boars on their property for hunters and some of 'em have managed to get onto our property."

"Looks like we need to do a little hog hunting and have ourselves a barbecue," Clint said. "We won't be able to use those pastures for anything after the hogs get through tearing it up."

After a few more minutes, Clint climbed into his pickup and drove toward the ranch house. He passed several ranch hands on horseback moving a herd of Brahmans from one pasture to another. He waved and drove through the gate they held open for him and continued up the road until he reached the ranch house.

He spent the rest of the afternoon in his office. It was

sundown when he stepped into the evening, the screen door banging shut behind him. He paused at the top step, listening to the sounds of the night. The crickets were busy and down by the pond the bullfrogs were warming up.

A light breeze stirred the leathery leaves on the live oak trees, causing their long, drooping branches to sway and bend, and sent their shadows dancing across the ground.

He stepped down off the last step into the muted colors of a soft summer twilight and walked toward the barn, careful not to step on the white prickly poppies that seemed to crop up overnight in the grass. He remembered how his mother used to watch from her bedroom window, and if he stepped on one prickly poppy, he would hear the tap of her reprimand against the windowpane.

He circled the flagstone patio, its perimeter defined by terra-cotta pots of geraniums, heavy with the showy clusters of vivid red blooms. Overhead, strings of light bulbs were still hanging where they had been for years, running from tree to tree in a crisscross pattern. He remembered the dances his parents would have out here under these same lights when he was supposed to be asleep.

He never knew, until after his father died, that his parents had known all those years ago that he was not sleeping. He almost laughed aloud when he thought of himself lying on his bed in his room on the second floor, with the lights out and his pillow in the open window, as he watched everything that went on, thinking his parents had no clue.

The ranch dogs came loping around the corner of the house to greet him, tongues lolling, and tails wagging. He gave each of them a pat on the head and said, "Let's go see!"

The dogs took off. A horse nickered softly and the dogs started to bark as they ran toward the barn. Clint followed, ready to start his rounds to assure himself that all was well, much in the same manner as he had with his father when he wasn't much taller than his dogs.

He remembered his dad saying he did the same with his father when he was about Clint's age, and his father before him. Clint found comfort in knowing some things never change, for he was one of those rare men who enjoyed his life and the work he did. He loved this land and its heritage. He felt connected to it, as an immigrant would feel connected to his homeland. This was where generations of Littletons were born, where they lived and died. Most of them were buried here, too, in the family cemetery, shaded by oaks and a stone's throw from the spring-fed creek.

He had never lived anywhere but here, in the same three-story, three-chimney ranch house his great-great-great-grandfather had started out of native limestone blocks, hand-chiseled to form walls eighteen inches thick. At one time, the Littleton ranch was one of the big Texas ranches, but over the course of years it was divided among heirs, until it was a fraction of its original size. It was still a nice-sized spread, ideally located about an hour's drive from Austin, and big enough to run all the Brahman cows Clint could take care of.

The ranch didn't support itself the way it had in his

grandfather's time, when cattle drives went all the way to Kansas, and ranching was profitable. Times changed, and the words "Go west, young man" evolved into the cautionary slogan "Diversify or go under."

Over the years, there had been some pretty tough times when he wondered if it wouldn't be easier to throw in the towel and sell out, but he always managed to find a way to hang on just a little bit longer. Everything changed when he opened the feed store, and made more money in one year than he had in five years of ranching.

He turned down a narrow trail outlined with smooth stones taken from the river and walked past the rich jumble that was once his mother's garden. The heavy, floral scent told him that it was still filled with roses, sunflowers, and lavender, only now they weren't as well tended as they once had been.

In the distance, a calf bellowed, and the dogs began to bay as they picked up the scent of something and disappeared in the brush. He stopped by the iron fence that surrounded the family cemetery, and his gaze rested upon the tombstone of his grandmother Cassandra, who had taught him to gather honey from each moment.

Here, in this place, he could feel peace flowing into him as easily as thirsty roots soak up water. He tucked a few straggling runners from heirloom ramblers now spilling over the iron fence and listened to the splash of water that spilled from a very old fountain, said to have come from a monastery in Spain.

His father was buried near the corner, next to his great-grandmother, and farther over were the letters of his great-great-grandfather's marker, so weathered they were difficult to read, not that Clint needed to see any letters. His father had seen to it that the words were inscribed upon his heart so he would not forget.

John Jacob Littleton
Born in Virginia, April 1779
Died in Texas, December 1852

His gaze rested upon the most recent gravestone, which bore his brother's name. Susan's stone should be there, next to Clay's, he thought, and her body too. She belongs next to Clay. He thought about Clay's death for a moment and the effect it had had upon his family. His mother had taken it especially hard, with a heart attack that almost killed her.

"Why is there so much tragedy in our family?" she asked him.

"I don't know. It just happens in some families—perfectly normal folk like us, who can find no explanation for it. Some families seem destined to have grief and tragedy stick to them all their lives."

"I've had enough grief to last three lifetimes. I want to die before it's time for anyone else I love to go. I can't handle burying another loved one."

Clint made his way through pale, shadowy patches of fading light that came sifting down through the leaves of old trees with impatiens nestled between their roots, while the perfume of blooming honeysuckle saturated the air about him.

He was thinking the moonlight was abnormally bright tonight, stealing color from everything it touched. It reminded him of the way the yard looked during the winter, when it was covered with a light dusting of frost.

He wondered if his sister had picked his mother up from her house in town and if they were on their way to the ranch. Virginia liked to be punctual. He turned back toward the house. It was dark now and the moon was full and yellow as an egg yolk, and it rested on the roof of the barn when he stepped through the back door and into the kitchen.

He thought about Ellery O'Brien and wondered how he was going to handle things with her. No doubt a discussion with his mother and sister would provide a solution. It was the main reason he'd invited them out to the ranch for dinner tonight. He had to tell them about Ellery's connection to Susan, and in turn, Ellery needed to know about Susan and Clay.

He heard the dogs barking and knew his sister and mother must have arrived. He looked in the direction of the rock barbecue pit and found his mother talking to Margie while she poked at a bed of coals he had started earlier.

"I was hoping to find a steak here," Margie said, turning toward him with a long-handled fork in her hand.

"You will in a couple of minutes."

True to his word, he soon had steaks sizzling while his mother and sister fussed about the kitchen, setting the table and clucking to each other about his style of housekeeping.

The sound of Margie's voice drifted through the open window. "It doesn't look the same as it did when you and Daddy lived here."

"I don't look the same either," Virginia replied. "He keeps a good enough house, with the help of the house-keeper."

It was a good meal, with a lot of shared memories, some of them good and some of them the kind that are always accompanied by pain. When they finished, they moved outside to sit in the lawn chairs. Clint served them each a glass of port.

Margie sipped hers. "You surprised me when you called and said you wanted to grill steaks for us. I can't remember the last time you did that."

"It has been a while."

"I don't think this is purely a family get-together," Virginia said. "What's bothering you, Clint?"

"I never can get away with anything around you, can I?"

"I'm surprised you keep trying."

"I hate to rush things," Margie said. "But if you want to talk about something, bring it up. I have to get home before too long. Jerry was snoring in the recliner when I left. He'll stay there until he petrifies, or I go home and wake him. What did you want to talk about?"

"Ellery O'Brien."

"Ellery O'Brien . . ." Margie repeated. "Isn't she the woman who ran over Brad's motorcycle?"

"Yes. After the accident, when I got a look at her, it struck me that there was something awfully familiar about her, but I couldn't pull it up. Yesterday, it all came together. She reminds me of Susan."

"You mean our Susan?" Margie asked.

He nodded. "I stopped by her house to thank her for getting the cycle replaced. While I was there, she told me she came here to find her twin sister. Then she asked if I knew anyone named Eubanks."

"Did you tell her about Ruth Anne and Lucy?" Virginia asked.

"She already knew about Ruth Anne. I told her about Lucy, and then she said her mother was the daughter of the Reverend Clyde Eubanks." Clint related the story Ellery told him about their birth and separation. "Can either of you tell me how many bank presidents there were in Agarita Springs thirty years ago?"

"I haven't a clue," Margie said.

"There were only two," Virginia said. "First State Bank was where Nathaniel Wilkerson was the president. First National Bank was the other one and Carter Rayburn was its president, but he was close to seventy, and already had five kids. It couldn't have been Carter."

"My thoughts exactly," Clint said. "Nathan Wilkerson must have been the father."

"But that would make her . . . Good Lord, are you trying to say this woman is Susan's twin sister?" Margie asked.

He nodded. "It shocked me as much as you."

"I don't believe it," Margie said.

"Don't be so quick to decide. Maybe Susan was a twin," Virginia said. "It could have happened, but how will we ever know? Anyone who knew the truth has been dead for a long time. What about this woman? Do you think she's making any of this up?"

"No, and I say that for two reasons. First, what would she stand to gain by claiming to be Susan's twin sister? Second, she looks too much like Susan for it to be a coincidence. I didn't see it at first, because her appearance is, well, her style is different. She's a television personality . . . a big-city woman loaded with ambition. Her hair is shorter than Susan's and very blond. She wears green contacts. She's probably fifteen or twenty pounds lighter than Susan was. She's got a Northeastern accent, an East Coast polish, an Ivy League diploma, and years in the media to give her self-confidence and poise."

"And Susan graduated from Agarita Springs High, was a quiet little music major at SMU, married her high school sweetheart, spoke with a Texas twang, and had never been out of the state. I see your point."

"You said something about television," Virginia said. "Doing what?"

"She was a television news anchor in D.C. when she learned about her twin sister." He told them how Ellery's father had told her about her twin sister shortly before he died.

"What a shame. That was quite a load to dump on a body when you are going to die and not be around to answer questions," Virginia said. "Makes me wonder why the old codger didn't leave well enough alone and hang on to it a bit longer."

"I guess he figured she had a right to know," Margie said, "although he sure took his own sweet time in arriving at that conclusion."

"Well, if she is Susan's twin, it's a crying shame she didn't learn about it before Susan died," Virginia said. "I know Susan would have been overjoyed to know she had a sister."

"She had Daniel," Margie said.

"A brother isn't the same as having a sister," Virginia said, "and I never cared too much for Daniel."

"He never had much to say," Margie said, "and shaking his hand was like grabbing a catfish on a trotline . . . cold and slimy. He's a cold fish, if you ask me."

"That doesn't mean he didn't care for his sister. Some people don't show their emotions as well as others, but you have to admit that he was terribly upset over the deaths of Susan and Clay," Virginia said.

Margie nodded. "Yes, he was, but that doesn't mean I'm not glad he's living in Austin and I don't have to run into him every time I go to town." Margie turned toward Clint. "Did you ever hear if the official copy of Nathan Wilkerson's will was legally certified as genuine and given to the executors or is it still tied up with the claim made by the Catholic church?"

Clint shook his head. "No, I haven't heard, not that I expect to. Nathan's will doesn't have anything to do with me and the courts in Austin are slower than they are in Agarita Springs. It might be another year or two before it's settled and the will is certified, thanks to the claim made by the Catholic church."

Virginia snorted at that. "I don't think the Catholic church has a snowball's chance in hell of getting any of Nathan's money," she said. "Everyone in town knows Nathan was a bit of a show-off when it came to his wealth. Just because he announced at some fund-raiser that he was going to give a million dollars to the diocese doesn't give them a valid claim against his estate."

"I don't think it does either, but the courts will have to

decide that. There's a lot at stake because Nathan was a very rich man."

"But not as rich as Daniel," Margie said. "I was never as surprised in my life as I was when Daniel formed that company of his and made himself a fortune."

"I read he is right up there with Michael Dell when it comes to income," Virginia said, "but I swear I never did understand exactly what it was his company did. I can't even remember the name of it."

"Manna," Margie said. "I know it's a software company that rivals Microsoft."

"It's an operating system that's not as susceptible to hackers and viruses as Microsoft," Clint said.

The room grew quiet. After a few minutes Virginia asked, "How did she take it when you told her how Susan disappeared, and is more than likely dead?"

"I didn't tell her anything about Susan," Clint said. "At least not yet."

Margie's mouth dropped. "You didn't tell her? Nothing? Not even about Clay?"

"Nope."

Virginia gave him a chastising look. "Clint, you should have told the poor girl and not leave her hanging on to her slim hopes. That is not like you. Try to put yourself in her place. That was downright cruel of you."

"Yes, it is cruel," Margie said. "I know you're prone to procrastinate sometimes, Clint, but when it's something like this—good Lord, the woman has a right to know. Susan was her twin sister, for crying out loud."

"Hmm, he does procrastinate, doesn't he?" Virginia said. "I guess I forgot about that aspect of Clint's personality. I agree with Margie. She has a right to know. Why didn't you tell her?"

"I wanted to tell the two of you first." He turned to his mother. "You almost died from that heart attack when Clay was killed. And you would have died with the one after Susan disappeared if we hadn't gotten you to the hospital in time. I was worried that if Ellery started digging up all these old ghosts it could be hardest of all on you. I didn't want to see you go through that. I thought if I had time to talk it over with you . . . to prepare you . . . it would make things easier. I can see by your reaction that I shouldn't have bothered. You seem to be taking this better than I am."

"Women are constitutionally stronger," Margie said. "I thought you had figured that out by now."

"I thought that only applied to you."

Clint could swear Margie had gotten more difficult since she'd dyed her hair red, but he didn't tell her that.

"Thank you for thinking of me," Virginia said, "but don't concern yourself over my ability to handle the bad along with the good. I've had a long time to toughen my old hide. I may look light as a feather, but on the inside, I'm made of pretty strong stuff."

"Maybe I'm not the best person to tell her something like this," Clint said. "I think a woman would do it better."

"Hogwash!" Virginia said. "You're just afraid you might have a crying woman on your hands."

"Or a thoroughly pissed-off one," Margie said. "I agree with Mama. Don't go pushing your mess onto our plates."

Virginia nodded. "It's too late to try and worm your way out of this one, Clint. You jumped into the middle of the fray when you withheld information, and don't think you can come sashaying in here and put me, or your sister, up to doing your apologies for you. You just girt up that big ole belt of yours, shine up your boots, go over to her house, and admit you were a scoundrel. And the sooner you do it, the better."

"Mother is right. You should go over there tomorrow and tell her what you know. And now, I need to be going." Margie stood and picked up her purse.

"Wait a minute," Virginia said, then turned back to her son. "Okay, Clint, I can tell that you haven't told us everything, so out with it."

"Well, there is one more thing," he said. "The house she rented . . . it's Clay and Susan's house."

"Oh, good Lord above! This is like a nightmare that won't end," Margie said. "Just how many turning points does this drama have?"

"I've told you all I know," Clint said.

Margie frowned. "Didn't you know she was the woman who rented it when you had that run-in with the motorcycle at the 7-Eleven?"

"I don't keep up with that stuff. That's why I have a realtor handling it. I was told the house was rented by a single woman with one dog. She agreed to the rent I'm asking, had good references, and paid for six months in advance. I didn't ask how many teeth she had."

"Does she know the house belongs to you and that you bought it from Susan not long before Susan was killed?"

"No, I didn't tell her anything. I told you that."

Virginia leaned back in her chair and started to rock. "I have a feeling we aren't even halfway through this drama."

"And how do you know that?" Clint asked.

"There are too many loose threads lying around that haven't been tied up. Susan's body hasn't been found. The police don't have a clue about the murderer's identity or a single suspect. We all know Clay's death was no accident. And now this woman shows up and we learn she's Susan's twin, and that she has a background as a television newscaster. Do you really think she's going to take all of this with a nod of meek acceptance, and quietly return to wherever it was she came from? No. I think she will start digging around until she finds what she's looking for and it will end up in the newspapers, and maybe even on prime-time television, which might not be a bad idea. Mark my word. Something is going to blow things wide open, and she will be smack in the middle of it. You just wait and see."

Margie gave a snort. "She was smack in the middle of it the moment she drove into town."

Twelve

After she left Starbucks Ellery drove home with her mind not on where she was going but on the sense of being weighed down by disappointment until she was stupefied by it. Her reaction to having no familial connection to anyone save the happy cousin she'd just met was difficult for her to deal with after having had such hopes and plans for her reunion with her sister. The sense of loss surged over her until she felt like every star, every planet, the sun and even the moon had come crashing down on her. She was overwhelmed by the immense and alien power of something she could not control, and now all hopes and joy lay buried in a silent tomb with the body of her sister . . . in a location only her murderer knew.

She pulled into the driveway and wondered how much worse could things become.

A moment later, she was sitting at her computer staring at the blank screen—which was how she felt . . . completely blank. She did not know where to go from here. The house closed around her in a comforting way and some of the anguish began to ease, and with it came the disappointment of an aching heart that could only be released by tears.

The ring of the telephone caught her off guard and for a moment she thought she would not answer it. But might be Lucy calling to check on her, she thought and picked up the phone. "Hello."

All she heard was the sound of someone breathing. "Lucy?" she said.

"*Lucy*," he mimicked. "Before it's all over you'll wish it had been Lucy."

"Who is this?"

"It's the man who will kill you . . . I will kill you just like I killed your sister. No one will know. No one will care. You will be as lonely in death as you are now. No one found her body and no one will ever find yours. You will spend eternity abandoned and alone."

She slammed down the phone. Terrified, she stood and found herself unable to move. Her heart beat painfully in her chest. Her mouth was dry. She was scared and wondered if he was on his way there to kill her.

She turned and ran through the house to make sure all the windows and doors were locked, then she poured herself a glass of wine and sat down to force herself to think rationally.

She picked up the phone next to her and checked the caller ID . . . UNLISTED. She took another sip of wine and another. Gradually, she began to think clearly. Whoever it was, his objective was to frighten her and it had worked.

He would probably get a thrill over reading about her threatening call in the newspaper, or perhaps he was watching somewhere, waiting and hoping to see a police detective ring her doorbell.

Well, she wouldn't give the cowardly bastard the satisfaction. Let the miserable little worm wither away from lack of attention. He won't get his kicks at my expense. But how did he know that her sister had been murdered? Was it someone who'd overheard her and Lucy talking at Starbucks? The only other person in town who knew she was Susan's sister was Clint Littleton . . .

She finished the glass of wine, carried the glass into the kitchen, and realized she was more angry than frightened. It was still early in the afternoon and she had more research she wanted to do, so she returned to her computer vowing not to answer the phone if the caller ID showed UNLISTED.

Merrily called and Ellery told her about the tragic news she'd learned from her cousin Lucy. Then she couldn't stop herself from mentioning the phone call because she still felt unsettled by it.

"I think you should call the police, Ellery. You don't want to dally with some schizophrenic tormenting you."

"What I don't understand is, why did he call me? There are only a few people in this town who know why I'm here."

"Maybe he isn't from Agarita Springs."

"Hmm, I hadn't thought about that, although I can't think of anyone in D.C. who would go to so much trouble to frighten me. Unless it was . . ."

"Sherman T. DeWitt," Merrily said.

"You know, it probably was Sherman. If anyone could find out where I was, he could, and he would love to scare the pants off me."

"He certainly has envied you since the two of you worked together and we both know what his kind of jealousy is capable of."

"Thanks for making me feel better about this . . . but how would Sherman know my long-lost twin was murdered? How could he make that connection between me and Susan when it took me so long to find out?"

"Ellery. You know that a snake he is, how he can wheedle information out of people. He even pays for it. I . . . Oh shoot, here comes my hubby, looking hungry and cross. I better mix him a double and shove it in his face when he walks in the door. Look, don't let that creep upset you. Call me later."

Ellery smiled. "Will do," she said, and hung up the phone.

She spent the rest of the afternoon on the computer and then took a break for dinner, which turned out to be a Margarita pizza from a local pizzeria called Tony's.

When she returned to her computer, she worked until nine-thirty and decided to call it a night. She had ordered a book on twins online and she wanted to finish reading it, so she shut down the computer. Afterward, she went around the house to turn on a few lamps. She decided to turn on the back porch light and made her way toward the door when she stopped suddenly and screamed.

There, a ghoulish, leering face was pressed up against one of the glass panes. She grabbed the wall phone and started to dial 911 when she realized there was no neck or shoulders below the face, which didn't move. She picked up a knife, walked to the door, and opened it. Taped to the outside of one of the door's upper glass panes was a lifelike mask, the kind a teenager would wear on Halloween.

She decided Sherman T. DeWitt had gone too far this time. Tomorrow she would call the *Daily Snoop* and lodge a complaint against him.

After she tossed the mask in the trach can outside, she opened a new bottle of wine, picked up a glass, and carried them to her room, having decided this was definitely a night to partake of the fruits of Bacchus.

Sitting at the kitchen table the next afternoon, Ellery stared at the bowl of soup in front of her. Bloodred tomato soup was a bad idea. She couldn't eat anything. The scent of Ma Liberté kept coming back to haunt her.

My liberty . . . did the name have to do with anything? Was the ghostly figure who appeared to her that of her sister? Was Susan searching for some sort of liberation because her body had neither been found nor buried?

Stop it, she told herself. This is how people go crazy. So she focused instead on Clint Littleton and the things he had kept from her. For some time she had been thinking about that, going over everything again and again, and she always came up with the same answer: He must be hiding something. But what could it be?

She dumped the soup in the sink and put the bowl in the dishwasher. She carried the coffee upstairs to her dressing room, where she changed into a pair of leggings and a T-shirt. She sat down to put on a little makeup and saw the dark circles under her eyes. She flipped the mirror over to 5X magnification and quickly flipped it back. God, she looked awful. If it was proof she wanted, that 5X magnification did it. She applied a little concealer to the circles, followed it with a little blush to camouflage her pale face. A couple of quick strokes of mascara and a dash of lipstick and she was out the door to put the leash on Bertha.

With Bertha at her side, she ran hard and fast to the center of town, circled the square twice and started back home. The light on the corner turned red. She stopped, jogging in place while she waited to cross Main Street.

Out of the corner of her eye, she saw a pickle-colored pickup, old and battered, as it came along beside her, slowed and pulled to a stop next to her. The back of the pickup was piled high with bags of feed, burlap sacks, and white blocks about a foot square. The entire load looked as if it might topple over any minute.

Already annoyed at him, she glanced at Clint Littleton sitting behind the wheel and experienced the same sort of vexation she used to feel when she conducted an interview with someone closemouthed and hostile. Truly, the man seemed to thrive on his nuisance value.

With an irritatingly jovial voice he said, "I thought most folks ran in the morning."

"I usually do, but today I didn't feel like it," she said as the light changed. Without another word she crossed the street. She ran about a block before he pulled up next to the curb and drove slowly alongside her. "I'd like to talk to you, if you'd stop a minute."

"Oh, I'm sure you would, but I'm not going to give

you the satisfaction of knowing if I accept your apology or not."

"I wasn't going to offer an apology but I would like to explain a few things."

"Listen . . ." She stopped and walked over to the pickup and tried to ignore the thought that, even sitting, he looked good in jeans. "Pay good attention to what I am saying so there will be no misunderstanding. You couldn't possibly explain enough to satisfy me, so don't come pulling up next to me looking like the Beverly Hillbillies in your wreck of a pickup, and think your good ole boy charm is going to get you anywhere, because it won't. You should have told me the truth about Clay and Susan."

"Mea culpa . . . I know I made a bad judgment call and I apologize for it."

"A judgment call? Is that what it was?"

His cell phone rang and when he answered it, she started up the block again. A few minutes later he was back, driving slowly beside her. "Sorry about that," he said. "It was my secretary, Carrie Lynn Bright."

"She can't be too bright if she works for you," she replied without breaking stride.

She ran several more blocks and was almost home when she noticed he was no longer following. She was filled with a sense of relief that he had finally given up. It was time for her to cool down, so she slowed to a walk. She was tired, but it helped to get the kinks out, and she felt better physically. Mentally, she was still exhausted.

She was relieved when she saw the gabled roof of her house just ahead, but then she frowned when she saw the pickle-green pickup parked in front of it.

His gall knew no bounds. She was really irritated now.

He was sitting on the front porch looking as fresh as this morning's milk when she walked up. She was too tired to think cleverly right now. She wanted him away from here.

The woman in her wanted to walk right by him and into the house without saying a word. The newswoman wanted to see what he had to say, what lies he could come up with to cover his ass.

She sat down on the step next to him. "All right, start talking yourself out of the hole you're in."

"That's not why I wanted to speak with you. I came to tell you about your sister, but I can tell you've already found out."

"I'm surprised you weren't clever enough to think Lucy would tell me. Well, of course she did. And she was kind enough to understand what I've been going through. She told me about Susan's death, and she told me about your brother . . . I'm sorry about what happened to him, by the way."

"Look, I apologized for not using good judgment. I know your hopes were built up and then dashed. I understand how devastating it must have been for you to—"

"I don't think you do. I think you're saying what you think you need to say in order to placate me."

"I don't placate," he said.

"Good, because if that's what you were doing, it isn't working, not that it matters because I don't trust you or anything you say and you have hardly given me a reason to, now have you?"

"I'm not as emotionally detached from all of this as you think."

She didn't buy that for a minute. "I need to get off this subject. I should look at everything through sterile, emotionless eyes, as you do. I shouldn't make a big deal out of it, is that what you think? Okay, so my parents and my sister are dead and I don't have any family left. I learned the awful truth so now I should go home to Washington. Isn't that how you see it?"

She came to her feet and made a point to have eye contact with him. She wasn't a nice little lady from D.C. who'd just moved to town any longer. Now, she was a hard-nosed, ballsy reporter and she was out for a story. "I am not going to meekly accept my sister's death and return to D.C. I'm going to find Susan's killer. And if there's a connection between her death and your brother's, I'm going to find it as well."

"I'm not trying to stop you. I'm offering you my help, if you want it."

"Help? After I've already found out everything with nothing but deterrents from you? Now you offer me help? You take the joy out of joyous, you know that?"

"Hey, I told you about Lucy."

She had forgotten about that. "You're right. You did tell me that and I am most appreciative because Lucy filled in everything else."

"Are you sure?"

"Of course I'm . . . What? Do you have something more to tell me?"

"I might. Did Lucy tell you that this house you're renting belongs to me?"

Now, that one did catch her off guard. "No, she didn't mention that."

"And did she tell you that I bought this house from Susan a few months before she died, or that she was the last person to live here before you?"

"I can't believe Susan owned this house. It's too coincidental."

"It's true. It belonged to Susan and Clay. This is where they lived after they married."

"Oh my . . . " Ellery had to sit down again. Things were falling into place so fast, she felt battered by the fallout. "That means this is the house where she was murdered . . . My God! I live in the house where my sister died. That goes beyond coincidence . . ." Suddenly, her head was spinning and she recalled the familiar image from her dream—a dream that was making more and more sense.

She recalled the scent of perfume. If it was proof she needed, the perfume provided it. No coincidence there. Was Susan trying to tell her something from beyond the grave? She shivered.

Her thoughts were interrupted when Clint said, "I think you knew the answer to that before you asked. You might as well know the whole story. The killer either was in the house or entered shortly after she returned home that night."

She saw this as the perfect opportunity to learn more about her sister's death, for who, aside from the police, would know more details than Clint? Ellery knew how the police were more prone to discuss cases with male reporters than with females and how they would often give that information using the old "off the record" comment. "How did it happen?"

"The first time he stabbed her was in the master bedroom upstairs. She managed to get out of the room and down the stairs."

Ellery cringed at the image that formed in her mind, but she had to play the reporter now and remove all emotion if she was going to continue. "How do you know how it happened?"

"I saw the crime scene with the chief of police."

"What about forensics?"

"The killer knew what he was doing. According to the detectives that investigated the murder, the crime was premeditated. As for the site, it was clean as a whistle. The only DNA they obtained was Susan's. The only other evidence was footprints . . . a size eleven shoe."

"That's it?"

"Yes."

"Didn't any of the neighbors hear or see anything . . . noises, a strange car, dogs barking . . . something?"

"We know Susan returned home from her book club around midnight. By that time all the neighbors were asleep. The police did interview everyone on the street, but no one reported hearing or seeing anything unusual. No one knew anything until the next morning about eleven o'clock, when Shirley Van Meter called the police. She went over to Susan's to return a book Susan had loaned her. She became concerned that Susan's car was in the driveway but she didn't answer the door after Shirley rang the bell and knocked on the door repeatedly. You could ask Shirley about it if you want more information."

"I would, but Shirley came over yesterday morning to tell me she was going to Houston for a week or so to visit her sister." She paused, thoughtful for a moment, and then said, "I wonder if she knows how very fortunate she is to have a sister to visit?"

Clint's features softened. "I know this has been difficult for you and you have no idea how sorry I am that you've had to go through all of this. I understand if you want to move out of this house and find someplace that isn't a constant reminder of your loss and the tragedy that occurred here. It has to be stressful for you. I don't want you to feel trapped in a nightmare. I'll arrange for someone to move you, so you won't have to deal with that. I'll even help you find another place, if—"

"I know you're concerned about me and I appreciate your offer to help." Tears welled in her eyes. "Naturally, this has been both heartbreaking and disturbing, but it would be the same no matter where I lived, don't you see that? The pain is inside me," she said, poking herself in the chest. "It isn't in the house or in anything anyone says. I don't want to move. I can't move. I don't know why, but I have a feeling this is where I have to be. I can't explain why. All I can tell you is, I feel closer to Susan here than I do anywhere else."

Ellery gazed off and after a few minutes she shook her head and said, "I have been through so many highs and lows in the past month, I'm beginning to feel like a thermometer."

He chuckled. "You sure don't look like a thermometer," he said. "Too many curves."

"They are dangerous curves as far as you're concerned," she said, trying to lighten up a bit and smile.

"Well, why don't you give me a glass of that Italian wine and let me try to distract you for a while from this sad business with a little polite conversation?"

"But why would you waste your time doing that?"

"It's hardly a waste of time," he said. "The way I see it, you are dug in here deeper than a fence post, so I don't see you pulling up anchor and heading back to D.C. anytime soon. And then there is the fact that we are sort of related in a roundabout way. After all, we'd be in-laws if Clay and Susan were still alive. Like it or not, we both have a personal investment in finding out what happened to your sister, and you know the proverbial saying, two—"

"Heads are better than one."

"Exactly. So, shall I pour, or do you prefer to serve your own wine? Or if you'd rather go out, we could go have a beer down at the Juicy Pig. The barbecue is good there."

"Hmm . . . such a difficult decision . . . Juicy Pig or Brunello di Montalcino."

Clint laughed softly and she found the sound so honest and human and appealing that she realized it was exactly what she needed at this moment.

"Let's stay here and get drunk. I don't have barbecue, but I can make a mean BLT."

His blue eyes glinted with mischief. "Just how drunk do you want to get?"

"Just drunk enough that I can still say no."

This laugh was even better than the first and she took

his hand and gave him a tug. He stood and followed her into the house. She found that listening to the leisurely tread of his boots on the hardwood floors behind her was comforting. She had never been around men like this, men who made one envision vast vistas with wide plains where lofty white clouds trailed the sun and lightning could strike at a moment's notice. She decided they had just come through their first summer storm, battered by peach-sized hail, and booming claps of thunder. The storm had passed, and they were still talking to each other . . . and in a deeper, more meaningful way.

She recalled the way he looked sitting in his pickle-green pickup, his long legs stretched in front of him, the worn jeans and blue denim shirt, sexy as hell. She liked the way his high cheekbones seemed to jut out beneath the brim of his hat, like the stony sides of a glacier. She could easily picture him on a horse, for even walking, he moved with the easygoing assurance of a cowboy crossing the prairie alone.

This made her curious about him and she wondered why a man of the earth like him had never married. She thought about the kind of loneliness he exuded that soaked through a person's skin, right down to the bone, like a cold winter rain.

Still wondering about him, she removed a bottle of wine from the wine rack.

She placed two glasses on the counter and while she waited for him to open the bottle, she allowed her gaze to roam around the room and tried to imagine her sister in here as she prepared dinner for Clint's brother. What had the kitchen looked like then? "When did you buy Susan's house?"

"A month or so before she died."

"Why did she sell it to you?"

"Susan didn't like living here after Clay died. She wasn't sure if she wanted to stay in town or move to Austin. She put the house up for sale but no one wanted to buy it. So I bought it from her."

"Is there anything still here that belonged to her?"

"No, I had everything redone. Of course the doors and things like that weren't changed, but the furniture and carpets and paint are all new."

As he'd done the first time they shared a glass of wine, he did the honors and carried everything outside, where they settled into chairs to drink their wine while they watched Bertha's antics until she settled down on the grass between them. Ellery figured this was a good time to ask the question that had been nagging her.

"Would it be out of line for me to ask you about Clay's death?"

"That depends on what you want to ask."

"Have you given up on ever finding Clay's killer?"

"No. I never accepted for a moment the ruling that Clay's death was a hunting accident, and I won't rest until I know the name of the bastard who so callously snuffed out a beautiful life and left a family shattered."

"How did Susan take Clay's death?"

"As well as anyone could expect her to, under the circumstances. She had good days and bad days, but she had an indomitable spirit, a strong faith, and the love and support of our family. Each day got her a little closer to the point where she would eventually think of Clay without hurting."

"What was she like? Did the two of you get along?"

"Of course we did. I'd known Susan all my life. She was like a second sister. All the Littletons loved her . . . everyone loved her. She was genuine, gracious, kindhearted, fun loving, had a beautiful smile and used it often, and more importantly, she loved my brother and made him the happiest man I've ever known. She loved to entertain and have friends over. She was talented in so many areas. I remember once I told her she should think about picking up a brush and see where her talent for painting would take her. She said, 'Clint, all I've wanted since I was in the second grade was to grow up and marry Clay.' I can also tell you that she would have felt the same way if she was given the opportunity to know you."

A sharp, piercing pain stabbed inside her and Ellery was afraid she was going to cry, so she quickly changed the subject and asked, "Did Susan believe Clay's death was an accident?"

"No, she felt the same way I did."

"Did the police have any suspects initially?"

"No. They ran the usual checks, interviewed half the town, but came up with nothing."

"Was there ever any kind of trouble between Clay or Susan and her brother, Daniel?"

"No, what made you ask that?"

"No reason other than the fact that he knew both of them and now they're dead."

"Everyone in Agarita Springs knew them, so that

doesn't move Daniel to the top of the list. Daniel had no motive for killing either of them. He got along well with Clay and he had no problems with Susan when they were growing up."

They talked on for a while until the faint chime of the grandfather clock drifted through the screen door and Clint said, "I didn't realize it'd gotten so late." He glanced at his watch and stood. "I think I've delighted you too long with my company, as my mother likes to say."

Ellery laughed and realized it felt so very good to do so. "I'm glad you came by and that we were able to have this talk."

He nodded, a corner of his mouth rising in a half-smile.

She stood up too. "I'm sorry for asking you to talk about this, but I had to ask those questions."

"I understand. I'm sure my mother and sister could answer more than I could. Let me know when you feel up to meeting them."

She nodded and they started walking toward the house.

"I hope I didn't act like I begrudge your asking questions because I don't," he said. "You've suffered a great loss. You have a right to learn all you can and to form your own opinions. I only hope I've been able to help you settle things in your mind a bit. If you find you need more answers than I can give you, you know you can always pay the county sheriff or the police a visit. The records are all there."

They stepped into the house and placed the bottle and glasses on the counter. She followed him into the family room.

He paused a moment and said, "I really do apologize for staying so long."

She thought about inviting him to stay longer, and then thought better of it. "No apology needed. I enjoyed having you here. I needed to talk to someone about all of this. Thank you for taking the time to answer my questions. I'm glad you came."

He gave her a smile that said he doubted the sincerity of that last comment. He picked up his hat that was lying upside down on the coffee table.

"I did enjoy your company," she said. "You're easy to be around and I like talking to you. Truly, I am very glad you were here."

"I'll probably do something before too long to make you want to take those words back."

She would have laughed, but the play of lamplight on the dark waves of his hair snagged her attention. The crease from his hat was still there. She noticed that the skin on his forehead, where his hat protected it, was a little lighter than the rest of his face.

She studied the way he stood there holding his straw hat in his hands and her heart flipped over a time or two. Who would have ever thought that she would find herself attracted to the rancher-cowboy type? Yet, here she was, feeling drawn in many different ways to a very masculine tall Texan. She even felt tongue-tied with not a damn clever thing to say entering her mind. "Why would I want to take my words back? Bertha isn't half as much fun to share a bottle of wine with."

Thirteen

LATER THAT EVENING, she thought about how there had been so much grief and suffering in the Littleton family and she wondered how Clint's poor mother had withstood it. She felt bad about asking him to talk about Susan's and Clay's deaths, but she'd had to know.

She thought about all she had in common with Clint and that set her heart to knocking again. She could not deny there was a very strong attraction between them.

Ellery felt it.

And she knew, judging from the way he looked at her, that Clint felt it as well. Suddenly, she put her hand to her head and asked herself, Good Lord, Ellery, why are you thinking about that at a time like this?

The last thing she needed right now was a man in her life, especially one like him. She needed to keep Clint out of her thoughts so she could stay focused . . . if she wanted to find the bastard who'd killed her sister.

Ellery spent the rest of the evening on the computer, answering e-mail and doing more research on twins and forensics. Several times she paused when she thought she heard a noise. It made her think about the frightening call she'd received and the mask taped to her door. She glanced at the telephone as if expecting it to ring. What if it wasn't Sherman T. who was harassing her? When she'd called the *Snoop* this morning, one of the secretaries had told her Sherman was on vacation in the Caribbean. But maybe he'd lied about his plans. Leaning back in her chair, Ellery looked around the room. She thought about this house having belonged to her sister—and how it made her feel protected somehow by the virtue of that fact alone.

It hadn't protected Susan though, had it?

She realized then that she was more bothered by the fact that this was where her sister had lived . . . and died . . . than she'd let on to Clint. She was engulfed with sadness, which was accompanied by a feeling of tightness in her throat and eyes.

She turned off her computer and went to the back door to call Bertha and let her in the house. It wasn't exactly that she was frightened, but more that she just didn't feel as if she were *alone* in the house.

In spite of her expectations that the dream would come again, she slept the night through and felt more rested the next morning than she had for several days. She remembered she needed to talk to Lucy, so she rolled over and picked up the phone and dialed her number.

"Hello."

"Lucy, this is Ellery. I apologize for calling so early. I hope you were up."

"Heavens yes. I'm glad you called."

"I'm sorry for rushing off the other day."

"Hey, don't worry about it. I understood perfectly. We all have our saturation points, and it was obvious you had reached yours. I'm so glad you called though. I've been worrying about you and cursing my stupidity in telling you everything in such a cold and callous way. I hope you will forgive me."

"Lucy, there's nothing to forgive. There isn't a nice way to tell someone her twin sister has been murdered. It wasn't the way you told me that was painful. It was learning what happened. You had to tell me. At least I won't spend the rest of my life looking for her."

"How are you doing?"

"I'm doing so well I want to take you to lunch. Do you have plans today?"

"Yes, some leftover tuna made into a sandwich. Your offer sounds so much better. I'm opening the fridge door right now."

Ellery heard noise in the background.

"As we speak, I am taking out the tuna and putting it into the cat's dish. Now you have to take me out to eat."

Ellery laughed. Lucy was like a ray of sunshine in her life. She was so upbeat and funny that some of it couldn't help rubbing off. Ellery felt better already. "Great. I have a lot to tell you, but it can wait until lunch."

"Shall I pick you up?" Lucy asked. "I've got several errands to run, so I'll already be out. It will be easy for me to stop by your house."

"It's probably easier for me to meet you there since I've got errands to run as well. As for lunch, I haven't a clue where we should go," Ellery said. "I'm afraid you're my first luncheon date in this town. Do you know a nice little place—one that women would like?"

"In other words, you don't want to go to Roy's Truck Stop."

Ellery laughed. "I would rather share the cat's tuna."

Anticipating some lunch counter or local café packed with men, Ellery was pleasantly surprised when she parked in front of a wood-framed house painted a delightful shade of blue. A second later, Lucy parked next to her. Ellery waved and waited for Lucy to join her.

"I think you'll really like this," Lucy said.

White flower boxes proudly showed their colorful stuff at every window. Wicker chairs of assorted styles and vintage were arranged on the porch. In groups of two, each had a table nestled in between. Wicker planters contained huge ferns that drooped lazily to the floor. Over the porch, a lavender sign proudly announced, in blue, rather artsy letters that this was THE TEA COZY.

Only one word would describe the inside and that was charming. It was furnished with Texas pine antiques, there were paintings by local artists on the walls, and each table had a unique tablecloth, topped with a milk-glass vase containing fresh flowers. "This is charming and absolutely perfect," she said to Lucy.

"And even better, the food is wonderful. Rhonda Carr and Renee Watkins own it, and they do all the cooking. They had a four-star restaurant in Austin, but sold it so they could move back home."

Once they were seated, they ordered tea, and then chatted while they looked over the menu.

After a while, the waitress put the hibiscus tea they ordered on the table, and asked, "Are you ladies ready to order now?"

"I am," Ellery said.

"You start then," Lucy said. "I'm still trying to make up my mind."

Ellery ordered the cold cantaloupe soup, and a radicchio salad, with pine nuts and balsamic dressing.

Lucy was still looking at the menu. She sighed and said, "This always happens to me. There are so many choices. I think I'll have the chicken salad plate."

"That comes with a cup of soup," the waitress said. "What kind would you like?"

"Tortilla soup, please."

They fell into the typical female conversation, interspersed with sips of iced hibiscus tea, but after a few minutes Ellery said, "I don't know if I told you that when I called Margaret Ledbetter, she was terribly rude to me. If possible, she was even more so when I went to see her. She told me on the phone to come at four o'clock, and then when I showed up, she wouldn't talk to me. She shouted at me from an upstairs window like a deranged person and told me to go away, then she slammed the window shut and left me talking to myself."

"I'm sorry. She was always such a dear, but she's been acting very strange with me as well. I don't know what's wrong. I began noticing it sometime after Susan disappeared. At first, I thought she was depressed over Susan's and Clay's deaths. Of late, I've started to worry that it might be Alzheimer's, because my mother started out that way. She would turn on me and say the most awful things. I knew it wasn't really her saying them, but it was still heartbreaking. After a while, I knew I would have to find a place that could care for her, if I was going to maintain my sanity and keep my marriage together. By the time I got her in the nursing home, my marriage was already damaged beyond repair. I hope Aunt Margaret isn't going to end up like my mother."

"Has she been to a doctor?"

"I tried to get her to let me take her. She refused and said there was nothing wrong with her mind. I decided to wait and see if things got better. They haven't. She is consistent, I'll say that, and always as cross as two sticks."

Ellery couldn't help smiling at Lucy's comparison. She loved the way people talked here, and how they still held to so many of their traditions, especially their wonderful sayings and the comparisons they drew.

"I'm glad I asked," Ellery said. "Understanding removes the hostility. Now all I feel is sorry for her . . . well, that and an urge to stay far away."

Lucy smiled and put her hand on Ellery's. "I can't tell you how very glad I am that you are here. It's nice to have some family close by, someone my age that I can talk to and confide in. Susan and I were cousins, but we were also good friends. We used to come to lunch here quite often. I miss her so much. After she was gone, I realized how hard it is to live where there's no family around. It's like being left out in the cold when you can see everyone else through the window."

"I hope we'll become even better friends." Ellery paused a moment, trying to think how she wanted to phrase her next words. Finally, she simply said, "I assume you don't know that the house I'm renting . . . it's Susan's house."

Lucy was obviously stunned and for a few seconds seemed to be at a loss for words. "The house on Live Oak . . . the one Susan and Clay owned?"

Ellery nodded.

"Good Lord! That is really weird, don't you think?"

"Yes, I do."

"Did you know it was Susan's house when you rented it?"

"No, I just found out."

"How?"

"Clint told me."

Ellery was thinking about the house; how it seemed so familiar to her. She remembered it had seemed familiar prior to coming to Texas. She wondered if this was some type of twin telepathy.

She saw the concerned look on Lucy's face and said, "I seem to be collecting coincidences, stacking them one on top of the other. How many can I add, I wonder, before it collapses?"

Lucy's expression seemed stiff, as if she were holding back tears. "I keep thinking if you get any more you'll turn tail and go back to Washington."

"No, don't worry. Nothing could make me leave now. Do you realize you are the only person who has offered to help, and the only relative I have, besides Hazel and Margaret?"

Lucy started laughing. "Then I'm glad you're renting." Her look turned more serious. "You know, I can't believe no one told you what happened there before you rented it."

Ellery was thinking the same thing and was about to say so, but the soup arrived, and they both fell silent.

After a while, Lucy said, "Listen, if this discovery has made you uncomfortable about staying in the house, I want you to know I would love to have you stay with me. There's plenty of room."

"Thank you, but I don't have any reservations about the house. Oh, I was a bit apprehensive in the beginning. If anything, I feel closer to my sister knowing I'm living in the same house where she lived. I think she was happy there. What about her marriage? Was it happy?"

"Oh yes. They were high school sweethearts . . . well, actually they were junior high sweethearts."

"That doesn't always translate to happily ever after."

A blank, helpless sort of expression settled over Lucy's face. "No, it doesn't."

"Lucy, I'm sorry. That was thoughtless of me. I forgot about your separation."

"Oh, that's okay. I'm not going to be separated much longer. Daryl filed for divorce two days ago."

"I'm not going to pry, but you have an open invitation to discuss it any time you feel the need to talk."

"Thanks. I'm sorry the dream ended. I'm not sorry Daryl is moving on. We were happy the first couple of years. Looking back, I don't know how I lasted eight more."

"You were the one who wanted the separation?"

"I wanted a divorce, but Daryl talked me into a separation. In the meantime he met someone else."

"Which immediately changed his mind and facilitated his filing?"

Lucy laughed. "Exactly. It's strange, but your comments make him sound so shallow. I never realized that about him until now. He really is a shallow person."

"I almost said 'superficial,' " Ellery admitted, and they both laughed.

Two women glanced in their direction.

Lucy lowered her voice and continued, "Some may disagree, but I think no marriage is better than a bad one. So now I'll be free of Daryl, but a divorced woman. They sort of balance each other out, don't they?"

The teasing tone was gone from Ellery's voice. "There is no stigma to being divorced."

The waitress brought their food and poured more hibiscus tea. "You two seem to be having a wonderful time," she said. "I love to see people enjoy themselves."

"I hope our laughter isn't bothering your other guests," Ellery said.

"It looked to me like they were all enjoying it. Who can criticize laughter, anyway?"

After the waitress left, Ellery took a couple of bites of salad before Lucy asked, "Were you ever married?"

"Almost. I made it as far as being engaged."

"What happened?"

"He was killed."

"How?"

"Edward went to work for the Securities and Exchange Commission after he finished law school. He planned to go into private practice after a few years. He was killed in a plane crash along with five other business associates. Our wedding was all planned and just a few weeks away."

"I'm sorry," Lucy said. "Did you say his name was Edward?"

"Yes."

She reached across the table and placed her hand over Ellery's. "Ellery, what was your fiancé's full name?"

"Carlton Edward Little the Third . . . why?"

"Oh, good Lord! Do you know what Clay's full name was?"

"No."

"Clayton Edward Littleton. That's almost spooky, isn't it? I mean, their names are so similar, and both were killed when they were still young."

Ellery rubbed her arms. "I can't deny it gives me a chill, but it doesn't surprise me. I've read twins quite often have a lot of things like that in common."

"I've read things like that too." Lucy paused and then said, "Oh, I almost forgot. Hazel is back from her trip to Europe. She came back early because her back was bothering her." Lucy frowned. "Although I've never known Hazel to have back trouble. Anyhow, she called today and I told her I'd bring you by to see her."

Ellery was jubilant at the news. "What are we waiting for, then?"

Lucy laughed. "Nothing. Are you serious? Because if you are, we can go now."

Ellery smiled. "Let's go." And they did just that as soon as they finsihed eating.

They drove to Hazel's quaint Victorian house on Thirteenth Street. When she opened the door, Hazel seemed thrilled to see Ellery and could not help exclaiming how much she looked like Susan.

Hazel was a small woman with mouse-brown hair, streaked with gray, and gentle gray eyes. She had lovely skin that had not been damaged by the sun, or covered with makeup. She wore a floral print dress that reached almost to her ankles and had a quaint white collar—the kind of dress Ellery hadn't seen in ages. She looked every bit the part of an elementary school librarian.

"I understand you went to see my mother and that she wasn't very friendly. I hope you won't judge her harshly because of it. My mother hasn't been herself of late. I've been worried about her."

"I understand," Ellery said. "Lucy said almost the same thing. Perhaps Margaret did not want to dig up old, painful memories."

"I don't think that was it," Hazel said. "I remember my mother talked about Claudia frequently and she always wondered what happened to 'poor Claudia's other little baby.' "

"You knew about that?"

"Of course, but we kept it in the family and never discussed it in front of anyone. It was painful for my mother and Lucy's to lose their sister. They did not want to talk about it to anyone outside the family."

Hazel changed the subject then and they talked about Hazel's trip. "That's terrible about your back and your having to cut short your vacation. When did you start having back trouble?" Lucy asked.

"Oh, it just came on all of a sudden and I felt I had to come home. I'm much better now." Hazel looked at Ellery and smiled. When Ellery commented on her lovely home, Hazel offered to show it to her. "That is, if you'd like to see it," she said.

"I would love a tour," Ellery assured her.

The house still retained much of its original charm,

with lovely stained-glass windows, French doors, and period lighting fixtures. A huge screened-in porch looked over a lovely yard and the kitchen seemed to have everything from the previous century, except a hand pump at the sink. Then Hazel gave them a tour of the upstairs with a guest room and a small sleeping porch off the master bedroom. They returned to the parlor a short while later to have coffee and lemon pound cake while they visited, Ellery answering Hazel's questions about where she grew up, her father Sam O'Brien, and her work in television. When Ellery asked Hazel about her biological father, Nathan Wilkerson, all Hazel said, shaking her head, was, "You'll have to ask my mother about him once she warms to you."

After another half hour of chitchat, Ellery couldn't help asking, "Don't you feel a little spooky about having such an address . . . 1313 Thirteenth Street sounds like something out of a horror movie."

Hazel laughed. "Lord, don't I know it. I've been teased about it for years. I just answer that someone had to have that address. Thankfully, I'm not the superstitious type. The way I see it, that many thirteens sort of cancel each other out, don't you think?"

"I hope so," Ellery said with a shiver. "I surely do hope so."

"You can't be superstitious either," Lucy said, "because you live in Susan's house." As soon as she blurted out the words, her face turned red. "I'm so sorry. I don't know why I said that."

"Don't apologize. It's something I've thought of enough, and truthfully, there are times when I think I must be out of my mind for staying, but I feel closer to Susan there than anywhere else. I don't know if I'd keep having those dreams either . . . if I moved to another house."

"What dreams?" Hazel asked.

Ellery told Hazel about the connection she'd felt to her sister even as a young girl, and how she began—after she learned about Susan's existence—to have strange dreams. "I thought I came here to find my sister. Now, I realize I came here to find her killer."

Hazel's warm and friendly demeanor changed suddenly, and the color seemed to drain from her face quite rapidly. She exhibited signs of nervousness. "You mustn't pursue such foolishness. No one knows who killed your sister. He could be living right next door. If you start poking around, you could very well end up dead like Susan."

Fourteen

ELLERY TOOK CLINT up on his suggestion that she pay a visit to the chief of police, but when she asked to speak to Jack Sherwood, she was told he was out on a call.

She noticed the name displayed on the desk about the same time Sergeant Carroll asked, "Could someone else help you?"

"I don't know." She explained she wanted to discuss the case of her twin sister, Susan Littleton.

He seemed surprised and looked her over, but all he said was, "Detective Roland Bardwell is the man you need to see. He investigated Susan Littleton's case. I'll let him know you're here."

A short time later Ellery was sitting in the waiting area and a man entered. He introduced himself. "I'm Detective Bardwell. I understand you wanted to ask me some questions."

Detective Bardwell had a face that looked like it was made out of leftovers. Nothing seemed to go together. His face was too broad. His eyes bulged a little too much.

His eyebrows looked like a couple of caterpillars had crawled across his forehead and parked. But he did have the most charming gap-toothed grin.

"Yes, I did want to visit with you," she said. She offered him her hand and gave him a brief rundown of who she was.

"I don't mind saying it's quite a surprise to suddenly learn that Susan Littleton had a twin sister."

"Believe me, it was quite a surprise to me as well," Ellery replied.

"Come on into my office. We can talk privately in there. Can I get you a cup of coffee?"

"No, thank you," she said, walking alongside him down the hall to his office. She seated herself in one of two chairs in front of his desk.

Detective Bardwell was getting close to not fitting into his chair. A quick glance across his desk explained why: assorted candy wrappers—although he did seem to prefer Butterfingers—an empty sack from Burger King, three crushed Coke cans, a large jar of M&M's, two bags of barbecue potato chips . . . unopened.

Bardwell reached for a yellow legal pad and pulled it across the desk until it was in front of him. He grabbed a pen out of a ceramic mug that said UNIVERSITY OF TEXAS, gave it a click to eject the point, and wrote something on the first line. "Would you mind giving me your particulars?"

She stared at him openmouthed. "My . . . what?" Surely he didn't mean what she thought he meant.

His face turned red and he cleared his throat. "That . . . um . . . would be your name, telephone number, address, and so on."

It was her turn to blush. "Oh, I see," she said, and gave him the information.

He wrote everything down, then he leaned back, and began to twirl the pen through his fingers without taking his gaze from her face. "Now, I know you said you were Ms. Littleton's twin sister, but I never knew that she had a sister."

"Neither did Susan. I only learned about it recently." She told him about her personal background, her work in television, and then explained a few details about her father's revelation before his death, and her subsequent decision to find her sister.

He was still writing when she said, "I hope this helps you understand the devastation I felt when I learned of her death and knew I would never know my sister. Naturally, I wanted to talk to you about her case. I didn't know her, but she was my twin and I want to know what happened to her. I want to find her body. I want to find out who did this."

"We all want to do that, Ms. O'Brien." His gaze never left her face. "You said you were an investigative reporter before you became a newscaster. You sound like you're hoping to return to your roots and start an investigation of your own."

"I don't intend to hang out my shingle and start taking statements and having interviews if that's what you mean, but yes, I am concerned and I do want answers."

"That's all?"

"Of course."

"Hold on a sec," he said, and picked up the phone. He punched in a few numbers with the eraser on the end of a pencil. "Hi, Karleen, I'd like you to pull the file on Susan Littleton for me. Would you mind dropping it by my office when you're done?"

When he hung up, his eyes were back on Ellery. "Your sister's case is still open, although it's not one we are actively investigating. What would you like to know?"

"Perhaps it would be easier to tell you what I do know and you can add to or correct it."

He nodded and she repeated everything she knew and followed it with some specifics she wanted to know about.

"Did you ever do any investigating on cases that the FBI was involved with?"

"A few times. Why do you ask?"

"Because it's evident you are quite advanced over the investigative reporters we have in Agarita Springs."

She smiled at him. "I cheat a little on the side, Detective."

"How's that?"

"I have a passion for crime novels and I'm addicted to forensic programs on television."

She got another glimpse of his gap-toothed grin before he said, "In regard to what we found at the crime scene, we conducted an independent, thorough, and complete investigation of this case that meets all accepted police investigative practices. We collected samples and ran the usual tests, but someone knew what they were doing. As I said, the place was pretty clean as far as evidence was concerned. We found a few fibers and fingerprints and sent them to the lab, but they came back belonging to friends or family members who were often in the house.

All the blood belonged to your sister and the killer went to great lengths to keep out of the way of it. Not one bloody footprint did we find. It was as if he had wrapped himself in a plastic bag . . . no hair samples were found other than those belonging to the victim. There was nothing to clue us to the murderer's identity. There were no fingerprints or handprints, save those of the victim, anywhere. We did find footprints in the carpet that measured to be about a size eleven shoe. The driveway is gravel, so no tire prints could be taken, that is, if the perpetrator drove to the crime scene."

"But you had suspects in the beginning, right?"

"The most promising suspect in the beginning was the yardman. Ms. Littleton had fired him the week before she disappeared for drinking on the job. After a couple of interviews, we moved him to the list of suspects cleared."

"Why?"

"He was in jail in Austin for drunk driving the night Susan was killed."

"Did you ever think Susan's and Clay's deaths could be related?"

"We looked at that possibility," he said, "at Clint Littleton's insistence, but there was nothing we found to lead us to believe there was a connection."

"Why not?"

"There are three things a good homicide detective looks for: motive, opportunity, means. We could not find anyone who had any motive to kill Susan and Clay. There is also the fact that Clay's death was ruled accidental, not murder. Secondly, there were no similarities in the ways in which the victims died to make us believe they were killed by the same person. Clay was killed climbing a fence, by his own shotgun, in broad daylight at the Littletons' ranch. There was no sign of a scuffle, or any sign that anyone else had been there. Your sister was murdered shortly after midnight, with a knife. And there was the time span between their deaths. If someone wanted them both dead, why didn't they kill both of them at the same time and save themselves a lot of trouble, not to mention added risk?"

"Did you ever suspect Susan's family members or friends might have anything to do with her death? I don't mean to imply I think anyone did, of course. I know that is where detectives usually begin their investigation."

"We talked to a number of people, including neighbors, family, close friends, acquaintances, and took statements from them. You need a motive to hang something like murder on a man and there was no motive we could find connecting any of them to Susan's murder and they all had tight alibis. And everyone knew how close-knit the family was."

"Who were the family members you checked out?"

"We talked to all of them . . . Clint, his mother, Virginia, his sister, Margie, and then there was Margie's husband, Jerry. There was nothing that made us interview them, other than the fact that they were family members. All of them could prove where they were the night of the murder."

"What about Susan's adopted brother, Daniel Wilkerson?"

"I remember talking to Daniel before we had a chance to call in any of the other people for questioning. He drove over from Austin as soon as he heard about Susan's death. He was all broken up over it and seemed to be taking it very hard. As he should, since she was his sister.

"While he was here, I asked him several questions . . . any names he could suggest of people who might have had a grievance against Susan, even when they were growing up and that sort of thing, but he couldn't think of anyone. Like everyone else, he thought she didn't have an enemy in the world. He put up a ten-thousand-dollar reward for information leading to the arrest and conviction of her killer."

"How did the investigation of Susan's death progress?"

"We quickly concluded it wasn't a random crime. Either the killer had followed the victim, or knew her movements. In this case, as we do in all similar cases, the investigation first concentrated on finding potential enemies, or those who could benefit from the victim's death."

Ellery was nodding in agreement.

Bardwell continued. "I'm sure that with your background you've heard the saying 'there are three major motives for murder: love, hate, and greed.' We easily eliminated the first. Her husband was dead and she was still grieving and definitely did not date. We found nothing to indicate she had any enemies, so the second was unlikely. So we focused on the third. We compiled financial profiles on family members to see if any of them were financially strapped, but all were in good financial shape."

A knock at the door interrupted the discussion and a young woman came into the office. "Excuse me for forcing an intermission, but you asked me to bring this over."

"Come on in, Karleen. This is Ellery O'Brien. Susan Littleton was her twin sister."

Karleen gave Ellery the once-over before she realized what she had done and then, to cover her embarrassment, she blurted out, "Your twin sister? Well, now that I know that, I can see the resemblance. I surely can. I'm sorry about Susan," Karleen said. "Everyone in town loved her. She was very active in volunteer and church work, and she had the most beautiful voice. She sang like an angel in the church choir."

Ellery felt tears coming to her eyes. "Thank you for sharing that with me. I want to learn all I can about Susan."

She gave Ellery an understanding smile, and placed the manila folders on Bardwell's desk.

Bardwell waited until Karleen had gone, then he opened one of the folders and began rummaging through it. "As you can see, we've kept everything from the investigation—the initial crime scene reports, the investigator notebooks, the suspect list, the interviews, and evidence reports. We don't have a ruling on the exact cause of death by the medical examiner since there was no body."

From time to time he would pull out a sheet and read bits of it to her, which led to some lengthy discussions. When he reached the end of it, he closed the folder and said, "I know you were hoping to learn more and I wish I had more to give you, but this has been a hard case to crack."

"How well did you know my sister?"

"Well enough that Clay punched me in the nose after a football game in high school for flirting with her. She was a cheerleader and I was flirtatiously harassing her while Clay was on the field."

She smiled at that, thinking these were the kinds of things she was so hungry to learn about her twin. "Were they happily married?"

"Oh yeah . . . if you could have seen them together, it was like there was no one else around—just the two of them. I always said if a woman ever looked at me the way Susan looked at Clay, well, there wouldn't be anything I wouldn't do for her."

"Why didn't Susan work since they had no children?"

"They were both pretty traditional in that regard and they liked being together. I'm sure you know Clay was an architect and a good one. They were comfortably well off financially, so Susan didn't need to work for the income. They belonged to the country club and frequently went to Austin for dinner and a movie . . . sometimes they went for the weekend to stay at the Four Seasons. Whenever Clay had a job that took him out of town or even out of state, Susan went with him. It was like they were inseparable."

"Where was Clay's office?"

"He had an office in their home. Susan answered the phone and handled the paperwork when she wasn't out volunteering in the community."

Ellery glanced at the clock on the wall and sighed. "I've taken up enough of your time, Detective. Thank you for filling in the blank spaces for me." She stood and offered him her hand. "You've helped me understand the circumstances and your investigation, as well as given me insight into who Susan was, and for that, I thank you."

Ellery was more than a little disappointed when she left. Although she did have a better understanding of things, by no means had she learned anything she considered helpful in locating Susan's murderer or her body.

What she did know was that someone out there had wanted her twin sister dead, and she was going to find out why.

Fifteen

ELLERY SAT AT HER DESK, staring at the computer screen, her thoughts not on the volume of e-mail downloading into Outlook. Her thoughts were elsewhere . . .

She'd dreamed again last night—the same dream, the same killer with the knife in his hand, and like the other times, the shadows had faded, revealing a little more of his face. She recalled how desperately she'd tried to make out his features more distinctly, but they'd remained blurred. All she could recall of the killer was a square-jawed face topped with dark hair. She knew his complexion was light and thought for some reason that his eyes were brown.

Not enough to pick him out of a lineup.

It was at times like this—when frustration was mounted upon frustration and she grew irritable at the snail's pace at which her investigation was moving—that she wondered why she couldn't have been born an only child, or why she was the type of person who always pushed herself to the very limit.

Ellery pushed a tumble of hair back and turned off the computer monitor. She lost herself in a few chores around the house, took Bertha for a walk, went to the post office, stopped by H.E.B., and spent a few minutes conversing with Lorraine in her driveway.

When she put the groceries away and checked messages, she returned a call from Lucy.

"Oh lordy, am I glad to hear from you. You won't believe what happened today. After I left the school, I stopped by to see Aunt Margaret, and guess who was sitting there with his butt parked right smack in the middle of her red silk sofa?"

"Who?"

"Daniel Wilkerson, in the flesh."

"You're kidding."

"I wish, but I'm not. I was so shocked I couldn't think of a damn thing to say, so I stood there in the hallway outside the parlor listening. I felt like a complete ninny when Daniel came over to greet me with a clammy kiss on the cheek."

"What was he doing there?"

"This is where it gets good. Daniel knows all about you . . . who you are . . . where you work . . . what you're doing here."

"How on earth did he find out?"

"Beats me."

"Did you ask him?"

"Of course I did, but he just gave me a wan smile and went on talking to Aunt Margaret, like I was some pissant. Daniel is rather arrogant. He made a fortune in computers."

"Well, I do want to meet him, since he is the perfect person to fill me in on Susan's life when they were growing up."

"I figured you'd get around to asking me how you could get in touch with him."

"I thought it best to contact him after I finished educating myself about Susan's death and Clay's too, for that matter. You know, I do find it strange that he hasn't tried to contact me. Don't you think it's a bit odd that he wouldn't at least be curious about me and how much I resemble his sister?"

"He was curious about you, don't think he wasn't. He was grilling Aunt Margaret when I arrived. I know this because I stood outside the door listening to them for a while before I entered the room. I heard him asking her questions about you, even after Aunt Margaret said she had never really talked with you, face-to-face, and did not care to discuss it. He did say something I found a bit odd. He said he thought she did the right thing by not talking to you."

"I wonder why he would say that," Ellery said.

"I haven't the foggiest. Maybe he thought it would be best for her not to be reminded of Susan's death. Aunt Margaret took Susan's death awfully hard. Sometimes I wonder if she isn't terribly depressed about it, but then at the same time, I think it's something else. I think I told you she hasn't been herself for some time now. She was never the reclusive sort."

"When you listened outside the door, what kind of questions did Daniel ask?"

"You know, the usual . . . what does she look like; do

you like her; how did she take the news that her twin was murdered; how long is she staying—that sort of thing."

"Hm," Ellery said, giving herself a moment to ponder all that Lucy was telling her. "Did he indicate why he was visiting Aunt Margaret?"

"For no reason in particular, according to him, that is. He just said he wasn't particularly busy at the office and decided to take a drive and see how Aunt Margaret is faring. I believe him. He does keep in touch with her—after a fashion. I guess eccentrics gravitate toward one another—you know, like magnets."

"Is he eccentric?"

"Oh Lord, yes."

"How so?"

"Well, he like to keep to himself. He doesn't seem to have girlfriends—or boyfriends." Lucy laughed. "But then I suppose a software genius—that's how he made his money—is bound to be introverted."

"Did he mention if he wanted to meet me anytime soon?"

"Yes, he was trying to talk Aunt Margaret into having a small cocktail party in your honor, but she refused. I don't know if you know it, but Aunt Margaret is tighter than a tick. She won't spend a dime that she doesn't have to . . . squeezes a dollar until old George hollers. But, back to Daniel . . . he said he was going to call you and take you to lunch or dinner because he was dying to meet you."

Ellery frowned at his choice of words. "I've decided to drop the word 'dying' from my vocabulary, at least for the time being."

"Don't blame you."

"Well, I guess I'll wait to meet Daniel until he calls . . . if he calls."

"You could call him, I guess."

"No, I've changed my mind. I think I'll wait and see how long it takes him to contact me."

"Oh, I'm sure he'll call soon. His curiosity is aroused. He is itching to compare you with Susan, believe me."

"Why don't we have lunch tomorrow? Or dinner," Ellery suggested. "Which is best for you?"

"Let's do dinner. I don't go out much at night and there is a really nice Italian restaurant here called La Pergola I want you to try. I'll make a reservation and call you back." She laughed. "I guess when one is without a man in one's life, one finds great comfort in good food."

"It's a date," Ellery said.

Sixteen

ELLERY WAS SOUND asleep the next morning when the doorbell rang. At first she tried to ignore it by rolling over and pulling the other pillow over her head. It kept ringing.

Determined bastard, she thought, whoever he is. She glanced at the clock. Seven A.M.? What idiot would ring someone's doorbell at seven o'clock in the morning?

If there was anything Ellery hated, it was being forced awake when in a deep sleep. She stumbled to the chair where she had tossed her robe the night before. She rubbed her eyes and looked at the clock again, certain she had misread the time. It was still the ungodly hour of seven o'clock in the morning.

The doorbell rang again and she started down the stairs. "Just a minute! I'm coming, I'm coming!"

She still had that groggy, "where am I, where's my coffee" feeling, but she woke up fast when she looked through the side window and saw Clint Littleton. She opened the door.

"You better have a good reason for waking me up."

"I thought you got up early?"

"Where did you get that crazy idea?" She said that because she did not want to tell him she'd slept later than usual because her sleep had been disturbed by nightmares once again. Last night the killer's face had seemed less blurred.

"You do the morning news, so you have to get up early."

"I get up early when I do the morning news in Washington, D.C.; I sleep late when I'm in Agarita Springs. I'm going back to bed. I'm still sleepy."

"Mind if I join you?"

She was about to tell him how flat that joke fell when he said, "Whoa! Not so fast! I picked up the newspaper for you."

"You drove all the way over here to pick the newspaper up out of my yard and hand it to me? Are you serious?"

"Yes, and you will be, too, once you see the article on the front page." He peeled away the rubber band and handed her the paper.

She yanked the paper out of his hand and pulled out the main section. The headline leaped off the page at her.

D.C. NEWSCASTER INVESTIGATES MURDER OF TWIN SISTER

She was stunned, until she read the name of the reporter below the headline . . .

"Sherman T. DeWitt . . . that miserable little worm.

He's supposed to be on vacation in the Caribbean. I might have known. But I still don't understand how he found out about my sister?"

"I take it you know him?"

"Oh yes, I know him. He was a fledgling reporter at WMDC with me when I first went to work there. From the beginning there was a lot of competition between us . . . more on his part than on mine. He was always making comments about women reporters—how they always quit to get married or have a baby, then whine when some guy gets ahead of them. I always ignored him, until he started making comments to me about my biological clock running out and things like that. I know why he did it, but I didn't fall into that trap. His jibes only made me work harder. When word began to circulate that WMDC was looking for a new cohost of the morning news show *Starting Point*, ol' Sherman T. was touting how he was the most likely choice.

"While he was busy bragging, I managed to get an interview with serial killer Ethan M. Aalderink, shortly before he was executed. During the interview, he confessed to all those murders that he swore he was innocent of during the trial. Sherman had me in his sights after that. Evidently it was the final straw because two days after Sherman blew up and called me all sorts of things, it was announced that I would be Chad Newberry's new coanchor on *Starting Point*."

"That wasn't the end of it, was it?"

"No, it wasn't. You know the kind who cannot let anything die—Sherman was a good reporter but he let his hot head and overinflated ego get in the way. I always suspected he was mentally unbalanced because the guy had no shame, no empathy, and excelled at playing mind games. Suffice it to say, he blew up when he learned that I would be doing *Starting Point*. He quit his job and went to WMAZ-TV. A week or so after he left, I found my car's windshield smashed; sugar was put into my gas tank a few days later. And when my tires were slashed, my executive producer told me not to bring my car to work after that. They assigned a driver to pick me up and take me home. No one could prove Sherman had vandalized my car but we all knew it was him. He ended up getting fired from WMAZ and is now working for one of those supermarket tabloids, the *Daily Snoop*." She considered telling Clint about the disturbing phone call and the mask, but something held her back. Instead, she glanced down at the paper in her hands and began to read.

Ellery O'Brien, the star of WMDC's morning news show, *Starting Point*, has become tabloid fodder since her move to Agarita Springs, Texas, a small town near Austin.

It seems that Ms. O'Brien has led a double life since the day she was born. When her father, Chevy Chase dentist Dr. Sam O'Brien, lay dying of cancer, he revealed that D.C.'s darling of morning television was not his daughter but the illegitimate offspring of a Texas banker and a minister's daughter. Another twist was added to this story when she learned she was separated from her twin sister at birth.

She has temporarily relocated to Agarita

Springs, where she began her search for her twin. It didn't take her long to hook up with wealthy rancher Clint Littleton. Now the story gets really interesting, for Clint Littleton is the brother of Clay Littleton, a well-known architect who was found dead at the Littleton Ranch three years ago. His death was ruled a hunting accident.

Clay Littleton was married to Ellery O'Brien's twin sister. Sadly for Ms. O'Brien, her sister disappeared from her home almost two years ago and her body has not been found. Foul play is suspected due to the bloody scene at the Littleton home the night she disappeared. Detective Roland Bardwell was in charge of the investigation. Bardwell said he believes Susan Littleton was murdered and her body disposed of elsewhere. "The murder weapon, a knife, was never found," he said. Police Chief Jack Sherwood was quoted as saying on the morning the grisly scene was discovered, "The condition of the house indicates something extremely violent occurred there, and we are treating this as a homicide case. At this time, we have no clues as to the location of Susan Littleton's body, which was removed from the scene prior to the police's arrival. We have not, as yet, come up with a list of suspects."

Ms. O'Brien seems to believe there is some connection between the disappearance and possible murder of her sister and Clay Littleton's death.

More eerily perplexing developments were soon revealed. Unbeknownst to her, the house Ms. O'Brien rented, sight unseen, before moving to Agarita Springs was none other than the home of her twin sister . . . the very house where the grisly murder occurred.

Vowing to find her sister's killer and solve the case, Ms. O'Brien has refused to leave the house that is now owned by Clint Littleton. It will bear watching to see if this influential anchorwoman will be able to dig up a suspect and enough evidence to charge someone with murder in either or both cases.

Rest assured that this reporter is as determined to continue reporting on this unraveling narrative until Ms. O'Brien solves the case or returns to her job at WMDC in defeat.

Ellery folded the paper and handed it back to Clint. "Return in defeat, will I? He doesn't know me very well." She paused a moment. "You know, what I don't understand is how he got wind of the story. I didn't tell anyone in D.C. except my next-door neighbor, who is my most trusted friend, and my boss at WMDC."

"Someone may have inadvertently slipped. Your boss could have mentioned it to his wife. Your friend's children could have overheard her telling her husband. A secretary at the TV station could have told someone in strict confidence. You may never know the identity of the snitch. Even the president of the United States isn't safe from leaks."

"I know. But how did he learn Susan Littleton is my sister?" She didn't meant to sound accusatory, but she supposed she did because Clint held his hands up defensively.

"Whoa! We Littletons don't talk to reporters, especially not about something like this that cuts so close to the bone." He paused, his expression dead serious. "The Eubanks clan keeps mum on this subject, as you well know. And I don't see anyone in the police department, who are all dedicated, loyal people, doing anything so low. I'm stumped."

"It's so disheartening to find your private matters making headlines," Ellery said with a sigh.

"You knew that sort of thing happened when you became a reporter and I'll wager you've spilled the beans on more than one case when you got wind of something."

She scowled. "If that was supposed to make me feel better, it didn't work."

He grinned. "Want me to try something else?"

"No."

"What does the *T* in Sherman T. DeWitt stand for?"

"Thaddeus. Sherman loves to remind everyone he is a descendant of Wellford Thaddeus Thorndale of the Alabama Thorndales, whoever they were."

Clint's rumbling laughter was infectious, and soon she joined in, thinking that laughter was the very best medicine.

He put the paper down on the entry table. "Why don't you ride out to the ranch with me? You need a change of scenery and it's a cinch you aren't going to go back to sleep now."

"I haven't had a chance to wash my face. I haven't brushed my teeth. I haven't even had a cup of coffee. I'm standing here talking to you in my robe and gown." She was about to tell him to take a hike and realized that wouldn't be very polite. Ye gods, she thought, am I turning into one of these kind and considerate Texans, where I worry about hurting someone's feelings with my harsh Yankee ways?

She must be, she thought, when the next thing she said was, "If I am going to be awakened at this wretched hour, I think I should be given enough time to at least make myself a cup of coffee and get dressed. If you'd like, you can join me . . . for the coffee, that is." She wanted to kick herself for the soft, smoky tone to her voice.

He must have liked it because there was a flirtatious gleam in his blue eyes . . . definitely flirtatious. "How long will it take you to get dressed?"

"That depends on how long we stand here yammering in the entry hall. Once I'm upstairs, I can be dressed and in the kitchen in fifteen minutes. Since you know where everything is in this house and you woke me up, why don't you make coffee? You do know how, don't you?"

"I know how to do a lot of things that might surprise you . . . and a few things that might please you as well," he added more softly.

She wasn't about to touch that last statement, although she was dying to know if what he was referring to was what she *thought* he was referring to. Instead, she ignored it and opened the door wider to allow him to enter.

The phone rang and Ellery hurried into the family room to answer it. "Hello."

"I'm sorry to call you so early, but I wanted to tell you about something in today's paper."

"Hi, Lucy. Clint is here. He just came by to show me the article."

"Are you okay?"

"Yes, just pissed as hell. If I ever get my hands on that good-for-nothing Sherman, I'll throttle him until his little bug eyes pop out of his head."

Lucy laughed. "Sounds like you know him."

"Oh, I know the good-for-nothing parasite. I worked with him at WMDC several years ago."

"Do you want me to come over?"

"I'm going to ride out to the ranch with Clint . . . he thinks I need to get some country air."

"It will be good for you."

"Why don't you come over after I get back? I'll call you when we leave the ranch."

"It's a deal. I'm glad Clint is there."

"Me too."

"Bye."

"See you later," Ellery said, and hung up.

Clint raised his brows in question. "Lucy?"

She nodded. "She was calling to tell me about the article."

"I imagine Shirley Van Meter will be next."

"No, she's still out of town. But my other neighbor, Lorraine, will call. No doubt about that."

"We need to get out of here," he said. "Don't answer any more phone calls."

She only had time for a quick shower. She combed her wet hair straight back and tried to ignore the fact that the ends were already beginning to curl. She was still fastening buttons as she walked to the bedroom door, in jeans and a white shirt that she left untucked. She was back downstairs in thirteen and a half minutes flat.

He looked up when she entered. "I didn't know there was such a thing as a punctual woman. My sister was always notoriously late. It drove me crazy when I had to wait for her every morning, so she could ride to high school with me."

"Comparing women could be dangerous to your health," Ellery advised.

He laughed. "A lot of things concerning women could be dangerous, but that hasn't stopped me from liking them."

The phone rang. She glanced at him and shrugged before she lifted the receiver. It was Merrily, calling to tell her about the article in the *Washington Post.*

Ellery related how it was in the local paper as well. They talked for a few minutes until Merrily said, "You be careful! That creep Sherman T. has a thing about you."

"Don't worry. At least now that I know for sure that it's him who's been harassing me, I know how to handle the situation. Thanks for calling. I'll talk to you soon."

Ellery hung up and turned around. Clint was standing at the stove, wearing her apron and frying ham and eggs. She couldn't help but smile.

It occurred to her that Clint Littleton treated women with polite respect, courtesy, and thoughtfulness that had nothing to do with sex or flirting—not that he couldn't flirt right up there with the best of them.

He was perfectly at ease and comfortable around women, and it was obvious he respected them as equals—something she attributed to his strong sense of family. In the short time she had known him she saw how he took family responsibilities seriously.

The one outstanding compliment she could hand him was he truly listened to what a woman had to say. He might not agree, but he did listen. She also realized he didn't have an arrogant bone in his body.

"I see you found the coffee . . . among other things."

"Kitchens are pretty predictable, so it's easy to find where everything is. You made it easier when you put most things in the same place Susan did."

That caught her off guard and made her realize that because he was close to his brother, he would have spent a great deal of time with Susan and Clay. He was the closest connection she had to Susan. "That's the kind of thing I miss not knowing. I think about it a lot—how twins are supposed to have this extrasensory connection that makes them do similar things like you mentioned, even if they've never met."

She jumped when the toast popped up. She took a knife out of the drawer and buttered four pieces of toast. "Do you always wear an apron when you cook breakfast?"

"Only when I'd rather not have grease splatters on my shirt. The coffee is ready."

She poured herself a cup. She picked up the toast and carried it along with the coffee to the table. She noticed he had everything set, napkins, silverware, apricot jam.

He carried their plates to the table. The apron was gone. "I hope you like your eggs fried." He sat down across from her.

"I like eggs cooked by someone else. I'm glad you decided to do this. I'm starving." She picked up a piece of toast and spread apricot jam over the top and took a bite. She took a sip of coffee and noticed over the top of the cup that he was gazing at her. "What?"

"Nothing." He shook his head. "I apologize for interrupting your sleep."

"Good, we've got that out of the way. Now, do you have a plan for finding out who snitched my family secrets to Sherman?"

"Oh, I think I'm going to pay a few of the local gossips and loudmouths a visit." Clint's easy tone belied the steely glint in his eyes.

Ellery felt a bit relieved. Clint seemed to be a prominent figure in Agarita Springs. If anyone could find out who was undermining her in this town, he could.

When they'd finished eating and washing the dishes, he dried his hands and said, "Now, why don't you ride out to the ranch with me? We won't be gone long."

She put her hand on her hair. It was dry and she could feel the curls, which she hated.

"You look good enough for me to invite you." He took the dishtowel away from her. "You won't see anything but horses and cows, and they're fashion blind."

"I . . ."

"This is your big chance. Have you ever been on a ranch?"

"I spent one horrible week on a dude ranch in Colorado. The cows didn't like me. The horses didn't either. I was the only happy guest when it rained for three days straight."

"Let me rephrase that. Have you ever been on a working ranch?"

"I saw the Budweiser horses when they were working."

"You don't leave a lot of room for a witty retort, do you?"

Ellery smiled sweetly at him. "If I had known you were capable of one, I would have."

Seventeen

H E WAS STILL laughing when he shut her door and climbed into his Range Rover.

"Just how many vehicles do you have?" she asked.

"Five or six, not counting the beat-up ones with no license plates we use at the ranch."

"Why so many cars for one man?"

"I wear a lot of hats. When I'm taking a pretty woman like you out, I'll take the Rover. For most of my driving, I take the black pickup. For hauling feed to the ranch it's the old green pickup. I've got an old Jeep that I use for hunting. I've got a motorcycle and a Mercedes convertible—I'm still trying to figure out why I bought it."

"You don't drive it?"

"Occasionally, when the weather is right and I'm not busy. Unfortunately, those two don't come together too often. It's a honey to drive to Austin or through the hill country."

She flipped the visor down and groaned at what stared back. She tried to do something with her hair.

"You look fine. But then, I think you look good any-time I see you. Those leggings you were running in were especially nice. I'll admit it started me wondering how long those legs of yours really are."

She popped the visor back up. "Are you flirting with me, Mr. Littleton?"

"I'm trying to, ma'am. I'm trying."

"You obviously haven't done it for a while."

He laughed. "You got that right. You might say that when it comes to flirting, I'm more than a little rusty. Like you said, it's been a spell since I tried my hand at it."

It had been eons since anyone had flirted with her as well, but she didn't tell him that.

He turned on the radio. It was set on a country station. A male singer with an unusual voice did a good job with a song called "Seminole Wind," and she found the words stirring and the melody touching, in a haunting way.

She turned her head to look out the open window, not minding in the least that her hair was blowing. She caught her reflection in the side mirror and saw her ponytail was whipping wildly, and the ribbon had come untied. She left the window down and retied the ribbon.

They fell into conversation easily, each of them making a few polite inquiries about the other. At one point, Ellery wished the trip to the ranch would take longer. The drive was a splendid surprise, especially when taken on a morning late in spring, when the countryside was at its magical best. A spectacular place, it was windswept, rocky, and bathed in the delicate, translucent beauty of the day. Color breathed life into the landscape. It reminded her of the rocky terrain of Provence; only the Alpilles were not lying in the distance.

It was not long before Clint pulled up to a barn and stopped.

"Well," he said, "here we are." He got out and came around to open the door for her and they walked to the corral.

Overhead, the sky was as pale and faded as a pair of old denims, with only an occasional cloud, white as whipped meringue, floating across her line of vision. She stared into the corral and tried to pet one of the horses but it snorted and whirled away. "See, I told you horses don't like me."

"You're complaining already and you haven't even put your foot in the stirrup."

"I am not a complainer and I don't think I want to ride. You ride. I'll watch."

He was already halfway to the stable by the time she finished her sentence. She occupied herself while he was gone by studying the horses and picking a few wildflowers.

When he reappeared, he was leading two saddled horses, a buckskin and a chestnut. "Are you going to ride two horses?"

"No, you're going to ride one of them."

"I told you, I'm not good at riding. I've only tried it once and I have no desire to try it again."

"I thought you never complained."

"I don't."

"You're doing a lot of grumbling for someone who doesn't complain. Now, get on the horse."

"You ride and I'll wait in the pickup."

"You're scared."

"I was thrown when I rode before."

"How did it happen?"

"Okay, I fell off. The stupid horse took off running, I couldn't stop it, and my butt started bouncing up and down until I was clearing the saddle by at least five inches. The horse made a turn. I went straight."

He shook his head and she could see he was working hard to squelch his laughter. She wanted to punch him.

He traced one finger down her arm.

She looked away. "I think it's time to start back."

"We've barely started."

"I don't think this is a good idea. I came to Texas to find out what happened to my sister, not to ride a horse."

"Call it what you like, but we aren't going anywhere until you get on that horse."

"I'm not getting on that horse," she said, and turned toward the car.

His arms were around her before she knew what he was doing and she found herself hauled up against him.

"Okay, so you're bigger than I am. I don't want to ride. Really."

"I didn't go to the trouble to work up to this point to let you go." His nose was a couple of inches from hers and she could really see now just how blue his eyes were . . . and those eyelashes—long and curled upward—Lord, any woman would be thrilled to have them.

This man was different, neither the type to joke innocently nor the political playboy type who was after a plaything or a quick lay. He had more than enough male drive and he knew how to use it to his advantage, but in an honest and forthright manner that miraculously bypassed teasing and mockery and went straight to a woman's favorable response center. The key was he made her feel desirable and feminine; he let her know he was interested in her; he was willing to wait until she was ready; he could press the issue; he knew when to back off.

All in all, he possessed a certain talent for perceiving the desires that lay in the hidden center of a woman's heart. He was alluring as hell and, boy, did he have the bait. So, what are you waiting for? a voice seemed to whisper.

His kiss caught her off guard. The moment his lips touched hers, she felt as if someone had ignited a bonfire around them; heat, hot and instantaneous as it beat down upon them with all the intensity of the molten sun overhead. He settled into the kiss sooner than she did and took the lead, drawing her closer, cradling her head with one hand, the other caressing her back, while he acquainted himself with her mouth, and she, not to be outdone, did a little investigative work of her own.

Soon, she was kissing him back and felt the pressing insistence of his kiss, warm, seeking, questioning, forceful but never rough. He was stronger than she was and could have used that against her, instead he used his gentle strength as a weapon; and she felt herself falling for him as surely as her body was warmed and receptive to the thought of making love with him.

When the kiss finally ended, she realized that inside she was still burning for him and it left her feeling as soft in the center as candy.

"That wasn't so bad, was it?" he asked, a satisfied grin on his handsome face.

Warmed by the sun and the heat of his kiss, she was soon doing two things that she swore never to do in her lifetime. She was on a horse and she was enjoying it.

They rode around the ranch for over two hours, splashing through creeks and down dusty roads, while he pointed out things and gave her a concise history of ranching. They walked the horses for a while, down a rocky trail that led to a narrow creek. When she complained her feet were hot, he told her to wade and cool her feet. He sat on the bank and watched her.

"You should try this. It feels divine."

"I'm used to the heat. It doesn't bother me." He stopped talking to watch her wade back toward him and laughed when she stepped in a hole and sat down with a splash.

She was having difficulty righting herself, so he pulled off his boots and waded toward her. He leaned forward to help her up and when he did, she pushed him hard enough that he lost his balance and fell to one side.

He wasn't as wet as she was, but he was wet enough. What truly surprised her was the sound of his laughter. "Was that to cool me off or for retribution?"

"Just a little old-fashioned justice."

"You don't like anyone to get the upper hand, do you?"

"Not if I can help it. In the newspaper business one cannot afford to let anyone have the advantage."

She was suddenly aware that they were both sitting in the middle of the creek with their clothes on having a conversation, as two normal people might do standing on a street corner, waiting for the light to change. She felt a little tug of admiration for the kind of man he was. There was a lot of depth to him and she found herself wishing she would be here long enough to really get to know him.

She wondered why no woman had scooped him up and made him hers. "Did you ever come close to getting married?" she asked.

"Once . . . a long time ago."

"College sweetheart?"

"Earlier. The first valentine card I ever gave was to her. It was in the first grade. It said, 'U-R-A-Q-T.' I gave her a twenty-five-cent box of candied hearts along with it."

"And you almost married her?"

"Almost."

"What happened?"

"My father wanted me to go to Yale. While I was gone those two years, she got tired of waiting and married my best friend."

"How long before she regretted it?"

"Two years."

"Tried to get you back, I bet."

"She tried. What about you? Did you ever come close?"

"Once, just like you," she answered, and then she told him about Edward and the tragic plane crash.

"We've both had our share of grief."

"Yes, but I do envy you, with your roots so firmly planted, while I bob along like an undocked boat, rootless and unattached."

"There's always a different way of looking at things," he said. "There's a lot of freedom in being a boat. You're able to drift and see what lies beyond the place where you are. When roots tie you down, you can only see what's around you. Roots mean obligations. They can be confining, even a burden at times."

He stood and helped her up. "I don't know about you, but my feet are beginning to shrivel." He offered her his hand.

She looked at his hand and then looked at him suspiciously. "You aren't going to get even, are you?"

"What do you think?"

She took his hand and waded back to the bank with him. They sat for a while on a rock until their clothes didn't squish when they walked. Clint gathered up his boots and leaned against a tree to pull them on. When she finished putting on her boots and turned to see where he was, she almost bumped into him.

The sight of him standing with his thumbs hooked in his belt made her feel out of place and uncertain . . . like a schoolgirl, really, with her first crush. She was too old for this sort of thing, although that didn't stop her from touching his lips with her index finger as she said in a teasing way, "This mouth is awfully silent. What happened to all those persuasive words you had earlier?"

She meant it as a joke, an icebreaker of sorts, to ease some of the stiffness that had come between them. She wanted that relaxed banter they'd shared earlier to return. But when she saw the way he was looking at her, she realized that was not going to happen.

He brushed the side of her cheek with the backs of his

fingers and brought them to his lips, to kiss the place where his fingers had touched her skin. Ellery felt as if she'd run into a solid wall. She was dizzy with a giddy feeling and her skin was burning as she looked at him and saw the way he was looking back at her. As if being encouraged by divine providence, the sun came from behind a cloud and she was completely dazzled by the brilliance of those blue eyes that contained all the fire of a glittering sapphire. She couldn't have moved if a rattlesnake had crawled up the leg of her jeans. Her mind was a complete blank . . . save for the mental gears whirring to process the seductive pull of those eyes.

God help her, she wondered if she could even talk.

He leaned forward without touching her and kissed her with a silent sort of ease, and she kissed him back. Suddenly nothing was relevant—not the reasons that had brought her to Texas, or the lost sister that made her stay. She was conscious only of the man who kissed her, while the cicadas hummed in the trees overhead.

She felt a huge disappointment when it ended and he said, "I guess I better get you home before Bertha tears up the house."

The mental image of that made her laugh. "I don't imagine Bertha has done much more than curl up in a patch of sunlight and nap." He didn't laugh and he didn't comment, but he sure was searching her face and gazing into her eyes as if looking for some answers to wordless questions.

She looked at her watch. "It's almost three-thirty. I didn't realize we were here that long."

They mounted the horses and rode back to the road.

After a while, a herd of grazing cattle stepped lazily aside as they cut across a pasture on their way to the part of the ranch that lay on the other side of the creek.

"What are those white squares scattered in the pasture?"

"Salt blocks . . . we put them out for the cattle. They don't get enough salt in their feed or by grazing."

"They eat it? Like they walk up to those blocks and take a bite of pure salt?"

He chuckled. "Cows don't have upper teeth in front, so they're out of luck when it comes to biting. They lick it—which is why the blocks are often called salt licks."

He was Cain, a tiller of the earth, but he was also Abel, a tender of herds. He loved this land with a passion she had not realized a man could be capable of. This was where he belonged, where his heart was. Here, with his bawling calves and hot, sunbaked land, his tractors and goose-necked trailers, and the miles of bumpy dirt road, surrounded by the smell of plowed fields, fresh air, and newly cut alfalfa curing in the fields. She saw he loved all these things with the single-minded devotion a mother would have for her young.

She saw the barn and stables up ahead. She yawned and rode quietly beside him and allowed the silence of this man, the solitude of this place, and the promise of this moment to ease her sense of displacement, and the bruised sense of separation lying fallow deep within.

And then she had a flashing glimpse of the face in her dreams and shivered as the sun passed behind a cloud.

Eighteen

W HEN THEY ARRIVED back at her house, she invited
him in for a glass of wine, which turned into three glasses
and a plate of hors d'œuvres.

They were sitting in the family room talking when
Clint looked at his watch and said, "It seems I'm always
overstaying my visit when it comes to you."

"There are worse things you could do."

"And a hell of a lot better ones too."

She raised her brows. "Oh really? I'd love to know, but
I don't think I better go there right now."

He didn't say anything. He picked up their glasses and
the plate of hors d'œuvres and carried them into the
kitchen. She stood and was about to follow him when he
returned.

He picked up his hat and said, "When I dropped by
this morning, I sure didn't plan on it leading to something like this."

She was about to say "something like what?" when he
said, "Oh hell," and tossed his hat back on the coffee

table. He turned to her with an expression so captivating, she wondered if she would ever have another moment like this. It was like every woman's fantasy come true, for when she gazed at him, she saw he wanted her as badly as she wanted him, and she lost her train of thought.

He wrapped her in his arms, a move that was neither gentle nor rough, but somewhere in between—strong enough to let her know his feelings were strong and gentle enough to allow her to respond.

The moment his lips touched hers, something in her mind said they were sailing down the river of no return. It was both surprising and overwhelming, and as far as kisses went, this one was so endearing, so intimate and tenderly full of feeling, that she melted against him. She had one thought before he kissed her again—that she could not believe that she might just have found herself a bona fide soul mate.

If she had followed her inner urging, if she had been a more aggressive type, she would have pushed his long-shanked body down on that sofa and climbed on top for the ride of her life.

He sure knew how to kiss a woman the way she liked it, with a sense of desperate urgency combined with practiced ease.

The kiss ended, and she was a bit giddy when she said, "My . . . I didn't expect you to do that any more than I expected it to affect me as it has. I think I need to sit down." She reached around him to move some of the pillows out of the way. Later, she would look back on what happened next and realize some of the best things in life happen by chance, with no forethought or planning. Some things were simply meant to happen a certain way and nothing could alter the outcome.

He had turned toward her about the same time she reached for the pillow, which put them in close enough proximity that she could hear the sound of his breathing as he whispered the words, "Now I know why I dropped by."

He took her face between his hands and the moment his skin made contact with hers, she drew in a quick breath and held it, as if afraid he would let her go the moment she released it. The intense, hopeful expression in his blue eyes drew her into another world, and she felt herself falling into the endless universe that was Clint Littleton.

His thumbs stroked the skin along her temples before he kissed her again. She wondered what he'd expected by coming here and if he felt the same arousing need to draw near—urgent and unavoidable—awakening within. She found herself hesitant to look deep into his eyes, for fear she would see the wrong answer in shining reply. But when his thumb stroked her lips and she opened her eyes to him, she saw all she needed to know.

She stared up at a face so close to hers, she could see the smooth texture of his skin, feel the warm wash of his breathing across her cheek. She took a deep breath, inhaling the smell of him, of starch on his shirt, and the scent of a straw hat in his hair. A need for him burned deeply and she said honestly, "I'm not any good at hiding what I feel."

"That's one of the many things I like and admire about you," he said with a gaze as honest as her words.

Slowly, without the awkwardness that usually comes with the letting down of barriers, she took his hand and brought it up to her breast. A long stretch of silence seemed to close the gap of intimacy between them.

In spite of her brave words and bold action, she felt a ripple of nerves at her daring dive into waters way over her head. It was a reaction that was counterbalanced by a warm wave of joy and the assurance that what she wanted, all she had thought about since that afternoon when she looked up and saw him in her back yard, was about to happen.

"Ellery . . ." he whispered as he spread his palms over her breasts and slid his fingers beneath the buttons of her shirt to open them with his thumbs. He leaned closer, to put his mouth against hers, and the feel of his shirt against her skin was her first indication that he had also unfastened her bra. Very smoothly done.

His kiss was long and promising, and Ellery's thoughts raced ahead and drew a response that in the past had only come with much more intimacy. Her hands worked at unbuttoning his shirt and then pushed the fabric apart. She placed her cheek against him, flesh alongside flesh, and rested the weight of her head there, content for a moment to listen to the vital force of lifeblood, balanced by the cadence of a beating heart.

He shifted his position to remove his shirt, and then with a burst of activity came the boots, belt, and jeans, while she gazed at him, capturing the moment in slow motion, tucking it away in her memory to play again later, after he was gone.

Her clothes were easy to remove, and she had no more

than done so when he shifted his position again, so that they were on the sofa and she was lying beneath him. She felt the weight of his breath, and wished she could absorb a small part of him through her skin. The soft pressure of his lips against her forehead forced the responsive closing of her eyes. Everything he did was slow and easy, for he seemed to be in no hurry, and more than content to learn the texture of her skin and the contour of her face with each kiss. The slowness was her undoing.

She felt his hands slide downward, over her bare arms, and the rippling of her own response like waves on the surface of disturbed water. Her soft body quivered against his firm smoothness that lay in such close proximity to hers. She felt at first shy and expectant, and then confident in knowing the exact moment it flowered into a bold wanting.

There was no need for talk. His body found its own way to communicate, an unspoken language more eloquent than any expressed with words. His kisses were long, and slow, as he took his time touching her, learning her response, and she discovered there is a wildness that comes with delay, a desperate yearning when you open and yield.

"Now," he whispered, and the meaning of the word washed over her and she opened urgently against him, until she felt the weight of him pressing into her, and a heat that rivaled the sun.

She arched her back at the quickening of her body. He pressed himself hard against her and made a sound of both anguish and expectation. They moved together, gasping for air, on the edge and out of control. She was hammered with a sensation so complete she could not control the sounds it triggered, or the lust it spawned.

Everything that peaks must wind down, and as the night melted black around them, she felt vulnerable and open in her nakedness until he covered her again, and made love to her again in that way he had that was both gentle and quiet.

When it was over she snuggled against him, surrounded by his calm strength and relaxed by his powerful gentleness. She did not know where this would lead. She had come here for a purpose and someone like Clint had never figured into the equation. The reason she came to Texas began to press down upon her like a gathering storm and she realized how precious and comforting this time with him, however brief it might be, was, and how endearing.

She did not remember feeling sleepy, and had only a vague recollection of walking with him to her room. It all seemed so right for her to open her arms and welcome into her embrace his naked body as it slipped into bed beside her.

She had no knowledge of when she closed her eyes and drifted into the safety and comfort that comes with the security of loving arms. "Don't go," she whispered.

"I'm here," he said, "for as long as you need me."

She smiled sleepily, wrapped his hand in hers and curled them against her breasts, holding it close. Her last memory was of the steady breathing of the man beside her, of the moon shining through the window, and a room filled with shadows, long and deep.

When she awoke, she saw the first pale streaks of

morning light, and saw too how it came into the room, long arms stretching into wakefulness to cover the shadows like a gossamer veil, until they grew faint and fainter still, and faded into the coming day.

She lifted her head from the pillow, and let it fall back when she saw he was dressed and watching her, something she found quite erotic. She wondered if she was brazen enough to drag him back into bed and take control, even as she reached for her blouse lying on the floor and slipped it on.

"Deftly done," he said.

She gave him a smile of uncertainty. His response was to lean toward her with a well-placed kiss on her lips and a slap on the butt that was as reassuring as it was gentle.

She sighed, leaned her head against his, and felt the rumbling of his laughter.

"Having previously seen you as such a ballsy newswoman, it came as quite a welcome surprise to see you also have a shy, gentle side."

"Well, after a stint as a ballsy newswoman, I am just as surprised that side of me still exists. The last couple of days I've been wondering why I chose such a different path in life than Susan . . ." She felt emotion welling up within her, and for one humbling moment, she was afraid she might cry—something the ballsy newswoman rarely did. "At times I wonder why I wanted a career at all, why I chose the roughest path, when there was a superhighway close by. Looking back, I truly wonder why I didn't do what Susan did—falling in love, getting married, and spending my life with someone I loved."

"Ellery?"

She shook her head. "I'm all right."

"I didn't come here to make you sad."

"I know, and you haven't. I've been stocking a well-spring of emotional reserves lately. When it gets full, some of the excess is bound to find a way out."

"Love isn't something you decide to do and then take action, like you open a trust fund. It isn't an empty box that you pile all your hopes into and then worry that at some point they will begin to fall out and you will be left with nothing. Everything will work itself out, in its own way."

"How do you know so much about love? You never married."

"No, but I can feel."

Suddenly, Clint's cell phone went off and it seemed to break the connection between them, and any further conversation. He flipped it open and glanced down. "It's my brother-in-law. He's at the feed store," he said. "I've got to take the call."

She forced a smile and a cheerful voice. "And I've got to take a shower and get dressed."

He punched a button. "Jerry, I'll call you right back."

He put his hands on her upper arms and rubbed lightly. "Are you all right?"

Ellery looked into his eyes, then looked away. "I guess I just feel overwhelmed. I don't regret what we did. But I just don't feel ready to get that close to anyone right now. I can't stop thinking about Susan, why something so horrible happened to her. I need to find out."

He took her hand in his and kissed it before he said, "I know. I'll let you walk me to the door."

A few minutes later, as she watched him climb into his

pickup, she imagined that when God created Clint Little-ton, he hadn't shaped him from a lump of river clay, but carved him from the sturdy trunk of a hard rock maple.

She watched until the outline of his car was swallowed into the early morning haze, then she closed the door and walked into the den. She gazed at the leather chair where he'd sat the night before. It still retained the im-print of his body and she thought there was nothing as empty as the place where someone you liked had re-cently been.

She went upstairs to shower, but found herself sitting on the side of her bed, her hand touching rumpled sheets, recalling a memory.

He had caught her unaware, as a cloud slips over the sun, and came upon her as quiet as night. A deep, abid-ing feeling for him welled up inside her and flooded her with every treasured memory of his existence. She felt as if a long-awaited view was gradually coming into her line of vision. And she was awed at the possibilities of what it might prove to be. But now, unfortunately, was not the time to find out.

No matter what happened or didn't happen between her and Clint in the future, she knew that for the rest of her life thoughts of him would dance across her mind.

Nineteen

CLINT CONVINCED ELLERY that she should talk to Detective Bardwell about Sherman T. DeWitt. He'd asked around town and no one had encountered the obnoxious reporter.

"Why should I go to Bardwell? I'm sure he'll think Sherman is a journalist who does what journalists do: He digs up stories and writes about them. Bardwell will think I'm an idiot for bringing Sherman to his notice."

"True . . . except for the fact that Sherman isn't your average run-of-the-mill journalist. There is a history of friction and ill will between the two of you, albeit all on his part. His kind of jealousy is dangerous. I don't think you want to wait until you discover the depravity that lurks in the depth of his heart and mind. Judging from the acts he committed against you in the past and his history of changing jobs frequently—whether by choice or request—he seems like the kind who will juggernaut his way through life with the basic belief that he's got a right and you better get out of his way, or else."

"How do you know he changes jobs frequently?"

"I told Bardwell about him and he did some research. He came up with some interesting revelations about your friend Sherman T."

Ellery was infuriated. "You went way out of bounds with that, Clint. My relationship with Sherman is none of your business. You had no right to talk to the police without asking me. You're pushing yourself into my affairs every bit as much as Sherman is."

"I'm trying to help you. This isn't a game you're playing, you know. Sherman has published information about you that could endanger your life, especially if what you think is true."

"And what is that?"

"If you turn out to be right about there being a connection between Clay's and Susan's deaths, then you could be next on the docket."

Ellery sighed. "All right, I'll call him, but next time you ask me before you take my matters into your own hands."

"Fair enough," he said.

Ellery went into her office, called Bardwell, and explained in more detail the animosity Sherman felt toward her and how it all came about. She also explained the things he did after he left WMDC.

"I spoke with a criminal psychologist about it last night," Bardwell said, "and he referred to the type as being a vengeful stalker. According to him, this is the most dangerous type because he has a mission to get even. They don't let old scores—real or imagined—go unsettled. If they feel wronged, eventually you will be subjected to payback time. Judging from the things I told him, he said it showed some characteristic marks of a paranoid narcissist, which he referred to as a mixed type. He said his idea was a controversial approach and not the way your average clinical psychologist is trained to diagnose. According to him . . . and I'm reading from my notes on all of this . . . paranoia of this type tends to be organized around aggression, from sadomasochistic violence to lingering hostile moods. On the narcissistic side you get envy, greed, power lust, an all-embracing sense of entitlement—that is a self-satisfying but incorrect justification for their behavior—as well as a pathological grandiose self. He said the writing of the article about you was typical of this type of personality. His exact words were, 'They are vengeful and will publish your private case details on the Internet or reveal them to others without seeking permission. To them, confidentiality is not an issue. People are objects to be used for their personal gratification. The feelings of others do not enter into the picture.' "

"Is that all?"

Bardwell's laugh was long and loud. "Does that mean you don't buy into any of this?"

"After the performance you gave, I wouldn't have the heart to say yes. Truthfully, though, I do think the things you said describe Sherman. It's been proven that he's a notorious liar and more than once he has misrepresented his credentials.

"After listening to all of this, I don't really see anything that makes me think he would necessarily engage in a criminal act against me."

"I think you're wrong there. This type is known for taking the path of least resistance or investment of self, whether being a con artist, cheating, lying, fraud, violence . . . you name it."

"What would you have me do, Detective?"

"Be diligent. Keep me posted on any contact or information you get on or about him. Do you have any idea where he's staying?"

"No. I called the *Daily Snoop* and was told he's on vacation in the Caribbean."

"Well, we know he's a liar. It won't be hard to find out if he's staying in Agarita Springs. I'll get someone on it and get back to you."

After she hung up the phone, Ellery could not stop wondering what Sherman T. was doing now. And when she would hear from him next.

Twenty

Ellery had difficulty falling asleep that night.

As soon as she switched off the light, she sat in the dark with her head resting against the headboard. She yawned and rubbed her eyes. She felt a mixture of weariness and a disturbing sense of presentiment—the kind one gets when one knows something evil is about to occur and is helpless to stop it. She did not know what it was, but she knew she was involved in it. She thought again of Susan's death and wondered who would have had a motive: Why was her sister killed? One thing seemed clear enough: She did not believe for an instant that it was a stranger who simply chose Susan as his victim. To the contrary, she felt strongly that it was someone who knew Susan; someone who had a motive for wanting her dead.

She thought about herself at that moment, sitting in the dark, weary from lack of sleep and tired from physical activity, her head full of gory images of a man holding a bloody knife—a man whose face became more and more recognizable each time she saw it. Now, the question looming in her mind was, would she be able to discover who he was, or would she end up like her sister before she could identify him? At that moment, she realized the progressive nature of the dreams were like an hourglass: Once the face was completely revealed, her time would have run out.

There was no way to stop the sand in the hourglass . . .

She slid down in the bed and rested her head against the pillow. With her eyes closed she kept seeing the face, the bloody handprints on the wall along the staircase. At the point when she thought she was about to drift off, she felt a cold draft, like the rush of air she sometimes got when she caught the metro at Dupont Station in D.C., and another train whooshed by.

Finally, her eyes closed and it was not long before she began to dream again. She was in her bedroom but there was a presence in the room with her. The air was getting colder, chilling her skin. The curtains at the window began to billow out and then, with a rush of air, they fell back into place.

A man stood in front of the window with a knife in his hand. His figure was shadowy, as it had been the first time she had seen him, but there was a new sharpness to the image—enough that she could tell he was tall and lean, with dark hair. She strained to see his face, but all that came into focus was the square outline of his jaw, and then his nose. It was a face that was familiar and yet it was not. Who are you? her mind asked, but the figure only smiled and his image began to fade and she was left with nothing but the memory that floated like dead leaves in a stagnant pond.

When she awoke the next morning, she felt apprehensive and disturbed by the memory of the towering man who strode after her like a living thing. No matter how she tried, she could not shake the image that washed across her mind in a painful wave.

She opened her journal and wrote down as much as she could remember about the dream. She knew now that the man was white, slender, and fairly tall. He was clean-shaven with dark hair and his jaw was square.

Hell, she thought, that description could fit half the men in town, including Clint Littleton. It could also fit Sherman, Detective Bardwell, and the benefactor in a painting at the public library.

While she showered she pushed the grim image from her mind and replaced it with the more pleasant memory of her recent lovemaking with Clint. She closed her eyes and saw his face hovering over hers, his eyes dark with desire. She stood under the hot water and let it run over her head to rinse the shampoo and felt a curling knot of desire low in her belly.

It remained there even after she dressed and had breakfast, so she decided to focus her energies on something that would, at least, yield immediate results. She went into the backyard to work. Bags of mulch were stacked on the patio. Two flats of vinca were still sitting on the porch. They had been there for three days. They were starting to droop.

When Mike the yardman arrived, Ellery pointed him toward the mulch and vinca, with instructions to mulch first, then plant. It didn't take him long to take care of both jobs. He was cutting away the dead branches on the willow tree that grew next to the fishpond when Ellery noticed there were still two bags of mulch left.

"Spread those around the fishpond," she told Mike. "Don't you think it would look better if we took it all the way over to the willow tree?"

Mike nodded, said, "I do," and began to spread the mulch.

Ellery's gaze rested on the willow. That part of the yard was depressing to her. The tree itself was so mournful; it seemed to be shedding silent tears of grief. Every time she looked at it, she felt a shiver. Perhaps it was the flower bed below the tree, for it was lifeless and void of color. It needed an infusion of cheerfulness. It was a focal point that had neither focus nor a point. It needed something— a bench, a hammock, some shrubs or flowers. Flowers . . . that was it! Tomorrow she would buy flowers.

After Mike left, she worked another hour. She could have stayed in the garden longer, but she had worked straight through lunch and now she was feeling hunger pangs. She went inside, opened the refrigerator and took out the chicken she was going to grill, and then decided she was too tired to grill anything, except Margaret Ledbetter.

She put the chicken back in the refrigerator. She took out the last bit of salad she'd made the day before, and whipped up an omelet of tomatoes, cheese, and mushrooms. She was almost too tired to eat and her body was beginning to grow stiff. She wondered if she would be sore tomorrow. She probably wouldn't be up to jogging with Bertha tomorrow so she left Bertha in the backyard where she could run around to her heart's content.

When she went to bed, she fell asleep within minutes. She was restless and changed positions frequently. A couple of times she talked in her sleep. She dreamed something was banging against the side of the house. She saw a flapping green shutter. She mumbled again and turned to her side.

She heard a loud bang, like a door blown shut by the wind.

It took her a while to wake up and to realize the noise did not come from a dream, but her house. This time she jumped when something hit the front of the house like a peppering of pebbles. She lay perfectly still. She wondered if someone was breaking into her house. She should have paid more attention to the feeling that her sister's murderer might decide to come after her. She had no security system, no lights outside save the ones on the porch, and no plan for escape if someone did break in.

The noise continued, but a different sound this time. *Ta-tap, ta-tap, ta-tap.* She couldn't pinpoint the location exactly, but then it didn't really matter. It seemed to be moving around the house now. She sat up and scooted back against the headboard. She couldn't make out much in the room. She wished she could turn on the light but she was afraid it would make her an easy target.

Target . . . bad choice of words.

She inched her way out of bed and moved slowly to the window that looked out over the backyard. She stood to one side and parted the drape barely enough to see out, but the yard was a black, empty space. She could not make out much of anything except the fairy statue in the fishpond and the drooping form of the willow. She tried not to think about the fact that weeping willows mean perpetual mourning when planted in a cemetery.

Cemetery . . . another bad choice.

She needed to think about this. She couldn't stand there trembling at the window while someone tried to break into her house. She needed to take some kind of action. If the intruder had a gun, which was highly probable, she wouldn't have a chance if she did nothing. If he came up to her bedroom, she would be trapped.

She dropped the curtain and turned away.

Ta-tap, ta-tap, ta-tap, the noise was louder now. It sounded like someone walking. It was inside the house and coming from one of the guest rooms down the hall. She pressed herself flat, with her back against the wall, and inched along it toward the door in the darkness. When she came to the bombé chest, she put her hand around the silent face of a bronze statue, light enough for her to brandish and heavy enough to crack a head. Not much defense against a gun, perhaps. But Ellery knew that at least she wouldn't wait helplessly in her room to be attacked.

She was almost to the door that led into the hallway when she heard a new sound. She held her breath and listened. It sounded like water running. It, too, seemed to be coming from one of the bedrooms down the hall. She inched closer to the door, so she could poke her head through the doorway, just enough to see down the gloomy hall. She saw nothing, but she kept her eyes fixed on the window at the end of the hallway. A stingy, diffused light would allow her to see a silhouette if anyone went into, or came out of, one of the rooms. She stayed in this position, not moving and starting to perspire in spite of the air-conditioning. She stared and listened, blinked when her eyes began to dry, then stared and listened some more. She felt the sweat collecting on her face, and then it began to burn her eyes. She blinked but they only burned more.

She was growing numb in places. She had pain in her neck from standing in this unnatural position with her neck craned awkwardly around the doorframe. She was wondering how long she should stay here like this, without hearing anything but the running water, when something crashed downstairs. She heard a door open and then close.

She continued to listen, still in the same position. She didn't hear Bertha barking at an intruder outside. She hoped the dog was all right. Dampness caused her gown to cling. The salty sting of sweat burned her eyes so badly she had to lift the hem of her gown to wipe it away. The tightly clenched muscles in her legs began to quiver and feel fatigued. She was starting to wonder if she was reading more into this than she actually heard. Perhaps it was only the wind playing tricks on her and making the branches tap against the house.

If she were inclined to believe in ghosts, she would have considered it likely that it was the restless spirits of Clay and Susan roaming about, perhaps going out for the night to search for those who murdered them.

When, after some time, she didn't hear another sound, she switched on the light and started down the hall. The sound of water was louder now, and she followed it until she opened the door to one of the bedrooms, where the sound seemed to be the strongest. She turned on the light and screamed.

Blood was running out of the bathroom and into the bedroom. The brilliant red stain was shocking and stark as it spread outward, onto the cream carpet. She did not know if there was someone still in the bathroom. She didn't want to wait around and find out.

She ran back to her bedroom, slammed the door, and twisted the lock in place. She grabbed the phone and dialed 911. When she hung up the phone, all she could remember was a calm voice assuring her that someone would be there in minutes.

She put on her robe and looked at her face in the mirror. She was deathly pale and her cheeks needed color, but right now, she didn't care who saw her with a pale face or with no makeup. All the perspiration on her scalp had caused her hair to curl tightly. She looked like a poodle with highlights. She ran her fingers through it and washed her face.

She did not leave the bedroom, but stood by the window, where she could see the driveway below. She did not unlock her door until she saw the play of flashing red and blue lights on her bedroom walls.

When she opened the door and stepped into the hall, she heard the doorbell. Before she reached the stairs, someone knocked loudly. She heard a voice call out, "Police . . . Ms. O'Brien . . . it's the police. Open up."

She opened the door and almost fell against one of the two officers standing there.

"Ms. O'Brien, I'm Sergeant James Worley. This is my partner, Officer Dave Plunkett."

"Upstairs," she said. "Go left at the top of the stairs . . . second bedroom on the right."

She sat on the front porch with her arms wrapped around her middle, and found an odd sort of solace in watching the lights of the patrol car hurl flashes of color into the night.

It meant she was not alone.

She heard someone approach and turned to see one of the policemen step onto the porch. It was Sergeant Worley. "We need you to come upstairs for a minute." He took her by the elbow and helped her to her feet.

James Worley was young—not over twenty-five or -six, but he knew how to ease the erratic thumping heart of a frightened woman who would never see thirty again. "It's all right," he said. "We checked the house completely. No one is inside. It isn't blood coming out of the upstairs bathroom. It looks like red dye. Some sick person's idea of a joke."

Red dye . . . Her knees buckled and her eyes began to water. She'd never felt more relieved or more like crying. Worley kept his hand under her elbow as they went up to the bedroom. Dave Plunkett was talking to the dispatcher. She wondered if he was calling for a photographer and someone from forensics—or would they even bother with that for red dye in a bathtub?

Ellery moved toward the bathroom and saw as she drew closer that it clearly wasn't blood. "I'm sorry. I should have turned on the other light and looked at it more closely before I panicked and called 911."

"You did the right thing. This is more than just a prank," Plunkett said. "Someone entered your home unauthorized and left a threatening message written with what appears to be red lipstick on the bathroom mirror."

She thought about looking at the mirror, but decided she'd had enough surprises to last a while. "I think I'll wait downstairs, unless you need me to stay here."

"No, ma'am," Worley said. "You wait wherever you feel comfortable."

"That would be the lobby of the police station," she said, and went back downstairs.

She was sitting on the sofa facing the window. She saw more flashing lights come down the driveway. She was almost to the door when it opened. Detective Roland Bardwell stepped inside.

"Oh, I'm sorry to barge into your home like this. I figured everyone would be upstairs. Are you all right?"

She was really glad to see him. "I'm a lot better now that you're here."

His eyes were kind, sympathetic. "Why don't you go make yourself a cup of coffee and stay in the kitchen until we finish up? You look about ready to collapse. I don't imagine the caffeine will hurt none, because I doubt you will get any more sleep tonight anyway."

"No, I probably won't." She started toward the kitchen and turned back to him. "Would you like some coffee?"

He grinned, and she felt uplifted by it. "Well, sure I would. Why do you think I suggested it?"

She gave him a weak smile—weak being all she could muster at the moment. His nod said he understood.

She made coffee and carried three cups upstairs. When she entered the bedroom, she saw Worley and some others who had come while she was in the kitchen making coffee. A woman was taking pictures. Another woman was dusting one of the windows for fingerprints and Ellery realized she had not noticed earlier that it was still open.

She glanced at Worley. "That's how he got in?" she asked. "But it's a second-floor window. Did he use a ladder?"

Worley shook his head. "No imprints in the garden to indicate that. Must have used a rope."

"I forgot I opened it earlier today to let in the scent of the honeysuckle."

"I've had all the windows in the house checked to be certain they're locked," Worley said. "I wouldn't open them at night anymore if I were you."

"Rest assured I won't." She handed out the coffee and placed the tray on the bed. She picked up the cup for Detective Bardwell and turned toward the door in time to see him walk into the room.

Bardwell took the coffee from her extended hand. "A big Starbucks cup," he said. "It ought to keep me revved up." He took a sip. "We'll be wrapping things up here pretty soon," he said. "Do you have someone you can stay with for the rest of the night?"

"I could call my cousin, Lucy Todd, but I would rather not bother her at this late hour. I'm sure I will be fine now. I doubt whoever it was will return tonight."

"When dealing with a criminal mind it is better never to make assumptions: A thief and darkness are close allies. I think it would be best if you didn't stay here tonight, but I can't force you to go," Bardwell said. "If you do stay here, I'll have a couple of policemen in a patrol car park in front of the house."

"Thank you, Detective."

She noticed that the lamp on the far side of the bed was shattered on the floor, and she remembered hearing something crash.

She shivered and put her hand to her head. For a brief moment she had a cloudy vision of a woman in this room, and then it disappeared before she could see much more than long hair and blood. "This doesn't seem like something a vengeful news reporter would do. It has to have been someone besides Sherman." She paused. "Do you think this might be connected to my sister's death?"

"It is starting to look that way," Bardwell said. "There's not another explanation for all of this, especially when you consider the message left on the bathroom mirror."

She had forgotten about the mirror. "What was the message? No, never mind, I think I need to see it for myself."

"Are you sure you want to see it? I can have one of the men clean the mirror."

"No, I want to know what kind of sick mind I'm up against."

"I will need you to come down to the station tomorrow and give a statement."

She nodded. "As long as it isn't too early."

He put the empty cup on the tray. "I'd say you've earned the right to sleep late."

She remembered she had not seen the message written on the mirror, so she walked to the other side of the bed in order to look into the bathroom without stepping on the soggy, red carpet. She sucked in her breath with a loud gasp when she read the large lettering in brilliant red:

You're Next

Dear God! The moment she saw it she knew Susan's murderer had been in her house tonight. The sight of the words slammed into her understanding and she froze in sheer terror. This was no scary movie with Johnny Depp losing his mind and killing everyone around him. This was the real thing. The pressure within her chest began to build until she feared she was having a heart attack. She did not realize she had ceased to breathe until she felt her mouth open and suck in a life-giving breath. She closed her eyes, feeling weak and sick, alone, and at the mercy of some unknown monster with no regard for human life.

How does one hold on to sanity?

The red lipstick seemed to jump from the mirror into her mind and she could almost feel the blood dripping off her body, just as it appeared to do beneath the letters. She rubbed her arms to ward off the chill that enveloped her like the cold breath of death.

Something is happening here . . . something I have no control over. Where is this nightmare going to end? Her hands were shaking. She wanted to scream. She wanted to run and keep on running until the nightmares stopped; until the mystery of Susan's missing body was solved; until the fiend who was doing this was behind bars.

Will it end? Or will the bony arms of death wrap around you as they did Susan? Will you be united with your sister in death?

"Susan," she whispered, "help me. Show me how to find you . . . Tell me what to do."

The smell of death was all around her . . . sweet, sticky, and evil. Had it come for her? Would she never leave this house alive? Was she so connected to her twin that she would follow her in death? She closed her eyes, leaned her head back, and breathed deeply.

"Are you all right?"

Bardwell's voice was like an oxygen mask forcing pure air into her lungs and clearing her head of morbid thoughts. She turned to look at him. "I don't know if I'm all right or not. I don't think the full impact of this has hit me. I can't deny I'm shaken. I guess I just answered my own question about whether this is related to my sister's death. It does make me feel good in one regard."

"And what is that?"

"We know the killer is close enough that he knows what's going on and why I am here. I know we are making him uncomfortable enough that he feels he has to threaten me. What I don't know is why. What would he stand to gain from killing me like he did Susan? She and I never even met, so I couldn't be connected to anything that went on in her life . . . unless it is because I look like her."

"We don't know for certain that it's the the same person who harmed Susan. It could be someone with a sick sense of humor, or someone who wants to send you back where you came from, instead of someone harboring malice with the intent to kill you. This may be the twenty-first century, but there are still people who resent newcomers."

"Yes, I've encountered a few of them around town." She sighed. "Well, whichever one it is, they messed up big time. I probably would have left before too long if I didn't get a break, but now I'm determined to remain here until we solve Susan's case."

Bardwell seemed amused. "Sounds like you've joined the investigation."

"Big time. But don't worry." she said, patting his arm. "Your job is not in jeopardy."

Twenty-one

THE NEXT MORNING, Ellery was relieved to open her eyes and realize she was still very much alive. She also realized it was raining.

She drew back the draperies in the bedroom and looked upon a palette of varying shades of green in the backyard. It was a good way to start the day, greeted by her favorite color. She noted how the newly mulched soil around the fishpond and willow tree still looked bare as a cupboard, and she thought it was too bad she hadn't got the flowers planted before the rain came.

While random thoughts drifted in and out of her consciousness, her gaze was fixed upon the willow tree for some time before she became aware of it. She thought it was a bit weird—how she would often find herself standing in this same spot looking at the willow, as if she were drawn to it in some inexplicable way.

Was it because Susan liked to stand at this very window and do the same?

Ellery had never realized before that there was something heartbreakingly sad about weeping willows. She was drawn to the way the canopy of droopy arched branches veiled part of the pond and surrounding flower bed. She observed the way the long branches swept the ground like a trailing garment and how the tree seemed to be sighing when disturbed by a breeze. She could see why they called them weeping willows—these mournful trees with their gnarled roots snaking above the ground. This one looked especially forlorn the way it stood off by itself, a lonely sentinel next to the fishpond, away from all the other trees.

Drip . . . drip . . . drip . . . Accompanied by the sound of rain, she watched the water run down the slender, drooping branches to splash into puddles below. Apparently melancholy tears weren't out of character for a weeping willow.

With a deep sigh, she turned toward her dressing room, where she put on a pair of navy pants and a sleeveless cotton sweater of the same color. She gave her face a little help, and brushed her hair out straight and loose. She was about to leave when her friend Merrily called from D.C. When she finished talking to her, Ellery dialed Lucy's number, but it went into voice mail, so she left a message.

When she finally made it downstairs and walked into the kitchen, the rain had stopped and the sun was starting to break through the clearing clouds. She made coffee. She poured a cup and picked up a piece of crunchy wheat toast, no jam this time. She carried it to the front porch. It was shady and cool. Everything smelled fresh after the rain. She sat on the porch swing to have her breakfast. She had always loved to sit on the front porch. It was something that went back to her childhood, when the porch held some sort of fascination that continued into her adult years. She remembered it as a place for playing with dolls when she was little; jacks when she was in elementary school; homework later on. She even had her first kiss while sitting in the porch swing.

She sipped her coffee and ate toast while she tried to think of a reason why she was being stalked. If it was related to Clay's and Susan's deaths, then what link connected the three of them? It didn't make sense. What did she have in common with two people she had never met? No one could have known about the twin link when Susan was murdered. Was it possible that Susan's link to Clay and her link to Ellery were not connected? No matter how she looked at it, she was left with questions that had no answers.

Back inside, she cleaned up her dishes and then sat at the kitchen table to make a list of things she wanted to do to make the house more secure. First she called a locksmith. It was two o'clock by the time he'd changed the locks and put dead bolts on the front and back doors. She'd have to tell the Realtor or Clint, the owner of the house, what she'd done. Maybe Clint had already heard through the town's grapevine what had happened last night.

The last group of calls went to various security companies, to have the house wired for an alarm system and to get motion detectors installed. She didn't intend to call so many, but many of them couldn't start the job for two to three weeks.

She was getting exasperated, so this time she explained why she needed it installed sooner, and her plea fell on a sympathetic ear.

"No one should have to go through that," the girl said. "I'll have someone out there next week. I'll call you back and give you the exact date and time."

She thanked her and hung up. She looked at the wall clock. It was four o'clock. It was too early to start dinner and too close to dinner to start a new project. She grabbed a can of Diet Coke, picked up a stack of mail, went back to the front porch, and took her customary seat on the steps. She had a perfect view right between the stone columns and straight down the street.

She had opened a few bills when she noticed a small speck in the distance was growing larger. As it drew closer, she thought it was too small to be a car, and then she heard the roar of a motor and the next thing she knew a red motorcycle was coming up her drive.

Clint came to a gravel-throwing stop in front of her. He removed his helmet and flashed her a wide grin. "Are you game for a little adventure?" he asked.

She eyed him with suspicion and hoped he didn't think he was going to get her on that dangerous contraption. "Just what kind of adventure did you have in mind?"

"I've been working out at the ranch since before sunup and now it's time for a little fun. Hop behind me and we'll go for a ride."

"Do I look that stupid? Is that your nephew's motorcycle?"

"The one you got for him, yes. I thought you'd like to

see what one of these beauties looks like before it gets run over."

"Funny . . . ha-ha."

"Come on. Hop on the back. You need a little diversion and excitement in your life. Put your arms around me, and I'll give you the thrill of your life." He tilted his head sideways and showed her what a trademark grin could do.

It did plenty. She felt as if she had swallowed something effervescent and was about to float off the top step. Oh, she bet he could give her a thrill all right; in fact, she was getting a pretty good one right now, by simply looking at him perched on that big red machine. She felt as if she were staring into a solar eclipse. She gazed into those aquamarine eyes and completely lost her train of thought.

She hadn't felt this way since junior high, when William Joseph Atchison, with the cornflower-blue eyes, had asked her to the St. Alban's dance. Of course, William Joseph Atchison turned out to be overly shy and a terrible dancer—he spent as much time on her feet as she did. But oh, the memory of having a hopeless crush on him for three months and then being asked to the dance put permanent stars in her eyes. To this day, there were some men who could look at her with that same shade of light blue eyes and she would feel all buttery inside.

"Climb on the bike. This is the best time of day to ride. It's not too hot."

She didn't budge.

"You aren't afraid to ride, are you?"

No, terrified was more like it. "I don't know. I've never been on one. I've always had too much common sense."

"You're kidding."

"I'm a city girl, okay? The closest I've been was watching an old Steve McQueen movie where he rode a bike over a fence and got tangled in the barbed wire."

"*The Great Escape,*" he said. "Great movie . . . a classic, really."

"I don't remember anything else about it." She noticed that even when wearing jeans, he was always impeccably dressed. She looked him over—yellow shirt tucked in properly, starched jeans, scuffed boots. She lost her concentration, because he was showing her how typically male he could be by revving up the motor as though he thought she would be impressed by cylinders, horsepower, chrome exhaust pipes, or the show he was putting on. She wondered if motorcycles even had cylinders.

The next thing she knew, he was off the bike and standing in front of her, looking as good as two Sundays come together. He took her hand and pulled her to her feet. "I'm going to get back on the cycle, and then I'll give you about three seconds to park your butt behind me."

She decided it would be an interesting tidbit to report about in her documentary. She could see it now, on the evening news, titled "A Moment of Idiocy in the Life of a Sensible Woman."

And then she surprised herself by deciding to do something purely idiotic for once in her life. She went inside to put her things away and came back out, locking the front door behind her. She made it as far as the motorcycle. She looked at the space on the seat behind him and had a memory of the girls in Italy riding behind the guys like this everywhere, which she always thought of as terribly romantic.

"I don't believe I'm doing this," she said. "I've always prided myself on being levelheaded and exercising good judgment."

"You are exercising good judgment. Now, put this on," he said, and handed her a helmet.

Helmet on now, she climbed behind him. She chose not to put her arms around him. But when he revved up the engine, eased up on the clutch, and the cycle shot forward with such force the front wheel rose off the ground, she changed her mind and almost yanked him back against her.

After a few seconds she relaxed, turned her head to the side, and rested her cheek against his back. She wasn't too happy about being on this devil-red machine, but she tried to focus on the positive, on how nice it was to be sitting this close to him. She remembered slow dancing in college and wondering if the guys could feel your breasts when they held you close. Now she was a grown woman, riding on the back of a motorcycle behind some Texas cowboy, and wondering if he could feel them.

If the news staff could see her now . . .

She wondered what it would be like if he didn't bring her back at all; if the two of them kept on driving toward the sun, Bradley's cycle eating up the miles and her without a care in the world. Maybe they would end up in Malibu, or perhaps they would head up toward Idaho, or even go as far as Jackson Hole, or maybe even Canada.

They could rent a cabin by a mountain stream and he would teach her to fly-fish, and while he cleaned the fish, she would gather "whatever" berries. They would swim naked in the stream, and after he dried her off, he would carry her inside and make love to her in a big iron bed with crisp white sheets. Afterward they would dine by candlelight on a dinner of fish and "whatever" cobbler.

Oddly enough, after what had happened at her house last night, all of this sounded remarkably sane.

"How you doin' back there?"

The sound of his voice snapped her back to the real world. They were no longer on Live Oak Street. She did not know where they were exactly, but she knew it wasn't the way to Malibu, or Jackson Hole. "So far so good," she replied. "Where are we going?"

He made a sweeping turn that almost tossed her off. He stopped and shut down the motor. The parking area was full of cars, SUVs, and pickups, but Clint had managed to find a spot for them to wedge into, with enough room to dismount.

She'd no more than pulled off the helmet when he took her hand. "Come on."

They walked around the corner and she thought they'd stepped into the 1890s. She barely had time to catch a glimpse of the name of the store when he opened the door and pulled her inside the Soda Fountain.

They sat in armless wire chairs with round seats at a table for two. It was next to the window, so she could watch those milling about outside, as well as try to imagine what a date must have been like back when these kinds of places were in fashion. Fascinated, she watched a soda jerk turn out creations she had not heard the name of in eons, if at all.

Clint handed her a menu. She almost tried a cherry phosphate but when she read that all the ice cream was homemade, she settled on a vanilla malt.

Clint wasn't so shy. He had a Dionne Sunday, which boasted five dips of ice cream named after the Dionne quintuplets. She gave him a taste of her malt and he fed her a bite of sundae and got chocolate syrup on her face. He watched her try to lick it off, then ran out of patience and wiped it with his napkin.

She considered telling him about the visitor she'd had the night before. She was surprised Bardwell hadn't told him. Not wanting to spoil the magic of this moment, she decided to tell him later. They talked for a long time before she realized the lights were on inside and it was dark on the other side of the plate-glass window.

Old-fashioned street lamps ran down both sides of the street and she wished she could stay here in this make-believe world, and not have to go home to see if she had had another visit from her new admirer.

Soon, they were back on the motorcycle again. She thought he was taking her home before she realized they were going the wrong way. Soon, the town disappeared behind them and they were heading down the highway. She was about to ask where they were going when they roared into another parking lot, this one displaying a big sign:

Lilly Langtry's

The place looked like a bona fide, genuine, authentic dive. The name was written with garish neon lights—

pink and blue, no less. Next to the name, a neon dance-hall girl did the cancan and threw her dress over her head.

Clint removed his helmet. He glanced at the one on her head. "You aren't going to wear that inside, are you?"

"You mean we're going in there?"

"I didn't bring you all the way out here to show you the sign. Think of it as a cultural experience. I bet they don't have anything like this in D.C."

She didn't say anything. She didn't need to. Her look said it all.

"People drive here from all over the state. This place is a legend."

She doubted that, but sometimes it was easier to simply give in. She removed her helmet and watched him fasten it to the cycle next to his and then they walked to the entrance. Clint opened the door and the twangy strains of a song floated over them. Ellery was about to step inside when she noticed a black stretch limousine pull up. She paused to watch a very civilized-looking man stepped out. He gave his hand to an attractive woman. Several others soon joined them.

"Let's go inside. Once those people reach the door, it's going to get crazy."

"Do you know who that is?"

"It's the governor and his wife, with their usual entourage."

They stepped inside and she stopped to look around. It was dark. The music was loud.

"You are inside a living piece of history," he said. "There aren't many old dance halls left. A lot of great bands have gotten their start here, and this is where some of country music's finest voices sang their first songs."

A band was playing what Clint called Western swing. The dance floor was as big as a gym floor, and it was packed with cowboys twirling and shuffling their women across the floor.

"Do you want a beer or would you prefer a cocktail?"

"A beer is fine."

He ordered two bottles of Shiner Bock at the bar, and carried them to a table near the dance floor. "You're watching some serious two-steppin' going on out there, mixed with some first-timers who haven't quite gotten the hang of it yet."

The first-timers were easy to spot. She sipped her beer, skeptical of a brand she'd never heard of. She took another sip. It was good . . . very good.

"Well, what do you think?"

She held the cold beer bottle against her cheek. "I think the creases on your jeans are dangerously straight."

She put the beer bottle down and traced her finger over the letters on the label. The band started another song with a catchy title: "Let Me Come Over There and Love You."

It was a bit hokey, and something straight out of a forties-era movie, but her gaze lifted and her eyes met his. They could have been Bogie and Bacall, Tracy and Hepburn, or shooting a scene from *The African Queen* for that matter.

He wanted. She wanted. And they both knew what the other one wanted. But the timing was all wrong.

It was simply destined to be one of those nights when

the principal characters had to yearn from afar, and cram enough sizzle into one glance to light up a couple of Christmas trees.

Robert Wayne Jasper walked into Lily Langtry's and waited for someone to take issue with that. There was a lot of liquor and testosterone in the place and the two didn't always mix favorably. That might have bothered a lot of men who feared being on the receiving end of some heckling bruiser's fist, but it didn't faze him.

He was like a junkyard dog. He didn't have to bite to frighten you away. It was the eyes. Whenever anyone looked into them they saw places they did not want to visit. He had been called a "creepy bastard" more than once.

He wasn't a big man, but his trim body was all steely sinew, his skin pocked with battle scars. He did not move like the average person, but fluidly, like water. He could defy physics with martial arts techniques, and had spent the early years of his life turning his body into a weapon.

Some people are said to be born bad and Robert Wayne Jasper was such a man—a habitual felony offender in the state of Texas, he served six months of a four-year sentence for burglary in Huntsville and an additional two months in prison for violating the terms of his parole. Three years later, after pleading guilty, he was sentenced on a hot, August afternoon, to five years for a second burglary conviction—although he got off easy, since he was guilty of another eight burglaries and two murders that the cops did not know about.

He was released in less than two years.

A year after his release, Jasper was dealing in drugs. He was also working for a bail bond office in Austin—to work off what he owed them for posting his bond for an attempted robbery.

When he finished work one afternoon, he left the bond office, walked up East Seventh Street toward I-35, where he was stopped by a man who got out of a new black Cadillac Escalade parked on the street. Jasper didn't know the dude, but in his business he encountered a lot of people he did not know.

"Robert Wayne Jasper?"

"If the money's right I'll be anyone you want me to be."

"I have been asked to perform a duty for someone," the man said, without introducing himself or the person who employed him. "Do you know where I might find a tight-lipped hit man?" he asked, and then laughed.

At first Jasper thought he was joking, but the man's expression turned suddenly serious when he said, "The job pays well . . . *real* well."

Jasper had been around enough to know that a hit that paid well would mean going back to prison if he got caught. But he also felt he was a lucky man. Didn't he have the word the words *heads* and *tails* tattooed on his fingers? And didn't he have a collection of lucky rattlesnake rattlers, wishbones, and horseshoes? Bottom line was, Jasper could use the money, so here he was at Langtry's.

He looked over a stack of empty shot glasses and saw where the chick from the East Coast and her cowboy dude were sitting and how they looked all lovey-dovey and lost in their own world. He wondered if they sensed he was there.

He bought a beer and carried it to a small table wedged in the corner not far away. He was glad to sit down. His feet were hot in these boots. He was probably the only Texan around who did not like cowboy boots or cowboy hats. He removed the hat and put it on the chair opposite him. He hoped someone would steal it.

He surveyed the area and located the three exits. It did not look like a troublemaking crowd—at least not yet. These cowboy types were usually well behaved, but the real test would come later, after they consumed a few longnecks.

When Ellery and her cowboy got up to dance, he took a few photographs. And now it's high-tech-toy time! He loved talking with his mind. He especially liked it when he saw a change in his victims, as if his thoughts had penetrated some barrier into their consciousness. Usually they took a look around, as if they sensed someone was watching. But the best was the look of fear that settled masklike on a face.

Ah . . . here it comes. She glanced around. You know I'm here now, don't you? Are you curious who I am, why I'm here?

After an hour, he decided it was time to go, and he left the beer untouched on the table. He purposely walked along the edge of the dance floor as he made his way to the exit. It warms the cockles of my cold heart to see the moment you sense my presence. You look around the room, but how can you see me when you don't know what I look like?

We go together well, you and I . . .
I am like the wind.
And you can feel what you cannot see.

Ellery never would have believed it, but she was having a great time at beer-guzzling dance hall. A while earlier she'd been tense and on edge, but now she was so relaxed, she wondered if it was Clint or the beer. Perhaps it was a combination of both. It felt good not to think for a change, to have fun and dance, and forget her troubles for a while.

Probably the biggest surprise of her life was to learn that country and western dancing was an absolute blast. Of course, it helped a lot that Clint was a good dancer, as well as an excellent teacher.

Later, as they left the dance hall, she couldn't remember when she had felt so happily energetic or enjoyed herself more and she wished the euphoria would last.

Everything changed the moment they pulled in front of her house and Clint stopped the bike. She sensed something wasn't right almost immediately. Nothing looked out of place and she saw nothing to alarm her, but something was off beam.

Clint must have noticed the change in her. "What is it?"

Her hands were shaking. "I don't know. I mean, I don't know of anything that's wrong, but I have this strange feeling that something is off kilter."

"What do you mean off kilter . . . with you or something with your house?"

She shivered and rubbed her arms. "I think he's been back . . . inside my house."

"Who?"

She remembered she had not mentioned anything about the incident last night to him. "I had a visitor last night. I heard a noise and realized someone was inside the house. I called 911 and had a house full of police officers, photographers, and Detective Bardwell."

"Why didn't you tell me before now? Dammit, why didn't Bardwell tell me?"

"I guess I was having so much fun, I forgot to mention it." She told him what had happened, and what the police had said. "I was fine all evening. I never thought about it the whole time I was with you, and then, the moment we pull in front of my house, I start acting paranoid."

She was about to thank him for such an enjoyable evening, when suddenly he was off the motorcycle before she could speak. He took her hand and helped her off. "Give me the key to the house. I'll go check everything out."

She handed him the key.

"You wait here."

"Stay here alone? Are you kidding? I'm coming with you."

"You would probably feel safer out here."

"Where I feel safer is with you."

His look melted her heart just a little more. "I wish you had said that earlier."

She asked in a voice that had turned husky, "Why do you wish I had said that earlier?"

He took her hand. "Don't play coy. You know why. Come on, let's go check everything out and then maybe I'll show you if you still haven't figured it out."

She vowed she would play the dummy and followed him up the steps, where she waited for him to put the key in the lock. He didn't, and that was when she noticed the front door was cracked slightly open. She scooted closer behind him.

They stepped inside.

The scent of incense drifted out to meet her. Ellery flipped on the light and screamed.

Clint took her in his arms and she buried her face against his chest. "It's okay. It's not real. It's only a mannequin."

She waited a moment for the panic to lessen before she looked at the terrifying sight of a woman hanging by her neck from the light fixture in the entry. Her feet were eerily moving from a slight draft coming through the open door behind them.

Ellery had seen her share of thriller movies, and read even more gruesome and terrifying things in dozens of bestsellers, yet nothing had ever affected her the way the sight of this did. She could see now that it was a mannequin, with long brown hair and glasses. She brought her hand up to her chest and took a deep breath. "I thought at first it was supposed to be me."

"No, it's Susan. Or rather, it's supposed to look like her, and the resemblance is close enough that anyone who knew her would probably see it."

She realized there was a note pinned to the dress about the same time Clint removed it. "What does it say?"

He handed the note to her. She read it softly. " 'Remember me as you pass by, as you are now, so once was

I. As I am now, so you will be. Prepare for death and follow me.' " She shuddered. Clint walked off.

She ran after him. "Where are you going?"

"To use the phone. We need to call the police."

While they waited for the police to arrive, they checked out the rest of the house, but didn't find anything out of order. When Clint saw the dyed red place on the bedroom carpet he said, "I don't think you should stay here, at least at night."

"I'm not going to let some freaked-out fruitcake get what he wants." She went to the kitchen and put on a pot of coffee. "He isn't going to run me off so easily."

"Do you think that's all he's trying to do?"

She gave him a cold look. "Don't you?"

"Either that or he has plans to do something more serious."

She opened the cabinet and took out several cups. "Oh, thank you very much. Just what I need . . . a reason to fear for my life."

"I'm not trying to scare you, but you have to face that possibility."

"I am facing it, dammit! It keeps me awake half the night. I jump at every little sound. I see the bastard's shadowed face in my dreams."

The police arrived and she was glad to see Detective Bardwell was with them. Once she greeted him, Ellery stood in the doorway and watched Bardwell circle the mannequin a few times before he spoke.

"Someone went to a lot of trouble to make this look like Susan Littleton," he said, "which tells us he knew her well enough to make this a damn good likeness. The question is why."

Ellery glanced at the mannequin again and felt light-headed and just a little queasy. She had to get out of here. She couldn't bear to look at the grotesque shape hanging in the entry hall a moment longer. "There's more coffee in the kitchen," she said, and listened to the drone of Bard-well's voice.

"It could be a stalker trying to use Susan's death to frighten you. It could be Susan's killer coming after you or trying to frighten you enough that you will leave town."

She added another one. "Or it could be some sick person with a warped sense of humor trying to have his moment of fame and good feelings about himself."

Ellery tried to gather her scattered thoughts. "What about you, Detective? Do you think this incident and the one last night are related?"

"I have my suspicions, but no evidence to back it up. When we get a crime scene report, something may pop up to connect the two. Do you know how he entered the house?"

"Look over there," Clint said grimly, pointing at a front window that was missing a pane. "He must have used glass cutters. Very neatly done. I didn't notice it when we walked up to the house."

"And I just had the locks changed this morning," Ellery said, biting her lip. When Clint turned to look at her, she said, "I was going to tell you."

Bardwell was still looking at the mannequin. "I'm sorry but we'll have to leave this up until the investigation on the premises is finished. Perhaps you'd be more comfortable in another room in the meantime."

She nodded in agreement. "I'll be in the kitchen," she said and departed.

A short time later, she sat at the kitchen table, her hands wrapped around her coffee cup. She heard the door open, the sound of someone entering. A photographer arrived about five minutes later, and began the routine of taking shots from every angle, while Detective Bardwell drank his coffee and wrote down the answers Clint and Ellery gave to his questions. When that was finished, he said, "You really should look into some kind of security system."

"I've already scheduled someone to do that. I'm having security lights put in the yard and in all the trees as well."

"You're on top of it," he said. "That's good."

"What do you make of this?" Clint asked.

"Right now we're treating it as a stalking case, and it could very well be your friend from D.C. He isn't registered in the hotel or any of the motels here in Agarita Springs, by the way. If it isn't your friend Sherman, I think it is someone you know, and he is trying to control you, make you afraid of him."

"Well, he's doing a bang-up job of it so far," she said.

"I know we talked over the phone about the criminal psychologist's theories, but I need to ask you some other questions. Whoever this person is, he is stalking you. Which brings me to my next round of questions for you. Can you think of anyone you know who might want to do this . . . a rejected boyfriend, an engagement broken off, a coworker out for revenge, aside from Sherman DeWitt?"

Her head was shaking before he finished. "No, I haven't really done any serious dating since my fiancé was killed. Mostly I had business dinner dates or attended black-tie functions."

"What about family members?"

"My closest family members are Lucy, Hazel, and Margaret."

"Have you been having any prank calls, or an unusual number of calls where the caller hangs up?"

"Well, just one, two days after I came to town. The same day I found that mask taped to the back door, but I told you about that."

Clint bristled. "You didn't tell me."

Ellery sighed. "I was sure it was Sherman."

Bardwell continued his questioning. "Have you noticed a particular car driving down your street a lot, or slowing down by your house?"

"No."

"Has there been anyone you noticed looking at you or following you around in a store, or anyone who appeared to be following you?"

"No, not that I noticed, although I do have a feeling sometimes that I am being watched. But it's only a creepy feeling."

"Anyone ring your doorbell claiming to be with the utility company or selling something?"

"No. I don't open my door to strangers."

"Good," he said and continued with a few more questions.

"You might prepare yourself for this type of thing, because it's fairly typical behavior of stalkers. I know you have your yellow Lab. You need to be aware that something could happen to it."

"What do you mean?"

"Victims tend to think a dog will protect them and put an end to everything, but all it puts an end to is the dog. A stalker won't hesitate to kill a pet, so you might want to consider leaving it with a friend or a vet."

She glanced toward Clint. "Would you take Bertha to the ranch tomorrow?"

"I know she's not much of a watchdog, but wouldn't you feel better if she were here with you?"

"They generally kill the animals immediately, isn't that right, Detective?"

"Yes, they do . . . generally."

"I'll give you a flyer we made up with a lot of information about stalking, and what you can do to help. It gives a list of things, like keeping a log of everything that happens, such as telephone calls. You need to remember stalking is all about power and control, and the perpetrator uses stalking to destroy the victim's sense of reality. It's a crime of terror that seems to be endless. He uses scare tactics to frighten you. All too often, this can lead to violence. Whatever you do, this is not something to be taken lightly." He paused. "I smell incense."

"I smelled it, too, when we first came in," Ellery said. "Only thing is, I don't have any incense."

"You do now," Bardwell said.

"What do you think about the note pinned to the dress?" Clint asked.

"Typical scare tactics." Bardwell looked at Ellery. "Was there anything about the note that reminded you of something . . . an incident, or perhaps a person?"

She shook her head. "No."

"Well, whatever he is, he's creative when he writes poetry," Bardwell said.

"It wasn't original," Clint said. "I've read it, or one similar, before. It was on a tombstone in a cemetery in East Texas. I heard that it originally came from an old grave somewhere in England."

Ellery gave Clint a quizzical look. "Are you a frequent graveyard visitor, or do you go only when there's a full moon?"

Bardwell laughed. Clint ignored it, which made Ellery smile.

"It's good to enjoy a laugh," Bardwell said. "I don't get to do that often in my line of work." He closed his notebook and stood. "It looks like the crew is finished and wrapping things up. I'll take the mannequin down and log it in as evidence. I'll send it over to the state crime lab tomorrow."

After the broken window was secured and the last car drove away, Ellery and Clint remained on the porch talking. "Are you going to be okay here alone?" he asked. "I really think—"

"Don't think, okay? I have to handle this my way. I would appreciate it if you would take Bertha to the ranch tomorrow, but if you refuse, I'll take her to Lucy's."

"Why are you being so hard-nosed? Why won't you let anyone help you?"

"I don't want help because this is my fight and not

yours. I can take care of myself. I doubt the perp will make a second call tonight. I'll be getting my alarm system next week. I can handle this. I will not let that bastard see me running scared."

"Gambling with your life isn't brave, it's foolish. You could be killed."

"And you could be asked to leave if you keep pushing me on this."

He put his hand out and cupped her face. "I care about what happens to you."

"Well, don't. I don't need this right now. I won't be distracted."

"All right, I'll take Bertha to the ranch with me."

"Thank you. I'm not trying to be hostile."

"You are, though, whether you're trying to or not."

"You need to understand that right now I feel terribly violated and angry."

"Stop pursuing this thing, Ellery. It's too dangerous."

"I'll ask for your advice when I want it, so you need to understand something right now. I intend to find Susan's killer—"

"By using yourself as bait?"

"If I have to, yes. This is important to me. You have to understand that."

"I'll stay here tonight."

"No." She started to say more, but when she looked into his eyes she knew she had said enough. "Would you like a glass of wine before you go?"

"I think you should come out to the ranch and spend the night."

"Now that's a great idea. I won't have to worry about

the stalker creeping up on me. I'll just worry about you slipping into my room."

He pulled her into his arms and kissed her hard. She was just warming up when he released her. "When I come into your room, it will be because you asked me, so there won't be any need to slip around, will there?"

"No, I guess not." She paused. "When and not *if*?"

He didn't say anything, but he didn't have to. His smile said it all.

"Do you want that glass of wine or not?"

"If that's all you're offering."

She did something totally spontaneous, which thoroughly surprised her. She came up on her toes, kissed him full on the mouth, and said, "It's all I'm offering right now."

"Is that a rain check?"

"What do you think?" She came up on her toes again to repeat the quick kiss, but Clint had something else in mind. His arms came around her and he gave her a kiss that told her a lot more about Clint Littleton than she had realized before—when he wanted to convey a message, he certainly knew the best way to do it.

But tonight was not the night for sex or for Clint to stay with her, so he left, with a promise to come after Bertha the next day.

Twenty-two

AFTER CLINT LEFT, Ellery closed the bedroom drapes and turned down the bed. It was past four in the morning. She was too tired to be frightened. All she could think about was bed and sleep. She lay down and sought her favorite sleeping position—one hand curled under her chin, and the other slipped beneath her pillow.

She gasped when her hand touched something hard and cold. Her feet got tangled in the sheet as she rolled from the bed, and she fell to the floor. She landed on her stomach. When she finally disentangled herself, she saw the gun: Black, shiny, and silent, it waited for her.

There was a piece of cotton twine tied around the barrel with a note attached. She picked it up and looked at the note. "Put this to your head and pull the trigger. So easy and you'll save us both a lot of time . . ."

She could tell the gun was not a real one, but it was a good copy. She stared at the gun in her hand and realized she shouldn't have touched it. Now her fingerprints would be on it.

Nothing could be done about it now. She opened the top drawer in the nightstand and placed the gun inside. Automatically her hand went to the telephone. She lifted the receiver a few inches and paused. What good would it do to call the police? They would lose sleep. She would lose sleep. And nothing would be solved.

She would call them in the morning. She turned off the lamp and fell asleep almost instantly.

He appeared, as quick as a fleeting shadow, in her bedroom. He moved closer to her bed and opened the drapes, allowing the moonlight to dance across her face. He spoke to her with his mind. *My, you do sleep like a baby, with your hand tucked under your chin. You were a pretty child, too, weren't you? Pampered, privileged, and pretty.*

Dear, dear, what have we here? Now, this is good, really good . . . a little skin showing. Homespun erotica. Did you do this to entice me? Tsk, tsk. Do not tinge it with romance. It would be a waste of time. I rarely go there anymore. I am impenetrable—neither transparent nor translucent. But lucky, lucky you, I brought my camera so I can capture this on film for you.

Click . . . click . . .

He looked at the long, slim leg for a moment before he ran one finger lightly down the length of it.

She stirred but did not wake.

Such a sound sleeper, aren't you, tucked safely away in your own little realm of distorted perceptions and altered states. Have you managed for a while to escape the tears and pain to innocently slumber in a world of your own? When you open your eyes, do you wonder if you're awake or still dreaming?

You will tomorrow . . .

But for now, you think you are safe here, in your little bed. Are you afraid to leave your dreams? Terrified of what might be out there if you do?

If you only knew . . .

So curious about me, aren't you? You want to know who I am and what I look like. Common sense tells you one thing, but what you see cannot be explained by the placid perfection of your logical mind. So you wonder, Am I dreaming, or am I mad?

Poor little Alice, you realize you aren't in Wonderland, and now you're worried, aren't you? If you can't clarify me, you are mad.

He pulled the sheet and covered her leg, and then he seemed to vanish, leaving nothing behind but a few haunting words.

"Don't you know there isn't a way out once you fall in the hole?"

Sunlight bathed her face. The rays coming through the bedroom window warmed her skin. Ellery's mind slowly came awake, but her eyes did not want to open. She didn't want to get up, but her face was growing uncomfortably warm. She should have closed the draperies.

That can't be right, she thought. Last night I closed . . .

Her eyes opened wide and she sprang into an upright position. She had closed the drapes last night. She remembered doing it. But now they were open. She left the bed and went into her dressing room. On the chaise longue a pair of her khaki Bermudas lay beside a white tank top. A pair of her panties and a bra lay beside them.

She put her hands over her mouth, but she couldn't stop the flow of tears. She was shaking so badly she slid down the wall to the floor. The marble was cool against her cheek. She couldn't stop crying.

When the phone rang, she staggered to her feet, doused her face with cold water and dried it. By the time she reached for the phone, it stopped ringing. She put her hand to her head. Was any of this real? Was she awake, or was she dreaming? She felt a prickling sensation at the back of her neck. Was he still here? Was he in the house with her?

Her knees threatened to buckle beneath her. She waited a moment for the dizziness to pass. This wasn't a dream. The clothes were still there, where he put them. She scooped them up with one arm and threw them in with the dirty clothes.

A piece of paper floated to the floor.

> *Your legs look so good in shorts.*
> *Wear these today.*
> *For me . . .*

Good Lord! Was he watching her every move? Was there no place she could go to have any privacy? She put her palms against her cheeks. She looked at herself in the mirror. She didn't know what was happening to her. She felt terrorized. Her mind wasn't working right. One minute she knew the threats were more than just words written on bits of paper, strategically placed. The next minute she thought a threat did not require words at all. The gun, although a fake, had certainly proved that.

She washed her face and brushed her teeth. She was putting the toothbrush away when the phone rang. She picked up the extension in the bathroom.

"Hello."

"Good morning. You were up late last night, so I let you sleep a while before I called you. Did you sleep well?"

The voice was like a shadow that passed over her and turned everything cold and damp before it slithered back into the darkness. "Who is this?"

"You know who it is. You have been waiting for me to call. Did you find the surprise I left for you? I hope you didn't think it was a real gun."

She slammed the phone down. She had to get out of there.

She dressed quickly in a pair of jeans and a black T-shirt. She would go to Starbucks, have a latte, and think about what she should do. Or should she go to the police first?

And Clint? She should call him, she decided, and then the phone rang again.

She hurried down the stairs and grabbed her purse from the chair where she'd left it the night before. She didn't bother to lock the door. Why bother? He could come and go as he pleased. For him, locked doors offered nothing more than a challenge.

The phone rang again.

"Leave a message, you bastard," she called out and slammed the door.

When she reached the car, she put her key in the lock and opened the door. She climbed in and shoved the key into the ignition. Suddenly she was paralyzed. She couldn't turn the key. And she couldn't release it.

Her heart thundered in her chest. What if he had put a bomb in her car? She had reported on such events dozens of times. She had read about it in books. She had seen it in movies. She knew the scenario. The key goes in the ignition; key turns to start the car; occupant is blown to bits . . .

Suddenly a loud explosion ripped across her consciousness, and blasted her ears. It rocked against the windows of the house. The fireball was huge, brilliant, and orange. Black smoke billowed up. She could smell gas and burning rubber. She could almost feel pieces of flying glass that pierced her skin.

Her head dropped against the steering wheel. She was shaking. She wanted to get out of the car, to get away from everything. She was afraid to move. This is what it does to you, she thought. You live with the fear so long until it becomes real and you cannot separate what is happening in your mind from what is going on around you.

She tried reasoning with herself because she had always been able to convince herself she could do anything if she reasoned it out. You've seen too many movies, Ellery. It's just your nerves. Go to town. Get a cup of coffee; surround yourself with people. There is safety in numbers.

Yes, that's what she needed—to be around people. She would go to town. Just turn the key, Ellery. Her hand trembled and she reached for the key. "Come on, start the car. Dammit, start the car!"

She couldn't.

She knew this could be the point where she crossed the line from sanity into that world of escape that lay beyond, in another dimension where none of this horror could reach her. Just give up, something inside of her said. Let go and it will all be over.

"No!" She pounded the steering wheel with her doubled fists. "No . . . No . . . No! You aren't going to win. Not now. Not ever."

Tears were running down her face by the time she got out of the car. She yanked her purse from the seat and hooked it over her shoulder. She started walking fast up the street. "To hell with the car," she said.

She was a few blocks from the center of town when an old woman, busy scolding her Chihuahua, ran a red light. The silver motorcycle coming from the opposite direction was already in the middle of the intersection. The driver swerved to the left. The front tire of the motorcycle slammed against the curb, next to Ellery. The tire bumped and scraped along the curb for several feet, burning rubber and brakes screeching horribly before it flipped on its side. It landed on the sidewalk less than a foot from her.

She screamed and started to run. She covered only a few feet before she tripped over a section of sidewalk, raised by a tree root. She fell forward, hit the sidewalk on all fours, and slid on her stomach.

"Are you all right?"

Someone helped her up. He wasn't much more than a kid, maybe sixteen or seventeen. He was holding a helmet in his left hand while he helped her to her feet. She could see his left arm was bleeding and there were scrapes on his face.

"I'm sorry I scared you. That woman ran a red light. I swerved to miss her. I'd offer you a ride, but all I have is my motorcycle, and I don't think it will run right now. All the gasoline has leaked out. Your arms are bleeding."

"So are yours."

She held her hands out in front of her and saw her scraped and bleeding skin. Both elbows burned like fire and her palms ached. When she held them out, she could see several places where small bits of gravel were gouged into her palms. They ached even more after she looked at them.

"Is there someone I can call for you? I've got a cell phone. I just called my brother. He's on his way over. Can we take you anywhere?"

She stared at the phone in his hand. She wasn't sure she could talk. She would rather sit down and bawl. No, you aren't going to do that. Get a grip. You're strong. You aren't going to let this get the best of you. She took a deep breath. She put her hand to her forehead and looked for a place to rest. "No, thank you. I've got a phone. I'll be all right. I'm just a little rattled right now. I think I need to sit down for a minute." She sat down on the curb not far from his motorcycle.

He sat down next to her. She opened her purse and handed him a couple of tissues. She took a couple for herself and began to dab at her bleeding arms.

"I keep trying to find something humorous about this," she said, wincing when she pulled a piece of gravel out of her elbow.

"We're getting a lot of strange looks," he said, "but I don't suppose that's humorous."

She looked at his dented vehicle and wondered why motorcycles kept recurring in her life. She started laughing then, at the irony of it all; at the number of cars slowing down to stare, creating a real traffic jam in town . . . probably the first in its history.

His laughter soon joined hers. "We probably look strange sitting here on the curb, bleeding and laughing like a couple of idiots," she said.

"I'm awfully sorry about this. I'd feel better if you'd let me call someone for you, or a taxi."

"Don't worry. I'm fine. You don't have to wait here with me."

The sudden roar of a loud engine cut through the normal noise on the street. They both looked up to see a black Range Rover make a hasty U-turn. It stopped against the curb a couple of feet from Ellery. The car door swung open and Clint got out.

"What are you doing here?" she asked.

"I was on my way to pick up Bertha when I saw you sitting here." He dropped down on his haunches in front of her. "Are you okay?"

She ignored her bleeding and stinging arms. "It looks worse than it is. I'm all right."

He glanced at the boy sitting beside her. "Hi, Justin. What happened here?"

"Hi, Mr. Littleton. It was my fault," he said, and started to describe what transpired earlier.

"Do you need a ride anywhere?"

"Thanks, but my brother is on his way here." He

glanced toward Ellery. "She's got some serious strawber-
ries on both her arms."

Clint was still looking at her. "Yes, I can see that she
does." He stood and reached for her hand. "Come on," he
said, and walked her to the Rover.

"Where were you going?" he asked when they were inside his car.

"I wanted a cup of coffee, and don't ask me why I
didn't make coffee at home."

"I wasn't going to, but now you've got me curious."

"I wanted to be around people, okay?"

"Fine with me," he said and drove to Starbucks.

"What would you like?" he asked, once she was seated.

"A latte and the most fattening thing they have in that
glass case."

He brought her the latte and a croissant with almond-
paste filling. It probably had eight hundred calories or
more, which made it taste even better. She ate the entire
thing, without offering Clint a bite. When she finished,
she licked her fingers and took a sip of coffee.

"Better?" he asked. "Do you want another one?"

"Immensely better, and no, I don't have room for another one."

"Do you want to talk about it?"

She turned toward him with a look that said it all. "If
living it is a nightmare, why on earth would I want to
talk about it?"

"Beats me," he said. "Come on and I'll take you home."

"I left to get away from home."

"I want to know what happened. You can tell me on
the way."

She told him everything: the gun under her pillow with the note attached; the clothes laid out for her in her bathroom; the telephone call. It took a couple of questions from him before she told of the terror she felt when she thought there might be a bomb in her car and how her fingers were frozen to the key in the ignition. She told him why she had walked to town and the stark terror she felt when Justin's motorcycle crashed next to her. She had thought someone was trying to run her down.

He made a call to Detective Bardwell, who said he would meet them at Ellery's house. When they arrived, Bardwell and two policemen were there. She related the story to him while the policemen searched the house, trying to find out how the stalker could have reentered the house the night before.

When they finished, Bardwell spoke with them, then returned to the family room where Ellery and Clint waited. "They did not find any signs of forced entry, but they did find a couple of gum wrappers and yesterday's sports page in the attic, so someone was there. I think he was still here when you came home last night and when we were searching the house. There are a lot of places in the attic where he could have hidden. He waited until you were asleep, then came downstairs and entered your room."

They talked a few minutes more, made arrangements to have Ellery's phone tapped, and then Bardwell left. When Ellery closed the door, Clint asked, "We need to get your cuts cleaned up. Where do you keep your medicine and Band-Aids?"

"I keep them in the bathroom like most normal people."

He kept his hand at her back as they went upstairs. "I need to look that up," he said.

"What?"

"To see if a grumpy disposition is normally the result of a terrorizing experience."

"Are you insinuating I'm grumpy, or are you calling me grumpy?"

"Both," he said, and opened the linen closet door. He pulled out an assortment of things and put them on the counter. "Come here. We need to wash your arms and hands first."

For the next half hour, he picked gravel out of her palms, cleaned the wounds with peroxide, applied Neosporin and Band-Aids in the places that needed them.

She looked at her reflection in the mirror. It was the first time she ever saw anyone wear an entire box of Band-Aids at one time. She looked like a mummy.

"What do you think?" he asked.

"I think you'll make a wonderful mother someday."

Twenty-three

DETECTIVE BARDWELL CALLED early the next morning
to tell Ellery they found out where Sherman T. was staying. "I made a call to the police in D.C. and they sent a
detective to do a little snooping. He called back to say
Sherman was staying at the Guest Quarters, so I drove
over to Austin and paid him a little visit."

"Oh, he is going to be angry at me now," she said. "I
better put my car in the garage before he can get to it."

"I can post a patrol car in front of your house."

"I'd rather not do that right now. It would only draw
attention and make my neighbors nervous. If things get
worse, I may change my mind."

"Just let me know."

"What did you ask him?"

"I asked typical questions about why he was here and
what made him write the article about you. I queried him
about his relationship with you and discovered what a
heartless, unbalanced woman you are. He has a bit of a
police record as well. Did you know that?"

"No, I didn't."

"It was nothing to warrant a prison sentence, but he has had more than his share of charges pressed for stalking, harassment, and a few other nice crimes, mostly against women."

"Power trip," she said.

Bardwell nodded. "I'll buy into that."

She was about to ask if he thought Sherman T. was the one harassing her, but Bardwell said, "There goes my other line. I'll keep you posted, and you do the same."

"Will do," she said and hung up.

After she hung up, Ellery finished the morning paper and was about to go for her run when the doorbell rang. She glanced at the clock and wondered who would be at her door at seven-thirty in the morning.

She put her coffee cup in the sink and went to the door. A red-faced Sherman T. DeWitt was standing on the other side.

His face was mottled with anger and his voice unusually high-pitched. "Listen, bitch, if you think sending the police to investigate me is going to make me tuck tail and run back to Washington, you're badly mistaken. I'm even more determined now. I'll follow you everywhere you go. You won't have a moment's rest. Every time you sneeze it will be in the paper. So why don't you do what you do best and keep screwing that rancher you're so fond of and stay out of my business? You'd be wise not to mess with me again."

"Always a bottom feeder, aren't you? Constantly trying to scoop a story, forever bound to sling your slimy sensationalism and thrive on the misfortune of others—that's your forte, isn't it?"

She must have hit a sore spot, for his voice turned shrill and so piercing she wanted to put her fingers in her ears. "You've always been jealous of me because you know I'm better at the game than you are."

"I don't play games, and unlike you, I don't disseminate facts and stoop to reckless, sleazy reporting. You better toe the mark, because if you slip and print one false accusation I'll haul your skinny ass into court for making false and defamatory statements and for reporting confidential information that puts my life in danger, and I'll name the *Daily Snoop* in the lawsuit. Now, get off my porch and don't come back."

"This isn't the end of it."

"I am quaking in my boots." She slammed the door and watched him through the side pane, to be sure he got in his car. It occurred to her that Sherman T. could also fit the description of the man she saw in her dreams. She was frustrated that she kept having the dreams, but and each time she did, more of the man's face became clear. However, it was a slow process and she wondered if she would ever see it completely—or at least enough of it to identify him before he tried to kill her.

Stalkers did not give up easily. He would come back again. She was certain of it. She just did not know when.

She didn't have to wait long to find out, for the stalker returned two days later. She returned from the grocery store to find all the faucets in the house were running full blast. Water was running out of the upstairs bathrooms, along the hall, and trickling down the stairs. The kitchen floor was covered with two inches of water.

Shortly after Detective Bardwell arrived, Lucy walked

in with Shirley. The had been discussing all that had happened to Ellery while Shirley was in Houston. While Bardwell and Clint talked in the study, the women were in the kitchen, sweeping and mopping up the mess.

"What about the upstairs?" Lucy asked when they finished.

"I've called a carpet cleaner. They have a vacuum that will suck up the water." Ellery was making coffee, which was becoming a regular pastime.

Shirley was leaning against her mop. "Any idea who is doing it, and why?"

Ellery told them about Sherman T. and added that she wasn't completely satisfied that he was the stalker. Something did not add up. Sherman T. was a pain in the posterior and vindictive as hell, but she just couldn't see him as a killer. And he certainly wouldn't have been responsible for Susan's or Clay's deaths.

"I don't know who it is," she said at last, "but I can tell you that he's in a class of his own. This isn't your run-of-the-mill stalker. This guy gives me that creepy-crawly feeling you'd get sleeping with centipedes."

"One thing I don't understand," Lucy said, "and that is, why does he keep playing with you like this? If he is the one who killed Susan and possibly Clay, why didn't he kill you the first time?"

Ellery did not have to think about that. "I think he enjoys it. He knows he can kill me anytime he chooses, but it's more fun and gives him a feeling of power to know he is controlling my life, that I'm afraid of what he can do."

"Sick bastard," Shirley said. "Now that Bertha is over

at the ranch, do you want me to bring Webster over to stay with you?"

Lucy and Ellery looked at one another and burst out laughing.

"I don't see anything funny," Shirley said in a miffed tone. "I thought I was being neighborly." She propped her mop against the counter and turned.

Ellery realized she was going home, so she said quickly, "Shirley, I'm sorry. You were being neighborly and Webster is good company. You know how much I enjoy him. It's just that when I think of a dog for protection it's more along the lines of a Doberman, not Webster. I'm sorry I laughed."

Shirley looked from Ellery to Lucy and back, and Ellery could see the indecision on her face.

"Please don't leave, Shirley, and don't begrudge my finding something to laugh at. There haven't been many opportunities for levity in my life of late."

Shirley nodded. "I guess you have to take your laughs where you can get them." She paused. "You know what? I've been thinking about Webster and I believe the problem is his name," Shirley said. "I ought to change his name to something more powerful, like Pit or Viper, maybe Hammer or Warlord."

Ellery did not say anything. It took every ounce of her willpower to suppress the laugh that beat against the back of her throat, demanding to be released. Lucy wasn't so fortunate, so she muffled her mouth and ran from the room.

Shirley picked up the mop and put it on the back porch to dry. When she returned, she said, "You said earlier that this guy has been busy this past week. What did he do?"

"He had black roses delivered to my house."

"Couldn't the police track that?" Lucy asked, coming back into the room.

Ellery shook her head. "The florist said they received an envelope with cash inside and instructions to dye roses black and deliver them. Naturally, the sender couldn't be traced. Initially I received several phone calls and when I answered, I could hear heavy breathing, or he would say things to try to frighten me."

"I guess he wouldn't be someone whose voice you could recognize," Lucy said.

"No, his voice was distorted, as if he were using a voice-altering device. He seems to have stopped the calls . . . he probably suspects that the police have tapped my phone."

She went on to tell them about the red dye in the bathroom, the lipstick on the mirror, the mannequin, and the toy gun.

"Stays busy, doesn't he?" Lucy said. "I wonder if he has a day job."

"How does he get inside?" Shirley asked.

"He knows I don't have an alarm, but that will all change soon. My alarm will be installed on Monday. The first time, I left the window unlocked. He broke a pane once and entered that way. Once, he hid in the attic and returned later, during the night when I was asleep. Another time the police found where he had been coming through the attic window. He must have climbed the tree onto the roof and then entered through the window.

Things should get better now, since the police have stepped up the number of times they patrol my house."

"I hope the alarm stops him," Lucy said.

"So do I," Ellery said. "I feel like I've called the cops so many times that I'm on a first-name basis with everyone there."

"Why do you stay here and take it?" Shirley asked. "Hell, the first time something like that happened to me, I'd be gone."

"No you wouldn't. You know how we women are. We cope. We get stronger the more you throw at us. You can push us so far and then we draw the line and make a stand," Ellery replied.

"She's got this wonderful ability to ride things out. Her strength of will is stronger than her fear, or common sense," Lucy said. "It's like Custer's Last Stand. You know she's outnumbered. You know she's going to lose. And yet, you have to admire her kind of guts."

Shirley looked skeptical, but being the skeptic was her chosen vocation and therefore quite predictable. "So what are the lard-butt police doing about it? Maybe we need to get Lorraine to start praying for them."

Lucy coughed to smother another laugh; Ellery was doing all she could to keep from laughing as well.

That didn't seem to bother Shirley. "Well, he's bound to strike again," she said. "You know you're walking on top of a volcano and it's got a mighty thin crust, don't you?"

Twenty-four

ELLERY OPENED HER eyes and looked at the clock. It was five after seven. She was supposed to meet Lucy at nine. She dropped her legs over the side of the bed and stayed in that position for a few minutes before she groaned and pushed herself to her feet.

She dragged herself into the bathroom and looked at her reflection in the mirror. One thing about mirrors, they never lied. "You look worse than awful," she said to her reflection.

It was true. She did look worse than awful. She truly did. Her hair looked like it had been zap-dried with a stun gun. It just lay there, limp, dull, and awful. She had a fading yellow bruise on her cheek from her fall the week before, and her elbows were all scabbed over and hurt every time she moved. People seemed hesitant to get too close to her in the checkout line at the grocery store.

She had to let her arms soak under the shower for a while before she could bend them enough to shampoo her hair. She cut herself three times shaving her legs. She was out of Band-Aids. By the time she did her hair and makeup and got dressed she was already running late.

Thanks to the kindness of Clint, who stopped by frequently, and her new routine of walking into town in order to burn up nervous energy, it was the first time she was in her car since her ordeal, but she didn't have any sense of panic when she opened the door and sat down. She put the key in the ignition and turned it. Nothing happened.

She tried again. Not even a click.

After several more tries, she went back into the house and called the filling station where she traded. Troy Watkins, who owned the station, answered and said he'd be right over.

She was supposed to meet Lucy in a few minutes, so she called her cell phone and explained she would be delayed. "I'll pick you up," Lucy said and hung up.

Ellery was standing next to the car when Troy drove up.

He pulled a toolbox out of the back of his pickup. "Good morning, Ms. O'Brien. Sorry you're having problems with your car."

"Hi, Troy. I just tried it again. It still won't start."

Troy tried to start the engine a time or two before he pulled the lever to pop the hood. "I don't think it's the starter. Sounds like the ignition, or maybe a loose connection, because it's not even turning over."

He opened the hood. He took a big step back and his arms went up in the air as if someone had told him to stick 'em up. "Whoa!"

"What is it?" Ellery looked under the hood. Lying near

the carburetor was a hand grenade with a note taped to it that said, "BOOM!"

"I don't think it's real, but there's no reason to take a chance. I think we should call the police." He pulled his cell phone out of his pocket. "Do you mind if I call them?"

"Oh no, I'm growing quite fond of having them over for coffee," she said and rattled off the number for him. "Speak to Detective Bardwell, if he's in."

Ellery took her usual spot on the front steps.

Troy closed his phone and put it in his pocket. "Roland said he'd be here in a flash."

It was more like ten or twelve flashes, but at least Detective Roland Bardwell put in an appearance. "What's this about a hand grenade?" he asked, getting out of his car. Ellery saw a box of Krispy Kreme doughnuts on the passenger seat. His shirtfront glistened with crystals of glazed sugar. He had a coffee cup in his hand.

Troy pointed under the hood. "I figure it's probably a fake grenade, but I'm a firm believer in safe over sorry."

Bardwell nodded and returned to the car. He came back with a cloth and a plastic bag. "You did right, Troy." He leaned over the carburetor and studied the grenade for a minute or two before he picked it up with the cloth and dropped it into the plastic bag.

"It will probably be like all the other things—clean as a whistle," Ellery said.

"My guess is you are right on target," Bardwell said, "but we need to run it through to be certain."

Troy let out a long, relieved breath, and Ellery could see he was quite shaken. "It sure does look like someone has a sick mind," he said and leaned over the fender.

While Troy tried to find the problem with Ellery's car, she spoke with Roland Bardwell.

Troy started the car, then killed the engine and closed the hood before he joined them a few minutes later. "One of the wires had been disconnected. It's all fixed now and you're ready to go."

In Bassinger's Bookstore, Lucy munched on a chocolate chip cookie while Ellery's expression was hidden behind a pair of sunglasses. Her coffee was untouched.

"Is your coffee okay?"

"What? Oh, I'm sure it's fine."

"Maybe it would help to talk about it," Lucy said. "You can't go around keeping all that inside you."

"I've talked about everything with the police until I'm sick of it. If this keeps up they will have to add on a room just to hold all the statements I've given."

"When I say talk, I don't mean go back over the same details until you're cross-eyed. I'm speaking of what the stress of all this is doing to you. You must have lost ten pounds since this started, and you were pretty slim to start with."

"I know. It's embarrassing when your leggings are loose."

"Better than having them cut off your circulation, like mine."

"I guess I haven't done a very good job dealing with everything. But it's hard to think about myself with so much happening. Every morning I ask myself what he will do today, instead of what do I want to do. Anticipating his next move has completely changed my life—if I can call it a life.

"He's like a hunter and you know he's there, but you can't react until he shoots, and by then it's already too late."

"Take off your glasses. I want to see your face so I can judge for myself how you're doing."

Ellery removed the glasses. She knew the loss of softness in the contours of her face was evident, and her skin didn't have the healthy, peachy glow it usually did. There were other casualties too. She was aware of the way her gaze kept darting around the room, but even when she made a conscious effort to stop, she could not. Her posture was different. The laid-back, relaxed body was gone, replaced by a tightly coiled spring surrounding an iron rod where her backbone used to be.

Lucy gave her a sympathetic look. "I don't think you should stay here any longer. I think you should leave town—go somewhere and not tell a soul. Not even me."

"I thought about it, but that would be giving in and letting him get what he wants. I've been through too much to quit. My mind tells me to get out, but my iron-clad will tells me to stand and fight. And I'm curious. Somehow, I know this is connected to Susan's death. I just don't know how—at least, not yet. I keep thinking that if I hang in there I'll know the truth eventually."

"Why don't you come and stay with me? Or I'll come and stay with you. The important thing is you shouldn't go through this alone."

"I don't want to involve anyone else. You have enough worries with your divorce. This is off the subject, but have you seen friendly Margaret lately?"

"I stopped by there a few days ago. She acted as if she

were afraid to talk to me. Truthfully, she looks as stressed as you do. I'm worried about her, but she refuses to see a doctor. She doesn't leave the house at all now. She even has her groceries delivered. I think I'll call Detective Bardwell. She was his eighth-grade math teacher. She is still very fond of him. He drops by to see her whenever he has time. Maybe he could talk her into going to the doctor."

Ellery put the sunglasses back on. "I guess we all have our problems, so that sort of balances things out, doesn't it?"

"No it doesn't," Lucy said, "because some have worse problems than others, and that's the unfair part of it."

They were interrupted by Ellery's cell phone. Ellery answered it on the third ring. "Hello?"

"Is this Ellery O'Brien?"

"Yes."

"This is Daniel Wilkerson. I think you know who I am."

"Yes, Lucy told me about you."

"I'd like for us to meet and wondered if there was a time I could drive over to pay you a visit, or take you to lunch. I feel like you're family and that we should at least be acquainted with one another. I'm sure you have a lot of questions about Susan and our early years. Perhaps I could answer some of them for you. After all, she was my sister and we grew up together. I'm willing to help in any way I can."

"That's so very kind of you, Daniel."

"What's your preference? Meet at your house or have lunch somewhere?"

"I've been a little stressed lately and not in much of a mood to go out. I think meeting at home would be more comfortable for me, if that is satisfactory with you."

"How about next Wednesday at two o'clock?"

"Wednesday at two is fine."

"I'm looking forward to meeting you."

"And I you. Thanks for your call, Daniel."

Ellery hung up and turned toward her friend. "I guess you know who that was."

"I knew he would call," Lucy said. "I told you he couldn't stand not knowing what you looked like and how much you favored Susan. I can't wait until Wednesday to hear what the two of you talked about." She paused and then laughed. "Actually, I think I already know. You'll talk about Daniel, because that's his favorite subject."

Twenty-five

Looking just like any other TV repair truck, the nondescript van drove slowly down Thirteenth Street, made a U-turn, and stopped at 1313. The repairman climbed out of the van and started up the walk.

He looked like any other repairman, with dark blue khaki pants and matching shirt. A SCOOTER'S TV REPAIR patch was sewn above the left pocket. A dark blue base-ball cap and sunglasses shaded his eyes from the glare of the hot Texas sun.

Across the street at 1312, Cassie Baxter had just let her dog outside for a few minutes and stood watching at the window so she would know when Hercules, her Mexican Chihuahua, was finished doing his business.

Cassie saw the van drive up and stop across the street. She found it odd that a television repairman would be stopping at Hazel Ledbetter's house, when everyone in town knew Hazel did not own a television. This was be-cause Hazel was a school librarian before she took early retirement last year so she could travel. In Hazel's mind, television could not compete in any way with a good book or a newspaper.

SCOOTER'S TV REPAIR . . . Cassie studied the sign painted on the side of the van and noticed it had an address on Burnet Road in Austin. She guessed he must be looking for another address and had stopped to make an inquiry, or else he had the wrong address to begin with.

About that time, Hercules scratched on the front door and she opened it to let him into the house. She caught a glimpse of the repairman as he climbed the two steps to Hazel's front porch just when Hercules darted through the door and she closed it behind him.

It was a little after two o'clock on a Monday afternoon when the repairman rang the doorbell and said to the woman who answered the door, "Cassandra Baxter?"

Hazel Ledbetter shook her head and said, "She lives across the street."

He flashed a smile and shook his head. "We've got a new gal answering the telephone and she probably wrote down the wrong number. Would you mind letting me borrow your telephone? My cell phone battery is dead and I need to call the store to give them the correct address so they will know where I am." He pulled a five-dollar bill out of his pocket and offered it to her. "Please take this for the long-distance call."

"Oh posh! Hazel said. "It costs a pittance to call Austin. Keep your money." She opened the door wider.

He stepped inside. "I sure do appreciate your doing this."

"Think nothing of it. There's a phone right here, in the kitchen," she said, and turned to lead the way, with the repairman following close behind. When she went through the doorway, she turned to the left to lift the receiver off the wall phone.

Before she knew what was happening, his hand came around and grabbed her chin and yanked it back, while the other hand, which held a twelve-inch boning knife, silently slit her throat with one fluid swipe that cut through her jugular and her larynx, all the way down to her spine.

Blood spurted with a pulsating hemorrhage and Hazel dropped to the floor about the same time the receiver hit the green linoleum.

A few minutes later, he walked slowly down the walk and opened the door to his van. By the time he climbed inside, most of Hazel Ledbetter's blood was spreading in an ever-widening pool across the floor.

He started the van and drove casually back down Thirteenth Street, looking just like any other TV repair truck.

Twenty-six

THE AGARITA SPRINGS police station received the call
from 911 concerning a call they took from Cassie Baxter.
Officer Dave Plunkett answered the phone.

"What kind of problem is Cassie having?" he asked.

"She said Hazel Ledbetter is her neighbor across the
street and they were supposed to go play bridge at the
country club at four o'clock. According to her, Ms. Ledbetter doesn't answer her phone or the door. Cassie
peeked through the glass window in the garage and saw
Hazel's car was there. She said she was worried because
there was a strange man at Hazel's house about two
o'clock. He drove a TV repair truck."

"What was so strange about that?"

"Hazel Ledbetter doesn't have a television."

"We'll send someone out to investigate," he said.

Rookie Officer Jimmy Thomas was dispatched to the
home of Hazel Ledbetter. He arrived at four forty-five. He
found the door unlocked and entered. He recognized the
smell of blood the moment he stepped inside the house.

It grew stronger as he headed toward the kitchen. He gagged a couple of times as he drew closer to the kitchen. As soon as he reached the doorway he saw the body. Hazel Ledbetter lay on the floor, sprawled on her back in a pool of blood. The gaping wound looked like an evil grin, drenched in blood.

He gagged, turned, and bolted from the house. He made it as far as the steps before he threw up in the front flower bed.

Detective Roland Bardwell arrived at the scene at 5:05.

He found Hazel's body in the kitchen, lying on the floor, her arms spread slightly outward, one hand close to the wall phone that was off the hook and resting on the green linoleum. Her throat had been cut from ear to ear, and he could tell from the angle of her head that it had almost been severed.

It took a strong arm and one helluva knife to do a job like that.

Nothing in the kitchen appeared to be out of place. There were no dishes in the sink, nothing out of the ordinary on the countertops. A tour through the rest of the house showed it to be in perfect order. Not so much as one of Hazel's lace doilies was out of place.

He stayed until the forensics team came and then he went across the street to talk to a tearful Cassie Baxter. When he finished with Cassie, he walked back toward Hazel's house. The ambulance had arrived to remove the body. Neighbors and curious passers-by were congregating near the house. A television van was parked in front of Cassie's house. The police had yellow tape in place.

He dodged questions by reporters and entered the

house again. He remained there until everyone had finished and Hazel's body was loaded in the ambulance. Once he left, he stopped by Lucy's and Margaret Ledbetter's to break the news, and then headed for Ellery O'Brien's house.

It was almost dark when he arrived, but Ellery was outside, watering the front yard. She turned when she heard a car and saw Detective Bardwell pull into her driveway. He wore a solemn expression when he stepped out of the car. "Evening, Ms. O'Brien."

"Good evening, Detective. What brings you out here this time of day? It's well past dinnertime. I would have thought you'd be home with your feet propped up by now."

"Could we step inside?"

A cold chill passed over her and she knew something was wrong, gravely wrong. She dropped the water hose into the flower bed, not bothering to turn it off. "Something hasn't happened to Lucy?"

"No, Lucy is okay."

She opened the door and waited for him to step inside, then closed it behind him. "In here," she said. "We can sit in the family room. Would you like something to drink?"

"No, ma'am. I just came by to deliver some bad news. Your cousin Hazel Ledbetter was killed a few hours ago."

"Oh, my God . . . no! No . . ." She dropped into a chair. "She was such a sweet person. She couldn't have an enemy in the world. What . . . how did it happen? Where? Do you know who did it?"

"No idea who the perp was at this time. We won't know the exact cause of death until the body is examined and a report issued. Unofficially, her throat was cut."

"Oh no . . . poor Hazel. She didn't deserve this."

"One thing about victims is none of them deserve what happens to them."

Ellery sat in a state of solemn disbelief as Detective Bardwell explained all the gruesome details, and when he finished she said, "This is entirely my fault. I should never have come here."

"I'm not so sure your being here had anything to do with it. I stopped by to tell Lucy on my way here. She was telling me how strange her aunt Margaret has been acting. She said Hazel was a bit strange, too, the day she took you over to meet her. She seems to think they might have been afraid of something."

"Like what?"

"I don't know yet, but I intend to find out."

"You need to give them time to come to grips with this before you go stirring up the pain all over again," Ellery said.

"My job is to save lives, not to spread goodwill."

She nodded. "Did you stop by Margaret's house as well?"

"Hazel was her daughter. She had to know, no matter how difficult it was to tell her. Lucy arrived a few minutes after I did. I think she is still there."

"Should I go over there?"

"No, Margaret is a bit standoffish of late. I believe it would be best to give Lucy some time alone with her. I told Lucy I'd advise you to stay away until she contacts you."

"I suppose that's best."

"I don't think you should stay here tonight."

Her heart began to pound. "You have reason to believe the killer is also after me?"

"I don't want to take any chances. Do you have a neighbor or someone here you could spend the night with?"

"I'm sure Shirley wouldn't mind my sleeping over there."

"Why don't you gather up your things then, and I'll walk you over to Shirley's house. I'll dispatch a patrol car with officers Jimmy Thomas and Ramon Dias. They'll be here all night in case you should need them."

"I'll go pack a few things."

"I'll wait at the top of the stairs."

She stopped and turned back to him. "You don't think someone came in while I was in the yard, do you?"

"This case has just been elevated up a notch, and I'm not taking any chances."

"What do you mean, 'elevated up a notch'?"

"I have no proof, mind you, and I'm just going on my gut instinct, but it could be that we've got a professional killer involved now."

Twenty-seven

TRUE TO HIS daily routine, Clint was up at five, but instead of going to the feed store after breakfast, he drove a couple of prospective buyers out to the pasture so they could look over a herd of heifers.

It was half past eight when he finalized the transaction and made arrangements to deliver the twenty-two heifers they selected to a ranch near Johnson City. Half an hour later, he was on his way to town.

He kept thinking about Ellery. For some reason he couldn't get his mind off trying to solve a problem that wasn't his to solve, as Ellery had so frankly put it the last time he'd tried to convince her to leave her house.

When he was a block from the feed store, he pulled over to the curb and stopped. Something wasn't right. He kept having the feeling he shouldn't go to work. He waited a minute or two, and when nothing came to mind, he pulled away from the curb. He drove on down the road for half a block, and made a U-turn.

He didn't know where this uneasiness was coming

from, but he would go by Ellery's to make sure nothing was wrong there. He tried to call her at the house, but she didn't answer. He called her mobile number, but she hadn't turned it on.

He switched on the radio for a little diversion. He heard half a song before the news cut in, telling him about Hazel Ledbetter's brutal murder the day before. He pushed down on the gas pedal and prayed Ellery was okay.

When he pulled in the driveway he saw her car and wondered why she hadn't answered the phone. He figured she was in the shower.

It wasn't until he rang the doorbell a number of times and she didn't answer that he began to worry in earnest. He tried the door. It was locked. He tried calling her again, but there was still no answer.

He decided to walk around to the back entrance to see if the door was unlocked. He rounded the corner of the house and saw her standing in the middle of the yard, not far from the fishpond, with her back to him. When he got closer, he saw she was barefoot and wearing her nightgown with a light robe thrown over it. The angle of the sun coming into the yard was to his advantage—so that it made her gown and robe transparent as tissue paper, and showed him just about everything any man would like to see, but not under these circumstances.

When he was a few feet from her, he called out her name so he wouldn't frighten her. She didn't move. "Ellery, what are you doing out here?" He walked in front of her. She stood statue still, with no spark of recognition in her eyes. He put his hands on her upper arms and gave her a pretty hard shake as he called her name again, only louder this time.

"Ellery! For God's sake, what are you doing out here like this?"

She looked at him with a sort of sadness that was heartbreaking. "Why are you out here?" he asked more softly. "You aren't even dressed."

She looked down at her feet, then back at him. He could see she was still dazed. He had never seen her so pale. Had she been sleepwalking, or was she distressed over the news about Hazel? "You shouldn't be out here like this. Come on. Let's go back inside. Where are your shoes?"

"I thought I saw him."

"Who? The stalker?"

She nodded.

"You shouldn't have come down," he said. "That was a very dangerous thing you did. What did he look like?"

Her head was pounding. "I . . . I don't know. I'm certain I saw someone down here, but when I arrived he was gone. Then I noticed there were no footprints." She turned her pale face up to him. "Do you think I'm losing my mind?"

"No, I don't. I think you're under a lot of stress. You aren't sleeping enough or eating enough. You've lost too much weight."

"Did you hear about Hazel?"

"I just heard it on the news. I called and you didn't answer, so I came on over. I was worried as hell about you." He took her arm. "We can talk about this later. Do you want me to carry you? How about a piggyback ride?"

"I can walk," she said.

"I know you can." He picked her up and held her in his arms.

She drew her head back to study his face, as if she would find the answer to her question there. "Why were you worried about me?"

"Damned if I know," he said. She didn't struggle, so he went on. "I had a feeling I should check on you even before I heard the news about Hazel. I called the house and your mobile, and when you didn't answer, I came on over." He kissed her forehead. "Do you know what? I kind of like having you this close."

"You may retract that statement after you pull your back out of joint."

"You aren't big enough to do any serious damage." He stopped at the back door and she leaned forward to turn the doorknob.

When he stepped inside and kicked the door closed, she said, "You can put me down now."

He lowered her to her feet. "Good. I hope you weren't expecting me to carry you up the stairs."

He watched her lean back against the table. He was standing a few inches away.

"You shouldn't worry about me. I'm not your responsibility." She gazed out the window to the backyard. "I know I've been acting a little crazy lately, but I'm not there yet."

"I may be, if you keep standing there in that nightgown. It's like you have nothing on, and it is damn well robbing me of all common sense." He came up behind her and put his arms around her.

She turned and placed her head against his chest. "I don't care and I wish I had taken you up on that piggyback ride."

"So do I."

Standing in the cover of the vacant lot next to Ellery's house, Jasper witnessed the tender little scene. He snapped so many pictures, he had to put a new media card in his camera. Now he would be able to take more digital shots . . . hours and hours of pictures all stored on a card smaller than a postage stamp. The things they could do nowadays.

He thought about the pictures he took of Ellery and her cowboy in the yard, and the climactic shot of Littleton carrying her into the house. All he needed was a horse and a sunset.

If that cowboy didn't carry her straight up to her bedroom and make love to her, it wouldn't be long before he did. He thought about all the great shots he'd gotten of Ellery coming outside in her nightgown, and looking like she was sleepwalking. He would load them into the computer later.

Clint put a plate with a slice of French toast in front of her. "Do you want powdered sugar, jam, or honey with that? And don't consider telling me you aren't hungry. You lose any more weight and you can audition for the skeleton at the Halloween Carnival." He walked to the refrigerator and waited for her answer.

"That's not until October. By then I should be either fatter, or dead. I'd like jam, please."

He yanked the refrigerator open. "That wasn't even borderline funny." He slammed down a jar of raspberry jam on the table in front of her.

"Now who is being grumpy?"

When he didn't say anything, but continued to bang things around, she spread jam on her toast. "This is twice you've made me breakfast, and I've yet to give you more than a glass of wine or a cup of coffee."

He carried the coffeepot to the table. Like everything else, he banged it down. "I'm not keeping a running tally."

"I am. That's the second thing you've slammed on the table."

He filled his empty cup. Hers was still half-full. "Do you want me to warm that up?"

"No, it's fine."

He put the coffeepot back and sat down across from her. "So, where are you with all of this?" he asked.

"How do you mean?"

"How are you holding up? Is it time to start looking for a place to secrete you away? What if we hired someone to stay here and protect you?"

"Why, Clint Littleton, are you worried about me?"

"Of course I'm worried, dammit. Everyone is. You're the only one who takes this lightly."

She looked down at the plate. "It's all a front because I'm afraid to admit I'm scared. I'm a strong person, but I'm also smart enough to know we all have our limits. I don't know if I'll come out on top of this or not. I keep hoping that if I hold on long enough they will catch him and then we may know the truth about your brother and my sister."

"I don't want information if it means putting you in danger. They're both dead and we can't change that, but you are alive, and I don't like the way you keep risking your life. It isn't worth it. You can't keep this up much longer. You know that, don't you?"

She nodded, but she did not look at him. She kept her gaze on something behind him. "I realize it every time the phone rings and I jump, or when I am sleeping and the slightest noise wakes me up and leaves me with a heart pounding too fast to go back to sleep. It becomes a reality when I want to go to the grocery store, but I'm afraid he will be there watching me. I know it because I am a prisoner and he has complete control over my life."

His chair scraped the floor when he stood. He picked up his cup and carried it to the sink. "It wouldn't be like that if you'd let me help you. You can come to the ranch. I'll move in here and stay in the guest room. I'll find you a safe place where you can be alone. I can put private detectives in every bedroom. You tell me what you want and I'll do it."

He came back to the table about the time she gathered her dishes and carried them to the sink. She placed them next to his coffee cup. She walked back to the table and paused, as if she wanted to say something. But she never did.

When she started to turn away, he caught her and pulled her into his arms. "I'm trying to help you, dammit, but you act so nonchalant I want to shake some sense into you. I know I'm new at this sort of thing, so you're going to have to help me a little bit. I know what this is doing to you. Each time I see you I become aware that a little more of you is gone. I know you wake up wondering if it will be the last day you have, because I sure as hell do. I honestly don't know how you've managed to hang in there as long as you have, except that I know you are unbelievably strong, and you've got about the most godoxious stubborn streak of anyone I've ever come across."

He was half propped, half sitting on the edge of the table. Her head was resting against his chest. He was looking down at her when she pulled her head back so she could see him. Now each of them searched the other's eyes for some hint as to where they should go from here. He was afraid if she searched too deep, she would see how desperately he wanted to make love to her, and how much he had come to care for her.

She was afraid he would see the longing in her eyes and know how she felt about him. Things would have been so different if she had come here and found Susan alive.

His hands were rubbing her back, but he was not aware of it. His mind was too focused on the feel of her pressed against him with almost nothing on. And that damn ribbon on the front of her gown was driving him crazy.

"Make love to me. I want to feel alive. I want to feel human."

He pulled the ribbon and the top of her gown gaped, but it didn't really reveal anything beyond luscious cleavage. It didn't take any more than that for him, though. Their kiss met somewhere near the halfway mark. His hand slipped inside her gown. She moaned and pressed closer, and responded to his kiss with a wildness he was glad to see in her.

He was kissing her everywhere and trying to undo the buttons on her gown. She began to help him and he took over the moment she shrugged out of it and let it drop to the floor. He turned so she was against the edge of the table. His hands went under her bottom to lift her onto the tabletop.

She wrapped her legs around him, but left enough room to attack the buttons on his shirt. As soon as his boots hit the floor, his jeans and boxers landed on top of them. Their lips met. He cupped her buttocks and held her against him and followed her down, until she was lying prone on the table.

Jasper was becoming bored with window peeking when there wasn't much to see. What's this? he wondered. Another session of their creaking, lumbering mode of courtship? He cooks her breakfast. Oh please, not again. Is that your only routine . . . cooking breakfast? Have you never heard of a change of scene? We are badly in need an infusion of some creativity here.

Things began to look more promising when she stopped eating and the conversation started to take on a more personal tone. He liked that. Bring in the emotion.

"You can't keep this up much longer. You know that, don't you?"

That's it! Punch up those words with feeling. Get into her head, man. Don't you know it's the quickest way to her bed? Oh, now look what you did . . . untied her ribbon. Things are looking a lot more promising now. Keep it up. Entertain me. Please.

Jasper was finding photography more and more to his liking. Click. Click. His camera was busy. They were slow to warm up, but once they got going . . . *Sizzling.*

Click. Click. Click. Nice, real nice, and so much feeling—you will be so glad when you see the pictures. Window-fogging stuff going on in there now. Woo-hoo . . . we're in the throes of passion now. Click. Click. Click.

He was having a hard time keeping up. Click. Things were moving so fast. Click. He was shooting pictures in rapid-fire sequence. Click. Click. Oh, this is the way it was meant to be. Turn on the heat. Somebody help me, it's getting hot in there.

When it was all over, and passions were spent, Jasper smiled. In the kitchen, no less—my, how creative. With her spread-eagled on the table naked, she made a nice centerpiece.

Lovemaking, like murder, was so much better when it wasn't premeditated.

Twenty-eight

HER FIRST THOUGHT after she awoke was that he had such beautiful hair. She wanted to touch it. She didn't want to wake him, so Ellery lay quietly beside Clint and watched him sleep. She was curious about something, though. How could he breathe with his face buried in the pillow like that?

She wondered why it was that the woman always woke up first. Or was that simply the way they portrayed it in the movies and wrote about it in books? She followed the long length of his torso and smiled. Men were so immodest. Not a stitch on and not a speck of anything covering him either. And he slept like a baby.

A lump formed in her throat. She thought about the first time she saw him, when she smashed that motorcycle and he was mad enough to spit nails. From that moment, she felt their destinies were braided together in a way she did not understand. She did not believe in love at first sight, but she did believe that there were those who met every now and then, who were meant to be together. And since that meeting, she had found herself falling a little more in love with him each day. Sometimes it was the way his eyes crinkled when he stared into the sun; other times it was the pride in his eyes when he talked about life on a ranch.

He had unbelievably smooth skin, and a great physique to go with it, slender but muscled in the right places. She trailed her finger over the veins in his biceps, and was distracted by how his back narrowed at his waist. Great butt. She recalled a painting she had seen of a group of cowboys leaning over a fence. She remembered thinking there wasn't a bad posterior in the bunch and wondered why that was.

She thought about their lovemaking earlier. What on earth had possessed them to make love on the kitchen table of all places? It had to be the most uncomfortable place imaginable. She rubbed her backbone and wondered if she would have blisters there tomorrow. If so, then Clint was bound to have them on his elbows and knees.

They were like a couple of sex-starved teenagers with more hormones than good sense. She glanced back at Clint and moved toward him, until she was close enough to slide one leg over his. That got his attention; he lifted his head and looked toward her. She wished she could spend the rest of her life waking up and seeing that boyish grin on such a sleepy face. "The sleep of the innocent," she said.

He propped himself up on one elbow and leaned over to give her a kiss. "But I was having some awfully wicked dreams."

"Maybe you better slow down. I bet neither of us will be able to walk today." She trailed her hand up and down his arm.

He picked it up and kissed her palm. "You may have to put a new coat of varnish on that kitchen table."

"Or your knees." She laughed. "At least you didn't wear your spurs. I can't believe we weren't even civilized enough to come upstairs. Anyone could have seen . . ."

Her hands came up to cover her mouth, and the dull throb of dread and fear returned. He'd been watching them this morning. He was watching them now. She could feel it.

She rolled over to get up. He caught her by the arm. "What's wrong? Why the sudden change? Did I do something earlier that you suddenly recalled?"

"No, but it's getting late. It's almost noon."

"Do you put a time limit on everyone, or just me?"

"There is no everyone, and if you believe that, I'm surprised you touched me at all. I don't deserve a comment like that."

He pulled her back against him. "No you don't, and I was way out of line. I'm sorry. I just woke up. I was thinking how good it felt to make love to you when suddenly you threw cold water all over me."

"Okay, let's say it's a draw, or a truce, or whatever you call it down here."

"How about we just forget it happened?"

She thought about that creep watching them even now, and she pulled the sheet over them.

He sat up. "You might as well tell me. I won't leave, or let you out of this bed, until you do."

She didn't say anything.

He rolled on top of her. "It's going to be all day in bed, then."

"It's him," she whispered.

"Him? Who?"

"Him . . ."

"Oh, you mean . . ."

She put her fingers over his mouth and whispered, "He was watching us this morning. He is watching us now. What if he took . . . is taking pictures?"

"You're getting a little paranoid, don't you think? How could he be watching?"

"I don't know how I know, but I know. I don't know how he does all the other things he does, but I am telling you, I can sense when he is around."

He did not believe her. She could tell by the look on his face. She didn't know why that upset her so much, but it did. She was peeved that he scoffed at her intuition.

He climbed out of bed. "That does it. You aren't staying here another night."

"This isn't the time to talk about that." She crawled out of bed and pulled the sheet with her. She wrapped it around her and went into the bathroom.

She took a long, hot shower. When she was done, she wrapped the towel around her head and walked into her dressing room. She stood in front of the mirror while she dressed in a jogging bra, thong underwear, a pair of jeans, and a white shell. Satisfied, she applied lipstick and let her damp hair hang loose.

When she came out, she glanced at the bed. Clint was gone.

She made the bed and went downstairs. She was about to punch in the alarm code and leave when Clint returned with a sack from Starbuck's. "Peace offering," he said. "I'm not trying to take charge of your life. I care about you—a lot—and your welfare is important to me. I'm trying to keep you alive, dammit!"

She put her arms around him. "I know you are and I know I'm not the easiest person to live with right now." She took his hand. "Come on, let's go have whatever it is in your sack that smells so good. I want you to tell me about Daniel Wilkerson. Tomorrow is the day he is officially paying me a visit."

They sat in the family room in two overstuffed chairs that faced each other, their feet propped on the ottoman between them. After a few sips of coffee and a bite of almond croissant, Ellery said, "Who is Daniel Wilkerson, the man? I've read on the Internet that he owns a high-tech company in Austin called Nostradamus Corporation, complete with its own big building on Tenth Street. But I don't know what it is exactly that he does, or anything about his background."

"Nostradamus was founded on the proceeds of something Daniel came up with . . . bear in mind, I'm no computer expert, but as I understand it, this idea is referred to in the tech world as 'computer code' . . . the language that computers are based upon. He named it Manna, and it's made him a fortune."

"What does Manna do? Is it like Microsoft Windows?"

"It is an alternative to Microsoft Windows in that it is an operating system, but it doesn't have all the glitches that plague Microsoft."

"Wow! So he's a self-made man, like Bill Gates or Michael Dell."

"Exactly. And like them, he started working on his idea in a garage while in college."

"Impressive."

"Yes, very."

"What about Daniel the person?"

"He's an introvert. He isn't comfortable around people, especially large groups. People around town used to say he was paranoid."

"Poor guy."

"Yes and no. You want to pity him, but there is something about him that just makes ordinary folks uneasy, although he's never done anything bad, at least not to my knowledge."

"All this sounds like a lot of computer folks that I know. A lot of them are loners and uncomfortable around people they don't know."

The conversation remained on Daniel for a while longer as Clint answered questions about Daniel's three failed marriages that produced no children. "He made bad choices when it came to women in that he always went for the trophy wife. All of them stayed for a while, and then split with the prenup agreement money."

Ellery did not say anything and Clint changed the subject. "I brought you a pistol. I want you to keep it in your bedside table. I thought we might drive out to the ranch, and I'll show you how to use it."

"I don't want a gun. I'd probably shoot myself instead of an intruder."

"If you are too stubborn to leave and insist on staying

in the house alone, then you need something to protect yourself. Do you know how to shoot a gun?"

"Yes." If she hadn't been angry, she would have laughed at his expression. "When I first started out, the station where I worked sent all the investigative reporters to a gun-safety class. Once we finished in the classroom, we moved to the firing range."

"I thought guns were illegal in the District."

"They are, but this place was in Maryland, or maybe it was Virginia; I can't remember now. I do remember the weirdest thing that happened. They even gave us lessons on how to handle a gun that someone else might have."

"You're pretty amazing, you know that?"

She grinned at him. "How so?"

"You just keep pulling rabbits out of that hat."

Twenty-nine

Daniel Wilkerson was a powerful, wealthy man with many business acquaintances, but no friends. In spite of his attempts to be jovial and good-natured, there was always an underlying feeling that deep within the persona of Daniel Wilkerson there lurked something slippery, insincere, and a just a little bit creepy.

He began life alone. An illegitimate child, he was rejected and abandoned by his teenage mother and put up for adoption shortly before his first birthday. It did not matter that he was adopted and raised by decent parents, or that they gave him a loving home and provided him every opportunity to succeed in life. No amount of love could ever undo the damage to his psyche, just as no one could understand that he had no identity when there were no others around to give him a sense of self.

He was a driven man, but he was not motivated by love, power, or fame. Money only figured into it because it was the means by which he could draw others to him. The primary drive in his life was his fear of rejection, of being alone. There was a black, empty place within him—a hole that he would fall into whenever things took a turn for the worse, or when he was swallowed up by stress.

Manna was a startling phenomenon, and it was his baby and his dream. He should have been content with that. Yet, in spite of his success, he could never shake the internal image he had of himself as the socially inept dud.

Even the socially inept can keep appointments and Daniel was punctual when he showed up at Ellery's front door at two forty-five on Wednesday afternoon.

He was not what she expected and apparently she wasn't what he expected, either, for when she opened the door, he blurted out, "My God! I feel like I'm staring at a ghost. You look so much like her."

She gave him a hesitant smile and offered him her hand, not because he was the type she would ordinarily be chummy with, but because he had grown up with Susan and could tell her more about Susan's childhood and teenage years than any other living person. "You have to be Daniel," she said.

He must have realized how he was coming across and tried to soften things a bit. "I apologize for the outburst. It's just that . . . well, I was prepared, but then I was totally unprepared for my first glimpse of you, and yes, I'm Daniel Wilkerson." He shook her hand. "Thank you for agreeing to let me pay you a visit."

If she had to describe him in two words it would be thin and nervous; if she had to compare him to an animal it would be a lizard, for he seemed ready to dart out of sight. She doubted this man had ever heard of inner peace. "Please," she said, and stood back to open the door wider. "Do come in."

His face, like his body, was long and thin; his jaw was square and his eyes were brown; and she was uncomfortable when she established eye contact with him for very long, but then, he was not the type to make or sustain direct eye contact with others. "I'm sorry, but I don't feel too talkative today. I'm sure you heard about Hazel Ledbetter's death."

"Oh yes, I did . . . Lucy called me yesterday. Horrible way to die . . . It's hard to reconcile that kind of random violence with a town like Agarita Springs. Hazel was a very nice lady. I'm going to stop by to see Margaret when I leave here. I know this is a terrible loss for her."

Ellery had never heard anyone say the right words with all the wrong delivery, for nothing about his voice, demeanor, facial expression—you name it—bespoke a man who had any empathy or feeling at all. He was devoid of any emotion. His words were sterile and cold, like a voice reading an article aloud from the newspaper about a sale at Home Depot.

Still, she was the perfect hostess, and when she offered him coffee, he accepted. "Have a seat here, in the family room. The coffee is made so I won't be gone long."

A few minutes later, she carried two cups into the family room and placed one on the table in front of him. "Well," he said, "I guess finding you had a twin sister surprised you as much as it did me when I learned Susan had a twin."

"I'm sure there were some similarities, although I do

envy you for having had the opportunity to know her, something I see as an incomparable loss."

"I'm sure Lucy has told you all about her."

"Yes, she has been a darling to tell me everything she can recall and to share her family photos. It's a very small part of my sister, but it is all I have."

He ignored that. "I suppose she told you that Susan and I did not get along so well when we were older."

"She mentioned you weren't terribly close, but then, a lot of siblings aren't, especially during their teenage years."

He didn't comment on that. "Our problem was different because I was adopted, and for that reason I was never accepted and was treated like an outsider."

"I know that must have been difficult for you." Ellery was ready to cut this visit short. She was tired and under tremendous stress. She felt sorry for Daniel, but she didn't care for him. She wanted this to be over and didn't bother to make any effort to soften her words, but rather spoke from the heart.

"It's easy to criticize the dead. I can't form an opinion on what you say because it would only be based upon hearsay. I have no intention of digging into your past or your relationship with Susan unless it helps me to know more about her as a person, although I would love copies of any photos you might have of her. Rest assured that I have no desire to dig into anyone's life. When I came here, I wanted only to find my sister and to get to know her. Nothing more."

"Now that you know that is impossible, why do you remain here? I would think you would have pressing affairs back in D.C. that need your attention."

She didn't like the way this conversation was going and her instincts and intuition told her not to reveal anything to him.

She glanced at him and realized he was waiting for her to answer, so she said, "Why do I remain here? I want to learn about my mother's family and as much as I can about Susan. I feel connected to her here, and especially by living in her house." She did not mention wanting to find Susan's killer.

He seemed taken aback by her frankness and honesty and his next words proved it. "You surprise me, Ellery . . . may I call you Ellery?"

"Yes, of course."

"You surprise me with your answer. It's common knowledge that you intend to find Susan's killer. It makes me wonder why you tried to keep that from me."

"That is a side issue, Daniel, and not the reason I came here. Of course, I would like to see the person who killed her behind bars, so he could never do something like that again. Do you have a reason for not wanting to know who killed her?"

"Of course I want to know, but I think the police are more experienced with that sort of thing than you are."

"Well, it may be one of those cases that is never solved."

"Does that mean you don't think the crime will ever be solved?"

"I don't know. I'm a television newscaster, not a detective. I don't solve mysteries."

His face relaxed and he shook his head. "I'm a software engineer. I don't solve mysteries either. A moment later, he stood. "I've stayed longer than I intended. I came only to introduce myself and to place myself at your disposal. We'll get together agin and I'll bring pictures of Susan. If there's anything I can do, or anything I can tell you, you've only to ask. Susan's death hit everyone hard because we all loved her. There isn't a day I don't wish I could turn back the clock to those days when we were younger so I could have another chance to be a better, more protective brother." He gave her a sad look. "It seems we do have something in common regarding Susan. We were both too late."

She walked him to the door and after he left she crossed her arms over her middle and thought she would not be surprised to learn he had some secret fetish that was allowed to roam freely in the privacy of his home—a fetish that sent three trophy wives scampering off with whatever wealth they could carry.

Unlike her reaction to Sherman's cruelty and urge to get even, when it came to Daniel, she was moved more toward pity and compassion than any real sense of fear.

A week later Lucy was thinking about Ellery and Hazel while she watered the flowers in front of her house. She heard a car and looked up in time to see Detective Bardwell pull into the driveway. She laid the hose down and left the water running. Roland was getting out of his car when she walked over to him.

"Hi, Roland, did you come to help with the yard work?"

"It's hot enough to ask for a dousing. Any idea what the temperature is today?"

"A hundred and one degrees is what they said on the radio."

Roland picked up the water hose and helped himself to a long drink.

"Why don't you let me get you a glass of ice water?"

"No time. I'm on my way to answer a call. I stopped by to say I paid Margaret a visit a little while ago."

"I don't suppose you could notice the strange way she's been acting lately, now that she's grieving over Hazel's death."

"No, in spite of her grief, I saw another layer there, and like you, I don't know what to make of it. I don't think it's Alzheimer's, though. Her mind seems as sharp as it ever was."

"Then what could be wrong? I am not making this up, Roland. I have never seen her so crabby and standoffish. It's as if she can't look me in the eye. She's always been a bit of a loner, but she is becoming completely antisocial. Did you see how long she stayed at Hazel's burial? She was one of the first ones to leave."

When Lucy finished, Bardwell spoke slowly. "I think she's frightened of something."

"Frightened? What could she be frightened of? Old age?"

Roland grinned. "No need to be afraid of something that's already happened to you."

"You're probably right. The reality of growing old is enough to frighten anyone. Thanks for checking on her."

"Anytime." He started the car, and backed out of the driveway. As he started up the street he gave a wave. "See you round like a doughnut."

She laughed and waved back, then finished watering. By the time she went back inside, she decided she would wait until around four o'clock, after Margaret's naptime, and pay her a visit.

It was half past four when Lucy walked all though her aunt's house before she found Margaret sitting on the back porch, having a glass of iced tea. Margaret was a tall, rather big-boned woman, not overweight, but with plenty of meat on her bones. When Lucy saw her, she was shocked at how much weight she had lost. She kissed her cheek. "Hi, Aunt Margaret. Isn't it a bit hot for you to be out here?"

Margaret looked at her with a startled expression, as if she had been jarred out of some kind of deep contemplation. She looked beyond Lucy to the door. "Are you alone?"

Lucy nodded and dropped into a nearby chair. "What are you doing outside on a day like this? It's hotter than blazes."

"I've got the fan going and a nice glass of peach tea. Why don't you get yourself one and join me?"

"Maybe in a minute. I wanted to talk to you first."

Margaret gave her a look that wasn't exactly suspicious, but not one that was very receptive either. "I don't know that I feel up to talking about anything."

"I want to know what's wrong. You're acting different. You're not yourself."

"My daughter was murdered. That would make anyone act different."

"I know that, but I'm not talking about grief, Aunt Margaret. I'm talking about the way you are becoming so withdrawn. Is something bothering you? Are you afraid of something?"

"There is nothing wrong with me."

Lucy was thinking she could give her a long list of things, but decided to hold off, at least for now. "Aunt Margaret, the bottom line is, I'm worried about you. You've been acting strange. You've lost weight. You always seem so preoccupied. You jump at the sound of a pin dropping. You don't even go buy groceries anymore, but have them delivered instead. Has anything frightened you?"

A change came over Margaret's face, and it seemed to lose all color. It reminded Lucy of the time she had on a bright lime-green dress and walked into a restaurant with weird lights that seemed to absorb all the dye from clothes.

Margaret picked up her glass and took several sips before she put it down. "I need to plant some fall flowers along that back fence and then I want to do a bench and little fountain with a brass plaque to honor Hazel."

Lucy wasn't going to give up so easily. "Okay, so you don't want to talk about it. Can you answer just one question? Does this have anything to do with the deaths of Clay or Susan or Hazel?"

Margaret kept her gaze fastened on her hands in her lap. They were trembling.

Lucy thought perhaps Margaret had slipped off into a brown study and hadn't heard her. But her appearance said she had not only heard everything Lucy said, but that she had a few answers. Margaret's shoulders were slumped forward. Her head was downcast, which made the wrinkles on her face and neck more pronounced. She appeared almost frail and weak, like she could shatter easily.

Lucy was baffled. She'd had no experience with anything like this. All she knew was that Margaret was reacting severely to her questions. She had come to ease her discomfort, not to cause her more. "Would you rather I leave and come back some other time?"

She didn't respond. Lucy tried again. "Aunt Margaret?" Lucy sighed. "Okay." She stood and put her hand on Margaret's back and touched nothing but bones. She wanted to help, but she seemed to make things worse. "I'm sorry I upset you. Terrible things have been happening to Ellery. Someone is stalking her. I don't want to upset you and I don't want Ellery to end up like her sister. I like her so much. If you knew her, you would like her too." She took a deep breath. "I'm just worried," Lucy said, "about both of you."

Silence . . .

She leaned over and kissed Margaret's cheek. "I'll be going now. Be sure to call me if you need anything."

She knew Margaret would not tell her anything, so Lucy left, careful not to say anything to agitate her further.

When she was back in her car, Lucy started the engine, but she didn't drive off. She was thinking about her visit with her aunt. She was beginning to agree with Bardwell that Margaret was frightened about something, but try as she might, Lucy couldn't think of a thing it could be.

Perhaps after losing so many family members in the last few years, Aunt Margaret was simply afraid of dying.

She put the car in gear and drove slowly down the street. She was too preoccupied to glance back at Margaret's house, and see her watching from the window. If she had, she might have seen the tears on a face that was not as out of touch with reality as it seemed.

Thirty

After the Sunday night news, Ellery clicked off the television. She should have gone to sleep because the news was mostly a bunch of human-interest stories. Her hand reached out to turn off the lamp, and seemed to freeze in midair.

She sniffed the air. She barely had time to register the thought that she smelled smoke, when the shrill blast of the smoke detectors confirmed it.

A second later, the alarm connected to the security system went off.

She grabbed her robe and ran into the hall. She could see smoke rising up the stairway. She rushed downstairs and followed the smoke into the kitchen. A great, undulating mass of black smoke was billowing upward from the stove. She grabbed a dishtowel and ran water over it, then covered her nose and mouth. She got close enough to see that a skillet on the stove was on fire. She turned off the burner.

She almost ran to the pantry and began shoving cans

and boxes around until she found the box of soda. She ripped the top off as she went back to the stove. She threw the entire box of soda all over the skillet and stovetop.

It smothered the fire almost immediately. In the distance she could hear a siren. She remembered the smoke detector had set off the security alarm. But why hadn't the alarm gone off when the intruder had come in? Had she forgot to set the alarm? Had her stalker figured out how to circumvent it? She opened the back door to let out some of the smoke.

Her throat was raw from smoke and coughing by the time she reached the front door. She opened it, and felt a fresh draft of air rush in. The fire truck pulled into the driveway. She walked out to meet them and spoke to the captain. "The fire was a skillet on the kitchen stove. I—"

Two of the firemen hurried inside. She continued explaining what had happened to the captain. She was about to tell him she'd doused the fire with soda when the two who had charged inside came back out. One of them carried the empty box of soda.

"Did you use this to put it out?" he asked.

She nodded. "Yes."

"I couldn't have done better myself. You did the right thing."

The other fireman spoke up. "Next time you want to be very careful about putting a skillet of grease on the stove and then leaving the kitchen."

She didn't bother to tell them she didn't put the skillet on. It was easier to let it go.

She stood on the porch and watched the fire truck

drive off. She watched it pass the patrol car coming her way, lights flashing. This was becoming a habit. Maybe she should see if any of them wanted to rent a room here.

Soon she was going over the details with two patrolmen. Later, after everyone was gone and she had locked the house, she went to bed. She glanced at the bedside clock. One-thirty on Monday morning. Thank God last week was over. She hoped the coming week would be better than last.

She ignored the thought that crept into the back of her mind and said, what will you do if it's worse?

Ellery was scrubbing the sooty residue in the kitchen when Clint stopped by the next morning. She told him about the fire and he insisted she have the alarm system checked. He stayed long enough to inspect the kitchen and to ask, "How are you dealing with all of this?"

"One day at a time. Actually, I think I'm coping rather well. I'm tired of the steady stream of things happening to me, but each one makes me stronger and more determined to resist." She put her hands around her mouth. "I said, each thing you do makes me stronger and more determined to resist. One of us is going to be forced to give up at some point. It isn't going to be me."

"What are you doing?"

"I'm letting him know I know he's listening."

"You really believe it, don't you? You think you can communicate with him."

"I bet you a steak dinner he has my house, my phones, and probably my underwear bugged."

He grinned and mussed her hair. "Why don't you have

Detective Bardwell check the place? They know how to find bugs."

"I'll mention it to him."

"I almost forgot. The postman came by when I was getting out of the car. Here's your mail."

"Just put it on the table."

Clint had been gone about an hour when Ellery picked up the mail and carried it to her desk. She started to leave it, and then decided to see what was in the large manila envelope. There was no return address. She suddenly had the strangest feeling that this was not something she wanted to see. Her hands were shaking when she opened it and shook the contents out on the desk. At least twelve eight-by-ten color photos fell out. They were all pictures of her and Clint in various stages of undress—some of them photos of them actually making love on the kitchen table.

She buried her face in her hands. "Oh no . . . please . . . not this . . ."

Was every aspect of her life to be violated? The room spun and the pictures were sucked into the twisting spiral. Even with her eyes closed she could see them spinning around and around, faster and faster.

"Stop!" she screamed, and slammed her hands down on the desk. She was breathing heavily. She could hear her heart pounding in her ears. She remained as she was for a few minutes until the calm began to settle over her.

She gathered the photos and stuffed them into the envelope. She hid them in the back of the file cabinet until she could decide how best to dispose of them. She went into the guest bath and washed her face, and reapplied lipstick. She did not want to tell Clint about the photos. The thought of anyone seeing them sickened her. She tried to make some logical sense out of something completely illogical. She faced something frightening, something she could not see.

She called Lucy and told her about the photos. "Don't mention it to anyone."

"The only way I'd tell is if they sent Johnny Depp to coax me," Lucy said.

After lunch, she drove to the nursery. She needed a diversion . . . something to think about besides death and dying. She was finally going to pick out plants for the area around the fishpond.

She had been there an hour when she realized she was enjoying herself. It was a beautiful day and nice to be out in the sunshine, around people, and having a good time.

She pulled her red wagon up one aisle and down the next, picking out plants as she went. She found so many she wondered if they would all fit in the back of her car. She wanted the area between the fishpond and willow tree to be beautiful and colorful. On impulse, she bought several climbing roses to put along the back fence.

Once she was back home, she unloaded everything and carried it all out back. She had no more than put the last container down when the phone rang. It took her a while to find where she had placed her mobile, but it kept ringing long enough for her to answer it.

She saw it was Clint's number. "Hi," she said.

"I was about to hang up. I thought I'd stop by to see how you're doing on my way home, if that's okay with you."

"I always think a visit from you is a grand idea," she said, and decided not to mention she was working in the yard. A lot of men seemed to have an aversion to yard work. She wondered if Clint was one of them as she made plans to enlist his help.

"I'll be leaving here in about ten minutes."

"Fine. If I don't answer the door, I'll be in the back."

By six o'clock the roses were all in the ground and watered. She turned her attention to the area around the willow tree and fishpond. Before she planted the new things, she trimmed the water lilies and water irises that were already growing in the pond, along with several grasses.

Then she planted wild thyme, geraniums, sedum, and ivy in the rocky areas around the pond. She followed those with the plants for the boggy areas—creeping jenny, marsh marigolds, and bog pimpernel—and lastly she planted lavender, where the ground wasn't so wet, yet still damp.

All that was left to go around the fishpond were what she called "fairy plants," which would provide lush little hideaways and nooks where it was said that fairies liked to hide. Since there was a fairy statue, she figured, why not? She sat back for a minute, her spade resting against her thighs, as she recalled how Sam had taught her about fairy gardens when she was a little girl. She wondered if there was another little girl living in their old home in Chevy Chase, and if she was as captivated by the magical lore of fairies and their gardens as she had been.

She studied the lovely bronze statue of a fairy pouring water from a lily. It stood in the middle of the pond. She wondered if her sister had put it there. Had she been fascinated with the magic of fairies and fishponds too?

She was studying the detail of the wings and the flowers wound in the statue's hair when Clint came around the side of the house.

"I know I'm later than I said. I seem to get tied up whenever I have someplace to go." He looked around and she knew he was thinking what a mess she had made with all the bags and plastic containers scattered about.

"It will look wonderful once I'm finished."

"You should have told me you were working. I could have come another time."

She threw a dirt clod at him. "That's why I didn't mention it." She sat back and pulled her gloves off. "Now that you're here, you might as well help."

"What do you want me to do?"

"Hand me that flat with the impatiens and primroses."

"Which are?"

"They're the ones on your left."

He moved them next to her. She removed a primrose from the container. "If you eat primroses you can see fairies."

"And do you indulge often?"

"I've never tried it, but I would give it a try if I thought it would make that invisible phantom that torments me visible. Why don't you take the impatiens and hand them to me?"

His expression when he looked at the flowers was one of a man who was obviously in very unfamiliar territory. "I'm not too good at getting the flowers out of those little plastic containers. I always end up pulling half the roots off."

"Is that by accident or by design?"

"Either way, it works."

She laughed and got to her feet. "Tell you what, I'll make us a drink, and then you can watch how easy it really is."

Inside, she washed her hands at the sink and removed two glasses from the cabinet. She put them on the counter next to the refrigerator and reached for the handle on the side where the freezer and icemaker were located. The moment her hand touched the handle, a stunning shock of electricity shot up her arm and vibrated through her entire body. She couldn't seem to let go for a moment, and then she made a shrieking sound, released the handle, and stepped back.

Clint was beside her in an instant. "It shocked me. For a minute there, I thought I wasn't going to be able to let go."

He picked up her hands. "They're wet. There must be a short of some kind. You don't want to mess with something like this. You were lucky this time. I'll call an electrician."

"It's six-thirty. Everything will be closed."

"I know someone who will make a late call."

Tommy Joe Hinkley needed only five minutes to find the problem. "This refrigerator looks better than it actually is. It's an older model and it isn't grounded. The conductors are exposed and they weren't protected from abrasion at the cutout hole. The cord doesn't have a strain relief on it. That's what caused it to fray like this. Your wet hands allowed the current to pass on to you. You were mighty lucky you weren't electrocuted."

"Can it be fixed?" she asked.

"I wouldn't attempt a repair like this on a refrigerator this old. My advice is, go buy a new refrigerator. Tomorrow. In the meantime, make sure you don't touch the handle with wet hands, or anything that's damp."

After Tommy Joe left, they sat in the lawn chairs out back and talked until dark. When it was time for him to go, Clint offered to take her shopping for a new refrigerator the next day.

"I never turn down an offer of help," she said, and walked to the car with him. He opened the door and gave her a kiss on the forehead. "I'm sorry I kept you from getting the rest of your flowers planted."

"That's the nice thing about unfinished work. It's always there waiting for you whenever you return."

Thirty-one

CLINT AND ELLERY drove to Austin to shop for a new refrigerator and it didn't take long to find one she liked. Only drawback was, it couldn't be delivered until the following Friday.

It was almost five o'clock when they arrived back at her house—early enough to finish the planting. He volunteered to clean up the containers after she emptied them, so she set to work keeping him busy. The plants were greatly reduced by the time Ellery worked her way closer to the willow tree.

There was a space of about six feet, which gently sloped up to a stone sitting-wall, with a woodsy garden beyond. It was her plan to arrange small plants toward the front, with a couple of rhododendrons and three azaleas farther back. Clint removed the larger plants from their pots and placed them where she wanted them planted.

She dug her spade into the dirt and began digging a hole for the azalea when her spade uncovered a piece of black plastic. It looked like the plastic of a trash bag, or the liner on the fishpond, which was probably what it was. Construction workers were famous for burying trash whenever they could.

She turned a hot, dust-streaked face toward Clint. She was about to ask him to help her pull the plastic out of the dirt when she had a better idea. "Why don't you go make us something cold to drink while I finish here?

He started toward the house. "Any preferences?"

"No," she called out. "Fix whatever you like. I trust you."

"Big mistake," he said. "I won't forget you said that."

"I hope not."

Once he was in the house, she put the spade down and pulled on the plastic. It gave a little, but most of it was buried deeper. Just her luck to find a piece of plastic that ran all the way to Hong Kong, when she was almost finished planting.

Clint came out of the kitchen door and paused long enough to catch the screen with his foot and let it close gently. He was walking carefully, as if he didn't want to spill a drop of the frozen margaritas he had in his hands. He carried them to the table and went back inside for napkins.

She picked up the spade and started digging again. Lord, she needed to let Clint do this. She put the spade down and tugged on the plastic. It gave a little, so she stood up and pulled with both hands as she leaned back. It was moving.

The sharp terror of her scream shattered the still quiet.

Clint took off running toward her. Ellery was hugging her middle and rocking back and forth, like someone wounded. She kept screaming and screaming.

When he reached her, he glanced down and said, "Oh God, don't look, Ellery. Don't look."

But she had already looked.

He pulled her against him and held her head against his chest. He let her cry, without saying anything, until the terror subsided and nothing was left but agonized sobs. "Come on. Let me get you to the house. We need to call the police."

"I know who it is," she wailed. "I don't want to leave. It's my sister. It's Susan. I know it's Susan."

"You don't know that for sure."

She pulled away from him. Her face was tear-streaked. "You don't understand. I saw long brown hair. I know it's Susan. One night, I thought I saw her standing here by the tree, only I didn't understand what she was trying to tell me. The tree . . . I've always felt sad when I looked at it; when it rained I saw tears."

"It's a weeping willow. Why do you think they named it that?"

She didn't say anything. He opened the back door and led her to the table. "Wait right here." He ran outside, picked up the margaritas, and carried them inside. He put one down in front of her.

She glanced at it and turned her head away. "I couldn't. Not now."

"You need it. It will help calm you. The police will be here soon."

"I am sick to death of police and giving statements. That's all we ever do. Why can't they solve this?" She laid her head down on the table and cried. Once she started, she could not stop.

Thirty-two

EVERYONE IN THE police force seemed to be at Ellery's house. Neighbors were standing in their yards. Some were brave enough to venture into Ellery's front yard, where they stood around talking in small groups. Vans and cars of the media were arriving, followed by curious townspeople.

Clint tried to get Ellery to wait inside, but she would not leave. She sat in a lawn chair on the opposite side of the fishpond and the willow tree. Her feet were in the chair and she had her arms wrapped around her legs. Her head rested on her knees. She never took her eyes off the site. She knew this was the closest she would ever be to her sister.

All this time she had been right here. I'm so sorry, Susan . . . I'm so very, very sorry.

She had seen a lot of gruesome things during her years in television—some firsthand when reporting, and others captured on film. But nothing could prepare her for the shock of discovering human remains while she was planting flowers, any more than it could soften the blow that the remains were those of her sister.

She could not get the image of her sister's hand out of her mind . . . the long, bony fingers, the index finger extended, as if pointing to her murderer.

Detective Bardwell was one of the first to arrive with the magnetic light on the roof of his car flashing. Three patrol cars followed, sirens shrieking. The second wave followed with police photographers and the forensics team, who apologized for removing several of the bushes Ellery had just planted.

While the photographer was taking pictures, the area was roped off with yellow tape. The excavation team arrived and began the slow, careful job of removing the soil around the remains. Occasionally Ellery would hear a comment.

"We've got a wedding ring on the left hand, and long brown hair."

A short while later more identification was called out: "Looks like the victim was wearing a blue satin nightgown."

Detective Bardwell went to the hole and dropped down on his haunches. "With the jewelry and clothes, I'd say we have more than enough here to make a presumptive ID. How much longer do you think it will be to complete the full excavation?"

"Another hour."

Bardwell spoke with Ellery and answered her questions about the condition of the body. "If it is Susan, will you be able to tell?" she asked.

"Yes, that shouldn't be a problem. Due to the heat and moisture content of the soil around the fishpond, the body was fairly decomposed, but things like teeth, bones, hair, and fingernails, as well as bits of clothing, were still intact."

Chief of Police Jack Sherwood stopped by for a while to speak with Bardwell and the forensics team. He inspected the gravesite and asked the two men doing the excavation a few questions. Afterward, he came to speak to Ellery, and to express his condolences.

"I know it's Susan," she said.

He obviously did not want to comment on that. "Whether it is or not, she was a fine, fine lady and her disappearance was a terrible loss to the community. I'm especially grieved for you. If it is Susan, I know it will be difficult to find closure on a relationship that had not really started. I know it doesn't seem fair. These cases never are. If there is anything I can do . . . if you need someone to simply talk to, I'm always available."

Ellery thanked him, and then she wrapped her arms around him and gave him a hug. He kissed the top of her head. "God bless you," he said, and left.

Her gaze wandered back to the roped-off area. She was not really able to see what was going on because there were too many police personnel milling about.

Someone handed her a cup of coffee. When she saw it was Clint, she leaned her head against his chest. He wrapped his arms around her and held her close, not saying a word, as if he knew she needed human contact more than words. When she did sit down, he sat next to her. He held her hand and scooted nearer so he could pull her close against him when two ambulance attendants arrived to remove the remains.

Clint touched her elbow. "It's almost over. Why don't you come inside now?" He took the coffee cup from her hand and helped her up.

Inside the house, she stood at the window and watched as the covered stretcher was placed in the ambulance. She took a deep breath and turned away. She was suddenly exhausted.

She had found her sister. Now, she wanted to find who had murdered her.

But first, she needed to rest.

Clint must have sensed how badly she needed a good night's sleep because he stayed with her that night and held her close while she slept, but he never closed his eyes.

The next day the men from the nursery came to replant the flowers. Once they were gone, she sat in the yard looking at the fishpond. The pure, unspoiled color of flowers, the splash of water from the fountain, the melodious sound of chimes carried by the wind soothed her bruised spirit. Susan could rest now. Soon she would be buried next to Clay in the family plot at the ranch.

Ellery thought of the stone bench she had ordered to mark the spot where her sister was found. She would have an inscription cut into the back of the bench, along with Susan's name. She had the perfect verse by a nineteenth-century French novelist picked out.

Every flower is a soul blossoming in Nature.
GÉRARD DE NERVAL

How sad that such a lovely setting should hold such a horrible secret. She sighed and placed her hands on her knees. It was over. She had reached the end of a long journey. She had accomplished a goal and done what she had set out to do. She had found her sister, yet she could not help asking, how can you succeed, and be defeated at the same time?

Thirty-three

W<small>HEN THE REMAINS</small> were positively identified as Susan Littleton, they buried her where she belonged, next to Clay, on the Littleton ranch.

Afterward, Ellery and Clint walked back to the ranch house, where friends and family were gathered. She left his side for a moment to speak briefly with Detective Bardwell. "I don't understand how she was buried at the house and none of the investigating team found the body."

"We don't think she was buried there until later—after the investigation was completed. A pretty good idea . . . he buries the body in the most obvious place—the murder scene—but after the search of the premises has concluded. He probably stashed the body elsewhere, then came back one night and buried her where you found her."

"What do you base that upon?"

"There were a couple of newspaper pages in the plastic bag. They were dated five days after Susan disappeared.

We have no way of knowing how long he waited to bury her at your house, but we do know she had to have been buried there on or after the dates on the newspaper."

Ellery turned away. She did not want to talk about death anymore. She located Clint and he tucked her arm through his. "Let's take a walk," he said.

They passed the rough-hewn quarters of an old building that he called a bunkhouse, and he told her some stories of the way ranching had been back during the days of the cattle drives.

She listened to the mellow tone of his voice as he pieced everything together like a living patchwork quilt.

"There are so many layers to your life and heritage," she said. "I could never get a true feel for what it encompasses in a single day. It would take a lifetime, and maybe not even then. I think true appreciation and understanding have to be bred into you."

"You have a lot of feeling and insight to realize that. It's impossible to explain to a lot of folk. I guess you hit on it when you said it's bred into you. My grandfather rode every day of his life, except for illness and the years he was off at war. He was ninety-six when he died of a heart attack, and he died only a few seconds after he finished his ride and dismounted. Dropped dead right beside his horse. It was the way he would have wanted to go."

"I never knew any of my grandparents, my sister, or my parents. You are fortunate to have so many memories of yours. Did you ever ride with your father?"

"Lord, yes. He taught me to ride. I was a year old when he put me on my first horse—not a pony, mind you, but a full-grown quarter horse, fourteen and a half hands tall. My mother almost fainted when she saw me. By the time I was six, he would snub up a horse that was green-broke and tell me to ride it."

The ranch house came into view and she saw what Clint saw, what he felt in his blood—something revered for its endurance and what that represented. It was a stately home, over a hundred years old, and it stood in the middle of open land. Three stories high, with dormer windows, three chimneys, and a porch that wrapped around the entire house, it did not need to compete for attention with hundreds of flowers, or the lofty dignity of a dozen magnificent oaks that shaded the sweep of lawn. It was a house that spoke of prosperity, constancy, and generations. A sense of time and eternity settled over her and she envisioned the children who had played in these trees, and grown to adulthood, and formed an unbreakable link between future and past.

This was where the Littleton women birthed their babies, buried their dead, and in between tended their roses with the same devotion they gave to their young. Now, as it must have been then, it was cool and inviting, right down to the assortment of rocking chairs scattered over the porch.

He accompanied her up the curving brick walk, but all she saw were her own imaginings that raced through her mind. She ducked under a low tree branch. Overhead, the breeze stirred and rattled the leaves and caused the low, sweeping branches of the live oaks to sway gently, like long, graceful arms.

"Why didn't you bring me here that day, when we came to the ranch?"

"I was waiting for the right time."

Her head flopped against his chest and his arm came around her. "I'm glad you saved it for now." She went up the steps ahead of him and waited until he opened the screen door. The moment she stepped inside, she could almost see calico dresses hanging in a wardrobe, jars of canned fruit that lined pantry shelves, dozens of well-thumbed books stacked in nooks and crannies, and time-worn quilts thrown across iron beds.

The hum of people talking reached her ears and the reason why they were here came to the forefront of her mind. "Where is everyone?"

"They're on the terrace out back. Before we go out there, I want you to meet someone."

"Who?"

"My mother."

"I thought you said she couldn't come to the graveside service. I thought that was because she was ill."

"In a way, that's true. She wanted to come, but I talked her out of it. I don't know how she would take seeing Clay's and Susan's graves. Her doctor was worried about the stress the funeral would put on her heart. That's why I invited everyone to come here afterward."

He led her down a hall, past the living room, and into a sunlit solarium. She saw a small, gray-haired woman. She was sitting in a rocking chair, asleep in a small patch of sun, with a lap robe tucked around her legs.

When Ellery saw her, she stopped to whisper she would wait in the other room.

"I'm not asleep," Virginia said. "I'm like a cat in a window, soaking up the sun. It warms my arthritis."

With Ellery standing slightly behind him, Clint gave his mother a kiss. "You like to make it sound like you're ancient, but the truth is, I always expect to catch you outside, jumping rope."

She opened her eyes. "I'm not opposed to the idea. It's the rest of me that needs convincing. Who is that tiny bit of humanity hiding behind you?"

"Someone you've been asking to meet," he said, and reached behind him to grope for Ellery's hand. "Ellery O'Brien, this is my mother, Virginia."

"Hello, Mrs. Littleton."

"Clint was right. I have been asking to meet you, and now I shall simply say, 'Welcome.' " She tossed aside the lap robe and, with Clint's help, stood so she could get a close look at Ellery. "Why, Clint, you didn't tell me she had Susan's face."

Clint looked at Ellery. "I never saw them as identical."

"Just like a man. He can't see beyond what is on the end of his nose." Ellery looked down into quite the most extraordinary gray eyes, so pale they were almost silver, and ringed with dark charcoal gray. She was so tiny Ellery wanted to hug her. She doubted she was over five feet tall. She could not help wondering how she had managed to have such a big son.

"Come on," Clint said. "Let's go outside. There are some others I want Ellery to meet, and I want you there beside us."

When they passed the family room, Virginia tucked her arm through Ellery's. "There's a grouping of family pictures on the piano you will want to see. Susan is in quite a few of them."

Ellery walked over to the collection of silver-framed photographs, and easily spotted the ones with her sister's face.

She picked up one of Susan on skis, with the word "Steamboat" written below. Another was a shot of what looked to be a family barbecue, with Clint looking devilishly good in a red shirt and Susan holding up her fingers to make horns behind his head.

Virginia patted her hand. "You must come again, when we have more time, so you can look through all the photographs, and Clint can show you the family movies. There are so many pictures of Susan. After you see them, we can talk. I can help you know her. It won't be the same, but it will ease the pain in your heart somewhat."

Ellery leaned over and kissed her cheek. "I would love to come. Thank you for understanding."

At last, Ellery could see what it was that made Clint Littleton so special.

Thirty-four

H E HAD DRESSED in black. He wanted to make himself invisible against the darkness that would surround him when he cut the power to the lights around the perimeter of her house.

His suit and his shoes were made of a special material that would leave no fibers to trace. His head was shaved, and as an extra precaution he wore a tight-fitting cap of the same material as his suit. His eyebrows were shaved as well, and his fingers had been painted with a gluelike substance that coated the fingerprints so they seemed to virtually disappear.

It was almost dark when he arrived and took his place of observation at the side of her house. After a couple of hours, he saw a car come down the street. Through the binoculars he followed the car's progress until he saw Ellery pull into the driveway.

It was nine-fifteen. She was home and alone in the dark.

He watched her get out of the car and go into the

house. He knew no one would be coming to visit her now, the day after her sister's funeral. Her cousin Lucy played bridge on Thursday nights and Clint Littleton was at the ranch because his mother had decided she wanted to spend a couple of days there instead of going back into town.

I've got Ellery all to myself, he thought.

He wasn't completely inhuman, however. He wished there had been another choice for him, but that's the way things worked out sometimes. In spite of what people thought, life wasn't beautiful. It was coldhearted and unfair. You had to grab what you could and do your best to hang on to it because there was always someone out there waiting and scheming to take it from you. It was a take-no-prisoners and give-no-quarter world. It wasn't fair, but it was the price you had to pay if you wanted to survive.

For a moment, he stood completely still, his gaze fixed upon something he did not really see, as if he were giving his heart, his mind, and his body time to become perfectly aligned for the task that lay before him.

It was the beginning of the end. The long-awaited moment had finally come. A sense of eagerness enveloped him, and left his eyes shining with expectation. A sweet taste permeated his mouth. He thought about the movies he had seen, and the excitement he felt at merely anticipating what was about to happen.

Movies were nothing like the real thing. He flexed and tightened his fingers. Blood rushed to his head. It was time to go. Soon all his problems would be solved, and before sunrise Ellery O'Brien would be dead.

*   *   *

After dinner, Clint picked up the phone and dialed his number to check his calls. There were only three calls. He deleted the first two and listened to the third.

"Clint, it's Lucy. I've been concerned about my aunt Margaret for months. She has been very reclusive, and quite unfriendly. I've tried to talk to her several times but she always clams up. This morning, I went to see her again. I told her Susan was buried at the ranch yesterday and I let her know I wasn't going to leave until she told me what was going on. It took almost two hours of relentless hammering at her before she finally broke down. I felt like a first-class heel, but when she started talking I was horrified. She is certain she knows who killed Hazel and Susan. Call me as soon as you get this message."

Clint dialed Lucy's home and cell numbers but she did not answer either one. When he hung up, he told his mother he was taking her back into town with him, and he dropped her off at her house as soon as they arrived. When he had Virginia safely inside, he drove toward the police station to see if he could catch Detective Bardwell. When he pulled into the station's parking lot, he felt like he had aged twenty years.

He parked his car, hurried inside, and saw Officer Dave Plunkett sitting at the front desk. Plunkett looked up to see him enter the building. "How are you doing, Clint? A little late for you to be dropping by for coffee, isn't it?"

"I'm okay, Dave. I'm looking for Detective Bardwell. Please tell me he's still here."

Clint had better luck than he anticipated, for according to Plunkett, "Yeah, Detective Bardwell is still here. He was getting ready to leave when Lucy Sizemore came in and said she needed to talk to him, that it was a matter of life or death. Must have been awfully urgent, because she's been in there for a while."

"Can you call him and tell him I'm here and would like to join them?"

"Sure thing," Plunkett said, and dialed Bardwell's number. A moment later, Clint headed down the hall for Bardwell's office and some answers.

Thirty-five

DETECTIVE BARDWELL HAD invited Ellery to the police station to attend a lecture given by a forensic pathologist from Atlanta. It was informative, long, and, due to air-conditioning breakdown, unbearably hot.

It was almost nine-thirty when she arrived home. She unlocked the front door and punched in the code for the alarm system. The house was cool, but she was still hot, so she turned the thermostat down lower, took a cool shower, and then slipped into a pair of jeans and a sleeveless shirt before she went to the kitchen for something cold to drink.

The new refrigerator hadn't arrived. She remembered to make certain her hands were dry before she opened the freezer and filled a glass with ice. She put the glass on the counter and opened the refrigerator to remove a can of Diet Coke. She paused to study a Tupperware container filled with tea. She couldn't remember how long ago she had placed it there, so she put it on the counter next to the Coke.

She filled the glass with ice and poured her drink, turned and bumped the container of tea with her elbow. It fell off the counter, bounced on the floor, and the lid came off. Tea spread across the floor.

"Well, hell," she said, wanting nothing more than to sit down and relax a moment. Instead of sitting down, she went to the laundry room and filled the mop bucket with water. She grabbed the mop and carried both into the kitchen. She leaned the mop against the counter and set the bucket nearby.

She poured the rest of the Diet Coke into her glass and was taking a couple of swallows when she thought she heard a noise. She ignored it at first, until she heard it a second time. She paused, listening. There it was again—a thumping, shuffling sound, as if someone were walking in another part of the house. She thought at first it might be Clint, but it couldn't be. Clint didn't have a key, and she'd locked the door when she came home. Besides, Clint always rang the doorbell.

At first, she tried to blow it off and say she was being paranoid. She knew she'd set the alarm system before she'd left for the lecture because she'd reset it moments ago when she'd come in. But this wasn't paranoia. Someone was in the house. An uneasy feeling crept up her spine, until she felt the bristling of her scalp and neck.

Heart pounding, her mouth dry as desert sand, she swallowed against the dryness sucking at her throat. A shuddering feeling of dread, laced with fear, swept over her. This was for real. The footsteps ceased. Her heart lurched and beads of sweat dotted her forehead. She did not have to turn around to know someone was in the room with her. She could feel it.

Slowly, she turned toward the door that led into the dark hallway and screamed.

Standing in the shadows of the doorway, like a creature that had crawled from the sea, was a man. He watched her with intense, piercing eyes that made her think there are people in this world who are born evil. He was the ghost who had haunted the dark perimeters of her home, entered her house, violated her privacy, crept into her dreams, and vanished without a trace.

Even before he stepped out of the shadows, she knew this was her tormentor, the man of her worst nightmares, the monster who'd stalked and terrified her, and that he had come here to take her life.

"Hello, Ellery."

Her flesh crawled. He was creepy, this one. He was dressed in a black outfit that resembled a diving suit, and it did nothing for his thin frame. A hoodlike cap was pulled over his head, so only his face was visible . . . a face she recognized. "Daniel? You frightened me. What are you doing here?"

"I think you know why I'm here . . ."

She didn't reply. She wanted to keep calm and use her head, but something was weirdly abnormal about him; something looked different, but what? She studied his person and then it hit her. It was the face—the freakish face. He had no eyebrows. She tried to decide if that had anything to do with why he was dressed as he was. He looked like a hit man in a frog suit.

"You don't mind if I call you by your first name, do you?"

Dryness closed her throat. She shook her head, unable to speak.

His soft-spoken, grave monotone scared her. It was the calm, calculating types you had to watch out for; the composed, unruffled exterior could make you forget you were actually standing in the eye of the storm, and that at any moment it could change into a whirling mass that sucked everything into its center.

Her gaze kept going back to his eyes. There was nothing there. No hate, no regret, no pity. No emotion at all. It was almost as if he were in a trance.

"You look remarkably like her, you know."

"Yes, you told me. You killed her. Why?" She couldn't bear to look at him. She was going to die. She understood that. He had come here to kill her, the same way he'd killed her sister. She might talk, and plead, and distract him to buy herself a little more time to live, but in the end, he would take out a gun or a knife and he would mortally wound her.

And then he would watch her die.

She would die here, in this kitchen, lying on the floor, terrified and alone, knowing the seconds she had to live were disappearing with each heartbeat that sent her blood flowing out of her veins and spilling over the floor, just like her sister.

Her mind would be alert, but her body would start to weaken. She would know she had only a short time left to live. Her breathing would grow faint. Her heart would start to beat slower and slower. Her eyes would close. Her spirit would depart. It would be over.

She was heartbroken to realize it took the reality of her

own murder to let her fully understand the terrible horror her poor sister had suffered. Something about that made her want to defeat him, made her want to live for her sister.

"It's really too bad you didn't get to see her when she was alive," he said. "There must have been a lot of questions you wanted to ask, and things you wanted to talk about. And now, knowing that will never happen, what do you feel? Cheated? Angry? Wounded? It doesn't matter, really, because whatever it is, you won't feel that way for long. You know that, don't you?"

His voice was dark as a shadow, vague and murky. It crept out of nowhere like fog and surrounded her, silent as a snake, seductive, and fatal. She hated the sound of it as much as she hated him. She never really knew what terror felt like before now, or that the will to live was so strong within her. "Why? Why did you kill her? Why must you kill me?"

Suddenly her fear began to subside. She wanted this bastard to fail. She wanted him dead . . . as dead as her sister. The flood of adrenaline into her system staggered her. She felt drugged, as if she had lain dormant for a long time and was just now coming out of hibernation.

Tears flooded her eyes. "You killed her . . . your own sister. And you killed Clay Littleton too. Didn't you?" She didn't realize she'd said the words aloud until she saw his smirking smile. She wanted to kill him with her bare hands, this pathetic, weird, pitiful excuse for humanity. She wanted to laugh and ridicule him, but not now. "You killed Hazel too, didn't you?"

"I hired someone to take care of her," he said bluntly.

"Why? Why would you hire someone? You had already killed Susan and Clay. What was one more?"

"I wanted an airtight alibi, and that was the best way to establish one. Let someone else kill her, while at the time of her murder I was in an airplane on my way to New York."

"Who was the killer? Where is he now?"

"He's dead, so his name is unimportant. But he did take some lovely photos of you."

"You killed him?"

"I couldn't let him live after killing poor Hazel, now could I? After all, she was family."

She wanted to tell him what a sick bastard he was, but she knew she had to keep from agitating him. "What did you have against Hazel? What did you stand to gain by killing her?"

"Stupid bitch confronted me and said she knew I killed Clay and Susan, so you see, I had to do it." His face became hard and his entire countenance changed, as if another person were inside him and had suddenly taken over. "It was an unfortunate set of circumstances, I assure you. It was not something I enjoyed, but necessity often dictates."

"What do you stand to gain by killing all of us? Why does killing me have anything to do with Clay's and Susan's deaths? I never met them. There were no connections between us. I didn't know who my real father was or that I was a twin until a few months ago."

"I'm surprised you couldn't figure that one out. Money. It's always about money . . . you know, 'the love of money is the root of all evil.' "

"I'm more surprised to learn you know a Bible verse.

Still, how could you gain anything monetarily by my death?"

"You may not have known about your father, but he knew about you. It would have behooved you to read your father's will. He left everything to Susan, with the stipulation that if you were ever found, it was to be divided between the two of you."

"And Clay?"

"Poor Clay. I regretted his death most of all. I liked Clay, but unfortunately, Susan loved him so much, she made out a will leaving everything to him in the event of her death. She told me so. Therefore, killing only Susan would not have helped me. They both had to die."

"And then I came along."

"Yes, poor, unfortunate little you. What a bad sense of timing you had, showing up here when you did. Your untimely arrival made things more difficult for me and, I'm sorry to say, tragic for you. But it will all be over soon. I am three fourths of the way there. Once you are gone, I will have the money."

"Why do you need to kill for money? I thought you were wealthy and owned your own corporation."

"Corporations, like people, have problems from time to time, and at this time Nostradamus is deeply in debt. So, you see, as much as I hate doing it, you have to go, dear heart."

"Why didn't you kill me at the beginning? Why did you use all those scare tactics when you knew from the start you were going to kill me? Why not do it and get it over with?"

"Setting it up to look like a stalker kept suspicion

away from me, and when your nemesis, Sherman T., paid me a visit, I knew right off he was the perfect scapegoat. He was already your enemy and seeking revenge. He stalked you once a few years ago. He was already stalking you when he followed you here."

"You won't get away with it."

"Wrong. I have already gotten away with it. And now, we must get on with the business at hand, so no more questions, dear heart."

At least she knew who he was and why he was here. No more mystery there. She had known from the beginning that her life was in danger, and she knew that at some point the stalker would try to kill her. Now, she was tired. She didn't want to talk anymore. She knew that even if she did put up a good fight, it would still end with her death.

Once you know it is inevitable, you stop trying to think of ways to save your life, she realized. You begin to think of ways to make it easier, or more comfortable, or to enjoy, at least, an honorable last moment. She faced him squarely. If she was going to be shot, she wanted to know when it was going to happen. She wasn't going to make any offers to him. Her luck had run out. Her gaze dropped to the gun in his hand, and back up to his face.

Something within her refused to give up. She didn't want to die. Not today. Not in the kitchen. And not because this man was more powerful than she was. Why couldn't she think of something—if not for herself, for Susan? Yet, as she thought that, she knew there was no way out for her. She was helpless. She could not match him in strength. If she had any defense to use against him at all, it would be pure luck or her own ingenuity, which seemed to be flagging. And with that thought came an idea. It was a long shot, but even long shots were better than dying. If she was fortunate enough, it just might work.

Her mouth was so dry. She glanced down at her glass. "Do you mind if I take a drink?"

His gaze shifted to the glass sitting on the counter before coming back to rest on her. "Oh, I see I interrupted you before you could finish your drink. Go ahead. I have plenty of time before I send you off for a nice long visit with your sister. Drink it if you like. I might even join you. What are you having?"

"Diet Coke." She was about to tell him there was another one in the refrigerator when he made an expression that turned his eyebrowless face into a hideous mask. "Hmmm, Diet Coke won't do."

"There is a bottle of vodka in the pantry."

"Get it."

She did as he said and placed the bottle on the counter.

As if he knew his way around, he opened a cabinet and took out a glass. "I don't like it straight. What do you have to mix with it?"

"There is orange juice in the refrigerator," she said, not bothering to tell him about the tomato juice in the pantry. She swallowed and stared straight into the round bore of his semiautomatic pistol.

He must have noticed, for he asked, "Were you expecting a knife? Did you want to die in the identical manner as your identical sister?" He still spoke with that clipped, clinical monotone that enveloped her like something cold and slimy. Her fists clenched at the thought of the evil he had wrought. She choked back the words she wanted to hurl at him. It was very hard for her to remain silent.

She felt numb as she watched him walk toward the refrigerator, the glass in one hand and the gun in the other. Her mind was blank with the reality of her own death hovering just beyond her reach. Please, God, she thought, please let this work. She knew she didn't have much longer to live. Once he'd had his drink, there would be nothing to keep him from finishing what he came here to do. Only the thought that she did not want to die replayed over and over in her head.

She did not want to die. She was scared, but she knew she had to remain in control; had to believe she at least had a chance.

"I assume the ice is on the left," he said when he stopped in front of the double doors on the refrigerator.

She nodded, her heart so heavy it did not seem to be beating at all. "Yes, the icemaker is on the left."

Everything seemed to shift down into slow motion after that, as if her heart were already anticipating the gradual weakening of her body that was soon to come. Please, she prayed, please give me this one chance.

She watched him put the glass down. His hand came up to grasp the handle. Suddenly she whirled into motion. She slammed her foot against the bucket as hard as she could and sent the bucket sliding across the floor. It sailed toward him and crashed against the side of his foot just as it tipped over. The water washed out in one big wave over his feet and spread in a wide puddle that extended beneath the refrigerator.

She heard a sizzling pop and then a cracking noise. His body jerked. He seemed unable to let go of the handle. Then suddenly, he was knocked backward.

He fell on his back, sprawled in a pool of water, his legs splayed. He lay there like a grotesque black lizard—cold-blooded and unmoving. She hoped with all her heart that he was dead. He'd gotten what he deserved.

Her knees buckled and she had to grab the counter for support. Her gaze fell on the pistol lying in the water near his feet. All the air in her lungs seemed to be going out, and none was coming in. It felt like all her circuit breakers were blown. Her system seemed to shut down. She couldn't think. She couldn't breathe. She couldn't speak.

She didn't know what she should do. She was afraid to take her eyes off him. Moments ago he had terrorized her and held her life in his hands. He didn't seem so powerful or so frightening now.

Although the water seemed to have stopped spreading, she knew better than to go near him. The refrigerator was still plugged into the electrical outlet, and as deadly as it had been moments ago.

He had not moved since he fell. Common sense told her that in all probability he was dead, but she was afraid to trust anything, even her own instincts. She needed to organize her thoughts and think about what she should do now.

Call an ambulance?

Call Clint?

Call the police?

Run like hell?

Running sounded good. She rubbed her forehead. Oh Lord, she was shaking too much to think. How could anyone survive the ordeal of almost being murdered like this?

She took one last glance at the body, to make certain he still had not moved. She hoped the bastard was fried, but if not, he would be soon enough where he was going.

She decided to call the police. Ellery knew she couldn't get to the kitchen wall phone because it was next to the refrigerator and she would have to risk walking dangerously near the water. She would have to use the phone in the family room. As she turned to go into the other room she saw a shape coming toward her, partially hidden in the shadows. She gasped and her body jerked to a stop.

For a moment she couldn't connect what she saw with what it meant. So many emotions clogged her throat, and she groped in the darkness of her mind for understanding. Until at last, it came to her softly, out of the shadows of her intellect, and she understood. Her knees almost dropped out from under her. Joy seemed to pour forth with each steady beat of her heart.

"Clint . . ." She let out a long-held breath. She was so glad to see him, to have him come in here and take charge. Her eyes filled with tears as she said, "He hasn't moved. I'm almost certain he's dead."

"Thank God. I was afraid I would be too late. Are you all right?" He was at her side immediately. His arm went around her to hold her close. He didn't move, but remained as still as the moonlight on a quiet bay.

"You're okay?" he asked again.

She nodded and he looked toward the place where Daniel's body lay sprawled in water. "I think you're right. He looks dead to me. Was it the refrigerator?"

"Yes, and you can't imagine how happy I am the new one didn't arrive because I'd be dead right now."

He held her close with his arms tight around her. "It's over." Clint looked back at Daniel's body. "Damn nasty business being electrocuted like that." He continued to study the still form. "Fortunately, I have no blood kinship to that miserable excuse for humanity. Ugly bastard, isn't he? What happened to his face?"

"It's the eyebrows." She thought for a moment she would cry.

Clint called Detective Bardwell on his cell phone. "It's Clint Littleton. I'm at Ellery's house. It was Daniel Wilkerson, just as Lucy said. He's here, lying in the middle of her kitchen floor and probably dead as a smoked herring. Yes, Ellery is okay . . . a bit shaken, but in good shape. Yes, we'll still be here."

"He's on his way?" she asked.

"Yes, and Lucy is at the station and she's coming with him. Come on, I want to get you out of here. We can go into the family room."

"I'd rather wait on the porch."

He chuckled and led her out of the kitchen, down the hall, and onto the front porch. She started to sit on the steps, then turned back to look up at him. "Stay here with me. I don't want to be alone right now."

"I wouldn't leave you alone for any amount of money," he said, and sat down next to her.

He put his arm around her and told her about Lucy's phone call, his subsequent trip to the police station, the visit with Bardwell and Lucy.

Ellery already knew about as much as he did. "Daniel told me he killed all of them. He told me about my father's will. Even after all those years, my father thought about me in the end."

"Did he mention that Hazel and Margaret found out, and that's why he had to kill Hazel?"

"Yes, I guess he had Margaret too terrified to say anything."

"He was taking money from her," Clint said. "Blackmail. If he had killed her, he would have been in deep financial trouble, because your father's will was still tied up in probate. So he would make his little trips over here, to dip his hand into her bank account and frighten the daylights out of her."

"I wonder how Hazel and Margaret found out," she said.

"Evidently Margaret suspected Daniel from the beginning and she mentioned it to Hazel. Hazel decided to go to Austin to find out about Nathan's will. She was looking for a motive. She must have put two and two together."

"What I don't understand is why he killed Clay first. It doesn't make sense."

"It makes perfect sense. By killing Clay first, no one would suspect it was for Susan's inheritance. After Clay was dead, he waited a couple of years and killed Susan."

"And I showed up and he had to get rid of me."

"Exactly."

"And I was thinking all along that it was Sherman T. Daniel said Sherman just happened to show up at the right time and Daniel used it to his advantage. He planned all those things so it would look like Sherman was the culprit. Then no one would suspect Daniel when he slipped in and killed me."

Clint nodded in agreement. "You and Daniel had no history aside from that one time when he came to meet you. I suppose he felt that kept him from being under suspicion."

"And Sherman would be arrested for my murder since he had a motive stemming from our problems in D.C., and the fact that he followed me here. What I didn't find out was how Daniel learned about Hazel's trip to Austin and that she'd looked into my father's will."

"Bardwell thinks Daniel probably found out through his lawyer or one of the clerks that helped Hazel when she wanted to see the will. He'll be checking out that side of things. Evidently, Daniel tried to get Nathan's money right after Susan died, but sometimes those wills can get tied up in probate for two or three years, which is what happened in this case. Judging from what Margaret said, I bet Bardwell will find out that Daniel and Nostradamus Corp. were heavily in debt and desperate for funds to keep operating."

"Oh, they were. He told me that himself. That's why he needed the money . . . to save Nostradamus." Ellery shook her head. "Poor Margaret . . . I'm sorry I thought such bad things about her."

"Don't blame yourself. You had no way of knowing.

Margaret brought it all upon herself. She should have gone to Bardwell."

As soon as he finished, she turned and put her arms around him. Then, with a sigh, she laid her head against his chest. "I guess this wraps everything up and I can start writing my documentary that will quickly turn into a murder mystery," she said, suddenly feeling sad to think she had nothing to keep her here any longer.

"Or you could write a love story."

"Which kind of love story?" she asked. "One with a sad ending or otherwise?"

"I was thinking otherwise."

She opened her mouth to say something but he silenced her with a kiss. "Hold that thought," he said. "I'll be right back."

Puzzled, she watched him go into the house. A moment later he reappeared with two glasses of wine. He sat down beside her and handed her a glass.

"Is this a diversionary tactic?"

He rubbed her neck. "No . . . a preliminary one."

"Preliminary . . . leading to what?"

"I was hoping it would entice you to come out to the ranch to spend the night."

"You needn't ply me with wine. There is no way I would sleep here tonight."

"I wasn't thinking about sleeping."

She turned to gaze into his eyes. "What were you thinking?"

"Oh, I don't know . . . wine and women. How would you feel about making a baby?"

"Don't people usually get married first?"

"That too," he said with a kiss to her cheek. "Whatever it takes to keep you here, forever."

She smiled, kissed him, then said, "That would do it, I think."

She decided at that moment not to tell him that she had been thinking of a myriad of reasons he could find to keep her here with him, if only for a little longer. Nor would she tell him that she liked his reasoning much better than her reasoning.

She knew then that there was more to her story and they would finish it together. But for now, she was content to sit on the porch, next to Clint, surrounded by the silence of the evening and the sweet perfume of life.

Fall in love

with bestselling romances from Pocket Books!